THE DARK HOLDS NO TERRORS

Shashi Deshpande

THE DARK HOLDS NO TERRORS

Europa
editions

Europa Editions
116 East 16th Street
New York, N.Y. 10003
www.europaeditions.com
info@europaeditions.com

Library of Congress Cataloging in Publication Data is available
ISBN 978-1-933372-67-9

Deshpande, Shashi
The Dark Holds No Terrors

Book design by Emanuele Ragnisco
www.mekkanografici.com

Cover image: Gustav Klimt, *Death and Life*
© The Gallery Collection/Corbis

Prepress by Plan.ed – Rome

Printed in the United States of America

CONTENTS

For my husband

You are your own refuge;
There is no other refuge.
This refuge is hard to achieve.
—THE DHAMMAPADA

The beginning was abrupt. There had been no preparation for it. There were no preliminaries, either. At first it was a nightmare of hands. Questing hands that left a trail of pain. Hurting hands that brought me out of a cocoon of blessed unreality . . . I'm-dreaming-this-is-not-real . . . into the savage reality of a monstrous onslaught. And then, the nightmare was compounded of lips and teeth as well. Hands and teeth? No, hammers and pincers. I could taste blood on my lips.

The hands became a body. Thrusting itself upon me. The familiarity of the sensation suddenly broke the shell of silent terror that had enclosed me. I emerged into the familiar world of rejection. My rejection that had become so drearily routine. I struggled to utter the usual words of protest, to say . . . no, not now, stop it. But the words were strangled in my throat. The face above mine was the face of a stranger. Blank, set, and rigid, it was a face I had never seen. A man I did not know.

Strangely, this brought an odd relief. The experience became the known instead of the unknown. It was my nightmare again, the nightmare that had, for some time, haunted me with fearful regularity. This was him, *the stranger who had come into my dreams for a few nights, leaving behind a fear that invaded even my waking hours. The stranger with the brown scarf whom I discovered standing that night at the head of my bed. And I, so frozen with terror that I could not move. Not even when his hands moved slowly, like some macabre slow-motion sequence, towards my throat. I tried to call out, to scream. Nothing issued* out of me but silence. Panic and terror mounted in me as the hands, deliberately, with a kind of casual cruelty, gradually tightened round my throat. Oh god, I was going to die!

And then he spoke. A voice that came from somewhere deep in his throat. Words carrying with them their own echo as if they had been flung into an enormous, empty cave. What was he saying? I never found out, because it was at that moment that I always woke up.

Now there was no waking. The dream, the nightmare, whatever it was, continued. Changing now, like some protean monster, into the horror of rape. This was not to be death by strangulation; it was a monstrous invasion of my body. I tried to move, twisting my body, wriggling under the weight that pinned it down. It was impossible. I was pinioned in a position of an abject surrender of my self. I began, in sheer helplessness, to make little whimpering sounds, piteous cries. The small pains merged all at once into one large one. And still the body above mine, hard and tense, went on with its rhythmic movements. The hands continued their quest for new areas of pain. Now the horror of what was happening to me was lost in a fierce desire to end it. I could not, would not, bear it. I began to fight back, hopelessly, savagely.

And suddenly, when I thought I could bear it no longer, the body that was not mine relaxed. The release was so abrupt it shocked me into an unfamiliar faintness. When the syncope wore off, I realised I was free. There was no weight pinning me down now. But I could not move. It was not just exhaustion, though there was that, too. It was more as if my mind had deserted my shamefully bruised body, disowning it, making it insensate.

And then the two came together. I knew where I was and what had happened. Panic and sensation came back simultaneously. I turned my head slightly, fearfully, and saw him beside me, snoring softly. No more a stranger, but my husband.

PART ONE

1.

It was the Krishna Sudama story* that suddenly came to her mind. That, and the illustration which had accompanied the story in one of her school texts, showing Krishna and his queen Rukmini running joyously to greet poor, ragged Sudama standing at the palace gates. As she knocked at the door, softly at first, then harder, she wondered why the story had come back to her now. She herself was certainly no Sudama in rags, bare feet and humility. She had none of these. Only a suitcase of clothes. She shifted it from hand to hand, finally putting it down at her feet, reluctant to knock again. She was not apprehensive, though not eager either, for the moment of confrontation. She glanced back at the rickshaw in which she had come. She hadn't paid the man as yet, as if keeping a route open for retreat. The driver, bored now, had got out of his seat and was yawning, a huge, animal yawn, arms stretched straight overhead. A different breed of men, she thought, from the tonga drivers who had brought her when she came home during vacations. That man would have carried her suitcase for her, knocked at the door with his whip, and cursed them for their tardiness in opening the door. This indifferent man . . . was he a symbol of the changes she could expect?

Here, though, there were no changes. There were still seven pairs of large stone slabs on which she had played hopscotch as a child leading to the front door. The yard was bare, as always, the ground beaten down to a smooth hardness, in

* For words and phrases followed by an asterisk see explanatory notes on page 265.

which nothing grew, not even weeds. There had never been an attempt to grow anything. It had merely been a place to dry things in summer. The tulsi* had been the only spot of green. But that had gone as well. Of course, it had served its purpose. She had died before her husband. Wasn't that what all women prayed to the tulsi for? For a moment she saw her mother standing in front of the tulsi, eyes closed, hands folded, lips moving. The memory was as violent as an assault and angrily she rejected it. Then she noticed the flowers in one corner against the wall. Hollyhocks, tall, colourful, and ridiculously incongruous in that place. Who could have planted them?

Deliberately she turned round and knocked again. Loud and long this time. Now, at last, there was the sound of approaching feet, slithering sounds of bare feet toughened by years of contact with the ground. The bolt was shot back with a loud groaning, protesting squeak. The doors opened with the reluctance of disuse.

They stared at each other. She smiled slightly to see the look of inquiry turn into a blank looking-at-a-stranger one. It was, she supposed, the unexpectedness of her presence. She felt a faint triumph as if she had scored something.

"Baba," she said.

His Adam's apple moved. His eyes moved from her to the suitcase at her feet, and then beyond her to the rickshaw standing on the road. And now back to her, with an awareness of her identity dawning in them. As if it was only by relating her to these other things that he could recognise her.

"Can I come in, Baba?"

He moved aside, composing his face into an expression of normality.

"I didn't expect you."

"No, how could you?"

"You didn't write."

He had changed. No, not just older. Something more profound than that. An alteration that made him not just the same man so many years older, but another man altogether.

"No, I made up my mind just two days back." She put the suitcase down. "I must pay the rickshaw man."

By the time she came back into the house, he had adjusted himself to her presence. Surprise was a thing of the past. Inside the house, the silence was palpable, throbbing and heavy. She felt herself enclosed, with an astonishing immediacy, in the old atmosphere of brooding stillness. As if something would happen sometime; not now, no, nothing now, but in some unknown future.

Nothing had changed. The same sagging easy chair, shaped to his body. The curtain of the inner door, made of glass pipes strung together to form a design, tinkled as musically when she moved it as it always had. The pictures on the wall were unchanged, too. A faded photograph of her grandfather whom she had never seen. One of a smiling Gandhi and Nehru, put up some time, perhaps, in a burst of patriotism. And a framed picture of Krishna as a crawling infant, chubby, solemn, with a hint of smile in the eyes. The whole done in a finely stitched embroidery, with a real peacock's feather stuck on the infant's head.

And yet there were alterations. An ashtray full of stubs. (Since when had he started smoking?) A stained cup with the dregs of tea standing in it. It was as if he had become an apostate, revolting against the pattern of living in which to leave a cup unwashed even for a minute had been a crime.

"You came by the Mail, I suppose?"

How safe, how comforting, to talk about trains . . .

"Was it on time?"

. . . and whether they are on time. He hasn't smiled at me as yet. But when have we ever smiled at each other?

"I don't know. What time is it supposed to arrive?"

"Ten-fifteen."

"Yes, it was on time. Maybe a few minutes late."

A few minutes more or less. Does it matter?

The familiar irritation, the familiar exasperation. To meet after fifteen years and feel only that!

"I'll have a wash," she announced. She felt crumpled and soiled after her night in the train.

There was an air of disuse to the bathroom. The boiler, which had been a shiny coppery red, a result of regular scrubbing with ash and tamarind, had turned a sullen dark. The stone floor seemed slimy. There was a plastic bucket and mug now in addition to the copper and brass buckets, which had the same neglected look as the boiler. As she soaped her face and hands . . . the same *Hamaam* still . . . the smell of the soap brought back her childhood more vividly than anything else so far. She went out, wiping her face and hands, and found him still sitting there, staring at her suitcase.

"Will you have some tea?"

"I'd like to. Shall I make it?"

"Don't bother. I'll get it for you in a minute."

She sat down on the divan, feeling all at once weary. Why had it seemed so important to come here, and at once? She thought of Abhi's tears . . . I want to go with you, mummy. I want to go. Of Renu's face and questions . . . Grandfather? What grandfather, mummy? I thought my grandfather was dead?

Why had the sense of urgency left her now? Was it because of him and the way he had looked at her? Or rather, avoided looking at her? She had closed her eyes, feeling herself swaying, succumbing to the sensation of still being in the train, when the tinkle of cup and saucer told her he was back. It was, she noticed, the "good" cup and saucer. As if she were company.

"You, Baba?"

"I just had mine. There's my cup."

He sat opposite her, not in his usual easy chair, but on the hard wooden one. The divan on which she sat had, she saw, given up all pretence of being anything but a bed. As she drank her tea . . . too sweet and strong . . . he sat gingerly on the edge of his chair, like an unwilling host entertaining an unwelcome guest. And that, I suppose, is what I really am. What gave me the idea I could come back?

She had, he thought, the look of a person expecting something. What could it be? He fumbled in his mind for something to say.

"I heard about Ai," she said abruptly, putting down her cup and saucer with a loud clatter.

"Oh!" Why had that not occurred to him? "Who told you?"

"Someone from this place. A patient."

She felt reluctant, remembering who it was, to reveal any more. He felt no curiosity, either, to know who it was. His curiosity was centred round her presence.

"Oh!"

She looked round. Quickly, as if guessing her thoughts, he said, "I should have put up her photograph. I've been thinking of it, but somehow . . . "

He gave her a small smile. The first smile she had from him. He seemed to be apologising to her for not putting up his dead wife's photograph on the wall. He rubbed at his wispy moustache. He didn't know what to say next.

"Baba," she said, "does it trouble you to have me here? Tell me if it does. I can go to a hotel"

He stopped the rubbing movements and pulled a cigarette pack from the lower shelf of the large table. With an unexpectedly elegant gesture, he lit one and put it in his mouth. Now he seemed more comfortable. Was that why he had been restless? Because he needed to smoke? Had it nothing to do with her, after all?

"When I heard of Ai's death," she went on, her voice harder and louder, "I thought I'd like to see you once more. But if there's any problem about my staying here . . . "

"No, no, nothing like that. But I didn't know . . . I mean, I never imagined . . . " His words trailed away. Suddenly she knew. It was his loyalty to the dead woman. He could not welcome her because that meant treachery to the dead. Yet when he spoke next, his voice was stronger. Stronger and more sure.

"What hotel? No, you stay here. Only . . . " and his eyes went round the place looking at it, perhaps, through her eyes. "I'm afraid things aren't very clean or comfortable. You may find it difficult."

"That doesn't matter. Where shall I take my bag?"

"Inside. Take it in. Go in."

He did not specify where. She peeped into the room that had been her parents'. It had been "their" room, but it had always seemed only his, so successfully had she managed to efface her personality from the room. And how powerful, how strong, she now thought, her mother had been to achieve that. How certain of herself she must have been!

Now the room had, in spite of being neat and clean, that indefinable air of being unoccupied. He had obviously moved out into the hall, she thought, remembering the pillow with its soiled cover, and the blanket folded into a square on the divan.

She went into the next room that had been her own. For a brief moment, she had a bewildering sensation of never having gone away. My room. They've kept it as it was. Then she realised that those were male clothes hanging on the wall. And there was no bed. Just a mattress rolled against the wall. An earthen jar with an upturned glass on it.

"That's Madhav's room," he called out from the hall, as if divining her surprise.

"Who's Madhav?"

"A student. In his first year in college. He's been with us for two years now."

She got out feeling oddly disturbed, as if the consciousness of her desertion had only just come to her

"Why don't you lie down for a while?" he asked her. "I must light the boiler before you can have a bath."

"Where?" she asked bluntly.

"Go and lie down in the *puja* room. That's clean. I clean it every day."

He brought her a straw mat and a pillow. It made her uneasy to have him tend to her. He had always been so much a man, the "master of the house," not to be bothered by any of the trivialities of daily routine. And yet he seemed comfortable in this new role, as if his earlier inactivity had been a giving-in to his wife's ideas, nothing to do with himself.

She was grateful for a chance to rest. She lay down and closed her eyes. There had always been a medley of smells in this room: was bare now, but pale ghosts of the old odours wafted about her as she lay there. These, and the tarnished silver mango leaves that hung from the top of the doorway, were the only indications that this had once been a *puja* room.

"Who looks after you, Baba?" she called out.

"No one. Madhav and I . . . we manage very well."

She smiled. Madhav. How easily he said the name. So unknown to her. And he had not said her name as yet.

"You know I have two children?"

It was easier to talk this way, without looking at him, without having him evade her eyes.

"I know."

"Who told you?" she asked in her turn. She pulled her sari down to cover her legs and shifted her head on the pillow. It was hard, but there was something comforting about its unyielding rigidity.

"Oh, somebody. I don't remember now."

He was imitating her reserve, unwilling to let her look at his cards.

"There's always someone who'll tell you things. I . . . We've always known everything about you."

Everything? No, by god, you don't! If you did . . . !

"A boy and a girl. That's right, isn't it?"

A boy and a girl. Don't you even want to know their names? She was angered by his indifference. It made her seem a remote acquaintance. Then she checked herself. What had she expected? What right had she to expect anything?

"Yes, one boy, one girl"

A family the right size. The right kind. Like the ads. A happy family. Healthy, happy, smiling, and in colour. But Abhi and his pains . . .

My tummy is paining me, mummy. Too much.

Now, Abhi, remember, mummy is a doctor. You shouldn't try to fool her. Just because you don't want to go to school . . .

No, mummy, it's really paining me. Terribly. I swear it is.

And there was Renu with her silences, her withdrawals.

Renu, what is the matter?

Nothing.

Why don't you talk?

I don't feel like it.

A happy family. With the skeleton locked firmly in the cupboard.

"Their names are Renu and Abhi," she said loudly, as if he had asked her for their names, as if she were speaking to a deaf man.

"Renu . . . ?"

"That's Renuka. And Abhi is Abhijit. She's nine, and he's five."

She could smell the kerosene now. A clatter as he threw chips into the boiler. A match striking. The hollow, hungry sound of the flames as they leapt up.

Flames . . . her first thought when she had heard of her mother's death had been . . . who lit the pyre? She had no son to do that for her. Dhruva had been seven when he died. She never said his name after that. Except that once . . . when I woke up sobbing at night and she called out . . . Dhruva? Saru?

My mother . . . she chewed the words reflectively in her mouth.

Remembering how it had been when the man had told her, baldly, crudely . . . Do you know your mother is dead?

2.

There is this strange new fear of disintegration. A terrified consciousness of not existing. No, worse. Of being just a ventriloquist's dummy, which smiles, laughs, and talks only because of the ventriloquist. The fear that without the ventriloquist, I will regress, go back to being a lifeless puppet, a smirk pasted on to its face.

Perhaps my profession functions as my ventriloquist. For, as long as there is a patient before me, I feel real. Between patients there is nothing. And yet I find myself taking more and more time between patients these days. As if it is restful not to be. To be nothing. When Nirmala peeps in, wondering maybe at the long pause between an outgoing patient and my bell, she sees me writing. Busy, engrossed, as if I'm writing notes on the patient who just left. But I'm only doodling. And always the same thing. One circle entwined in another, one circle entwined in another. Ending up sometimes with a complex, intricate pattern of a strange, mystifying beauty. Once I found myself cutting a piece of paper, telling myself . . . these are bits of my mind falling on the ground. And there was Nirmala's face looking at me from the door. Saying in an astonished voice . . . What is it, doctor? And the fear in me that my mind had indeed gone. That it was lying there in strips on the ground. The time it took me to come out of that fear. It seemed hours, though it must have been just seconds. And then saying in that cold, it's-none-of-your-business voice, "Send in the next patient, Nirmala."

"Yes, doctor."

Relief in her voice, as if she knew me again. As if things were normal again. But never any relief for me. Always the fear that one day Nirmala would look in and find no one behind the table. Just a white coat containing nothing. Emptiness. The mounting terror that one day there would be no ventriloquist giving me the right lines to say, the right faces to make.

Now, where is it paining you? Show me.
Put out your tongue.
I'm not going to hurt you. Don't be scared.
Tch, tch, such a big boy and scared of the doctor?
Be a brave girl, now.

And behind this fear the uneasiness that comes from losing something. No, not losing it, but being unable to find it because I've hidden it to keep it safe. Hidden it so well that I can't find it myself now. And each day the thought . . . I can't go on.

Yet, surprisingly, I invariably did, until that day.

"Some new patients, doctor," Nirmala made a face at me, the two of us allied against the whole world of stupid patients.

"No appointment. Not referred by anyone, either. They say you know them and you'll see them."

"What's the name?"

She gave me the slip. I stared at it. Why today after all these years? Why now? Well, why not?

"All right," I said at last. "I'll see them. But keep them to the last."

Some time to prepare, to arm myself, to get back into the pose, to be nothing but the complete professional woman.

I don't know what I did, what I said, to the other patients. I suppose, like any other well-trained animal, I was capable of making the right noises, the right gestures automatically. I must have felt and prodded, auscultated and screened, frowned and smiled, written out prescriptions and investigations. I can remember nothing. Only the pang of hatred that shot through me at the sight of his face when, all other patients gone, I could no longer keep them at bay, and they entered.

There were three of them. He, his wife, and, yes, their daughter, Manda, carrying a child in her arms. Manda had been scarcely seven or eight when I had last seen her.

For a moment it seemed the ventriloquist had truly deserted me as I struggled to find the right thing to say. And then the child began to cry. It was like a coin being dropped into the slot. I relaxed. It was easy now. I was in charge. No, not I, really, but the dummy in the white coat.

"Sit down." I smiled at them like I would at any other parents. "It's Manda, isn't it? Your kid, Manda? What's wrong?"

"And how are you, Saru?" the mother asked, not intimidated, obviously, by my purposefully professional air. And why was he silent? "It's so long, isn't it, since we met? You know we're in Bombay now? It's nearly five years since we came here. We're staying with Suresh . . . he's in Andheri. And Manda got married two years back. Her husband is a lawyer. This is her first child. A son." She beamed.

"First child?" I interrupted her adroitly. "What's the matter with him? Let me see."

Even as Manda began unwrapping the child from his multitudes of wrappings, he cleared his throat and spoke for the first time. And now he struck me, not as dignified . . . why had I thought him that? . . . but pompous.

"I wouldn't have recognised you, Saru. You've changed."

Changed? Yes, maybe. I'm more elegant, more sophisticated, I know how to dress, how to carry myself. All just a veneer. Behind this, there's nothing.

I smiled with what I hoped was complacence. "Well, it's been so long . . . "

And then it came, the dreaded question I had been waiting for, braced myself for.

"How is Manohar?"

It was surprisingly, unexpectedly easy to reply. "Flourishing." And then, determinedly, deliberately I turned my back on him.

I said to Manda, "Bring him here. How many months? Ten? What's wrong?"

I could feel, if not see, his air of dignified cordiality crumple into bewilderment. I hardened myself. What business was it of his? And if it was, I was not prepared to let him get off with just a few trite remarks.

You've changed. By god, I have. And would you like to know why? Shall I tell you? Will you tell me what to do this time? If you have any sense of justice, you should. After all, it was you, wasn't it, who said then, so glibly, "Go ahead, Saru. Get married and to hell with all of them. I'm with you both, remember."

Yes, I remember. If it had not been for you, maybe . . .

There was no more attempt at friendliness after that. I finished my examination, gave instructions and wrote down the prescription with the impersonal air of any doctor. But when leaving, he looked straight into my face, as if he had waited for this, to gather all his strength into one blow, and said . . . "Do you know your mother is dead?"

"My mother?"

All defences down now. The battle for a while given up, won by a frightened girl who stammered . . . My mother? But I would not give up so easily. I struggled until the frightened girl vanished.

"When?"

"About a month ago, I suppose. She died here in Bombay, you know. I was at the funeral. She didn't send for you?"

I shook my head, my hand reaching out to put back the pen

I had been writing with. My fingers, I noticed, were steady. Not a quiver in them.

"Why should she? You should know that."

You, who brought me my mother's last message. What was it she had said? The words should be etched in my mind, but, oddly enough, I have forgotten them. I can only remember that she cursed me as no mother should.

A corner of my mind registered the fact that I was late. I was delaying others, too. Nirmala, who would sulk, her painted lips looking ugly in discontent. And Vasant, making faces at my door, shrugging meaningfully at Nirmala, thinking . . . Why can't she lock up herself? Why must I wait?

"But I thought . . . maybe when she was dying . . . "

"Yes, to be as adamant as that! I can almost admire her now, can't you? To be so unforgiving to your own daughter . . . your only child!"

The mother, stuffing one more dirty nappy into her capacious bag, was indifferent. But Manda, her anxiety about the child temporarily allayed, was taking it all in eagerly. Drama. Something her own life lacked, perhaps. A husband chosen by her parents. A wedding in the midst of approving relations. Bowing down dutifully to all of them. Receiving their blessings. A child at the first lawful moment. In-laws and parents, proud and approving. Grandparents, uncles, and aunts or the child who slept in her arms.

Mummy, why don't I have a grandfather? Like Sangeeta's grandfather? Why don't I have one?

Your grandfather's dead, Renu.

But Sangeeta has two grandfathers. Where's my other grandfather?

"What was wrong with her?" I asked, as indifferent at any stranger.

"Cancer. Of the stomach, I think I heard someone say. They brought her here to Tata."

Cancer . . .
Doctor, it isn't cancer, is it?
Can't you do something for this pain?
I'll be back at work soon, won't I, doctor?
How long, doctor? How long?

"But it was too late by then. They didn't even admit her. In fact, your father was to take her back home when she died. Somewhere in Goregaon. I believe it was her sister's house she died in."

Her sister. I did not know it as a child, the knowledge came to me later, that she had quarrelled with all of Baba's family after his father's death. The quarrel, I learnt much later by putting things together, had been over a trivial piece of property. An old house that had nothing but nuisance value. Yet it left its mark on our lives. We never had uncles, aunts, cousins like other children had. There was just this one aunt . . . her sister.

That night I told Manu about it.

"My mother's dead," I said.

"Your mother?" His eyes searched my face. He seemed reassured by what he saw. Or perhaps, by what he didn't see.

"Who told you about it?"

"Your Prof. Kulkarni."

"Where did you meet him?"

We were in the bedroom, he on the bed, I on the stool in front of the dressing table, plaiting my hair. He spoke to my reflection and my reflection answered his. This way it was easy. Safer. And we were, in the mirror, like two people posing for a photograph of a well-furnished bedroom. With the caption, perhaps, reading . . . "Mrs. . . . prefers pastels. The one startling touch of colour is provided by the bedspread."

"He came to my rooms today. With his grandchild. You remember Manda, don't you? It's her child."

But he was interested neither in Manda nor in her child. And he seemed to have already forgotten my mother.

"Did he ask you about me?"

The mention of the man's name brought back the man he himself had been. Standing in front of the mike that day. So sure of himself and his attractions. Even now, for one brief, deceptive, illusory moment he looked like Prof. Kulkarni's favourite student. The man I had seen that day at the inauguration of the Literary Society.

After that my mother was forgotten. What is a mother if she casts you off? We had lived fifteen years without mentioning her. Why should she matter dead, when she had never mattered alive? But at that moment I knew I had to go back. I would go home and meet Baba.

"Why do you have to go?"

He had been flabbergasted.

"Did they let you know when she was ill? When she was dying? When she was dead?"

"No."

"Then why do you have to go?"

"I don't know."

"Oh, come on, Saru, there must be some reason. After all these years, why now?"

Tell him. This is the time. Tell him why you have to go. But his eyes, puzzled, groping, pathetic . . .

"And what about your work? Your patients?"

"That's no problem, After all it's only for a few days . . . "

Is it?

"I know. I suppose you want to be forgiven."

Forgiven? I began to laugh while he stared at me in astonishment. Forgiven? I want nothing so complicated. My wants are simpler. To sleep peacefully the night through. To wake up without pain. To go through tomorrow without apprehension. Not to think, not to dream. Just to live.

And to do that I must get away. Yes, that's why I'm going. To get away from this house, this paradise of matching curtains and handloom bedspreads. This hell of savagery and submission. But what if I carry my own hell within me? Then there is no hope for me at all. But that, too, I have to know. And therefore I am going home to my father. To tell him that I know my mother is dead. That I know she died unforgiving.

"What's the matter? What's so funny?"

"Nothing. The idea of forgiveness. It's so stupid."

3

S trangely, she fell asleep there, on the hard ground, in that stuffy room. She was exhausted, though she had not realised it herself. It was a kind of accumulated fatigue, and later, when she thought of it, she wondered how she had gone on for so long with her relentless routine . . . hospital, teaching, rooms, visits, home, children. And the nightmares.

Now she woke up feeling not refreshed, but resentful, as if someone had woken her up prematurely. And then she realised what it was that had awakened her. Low voices that, nevertheless, carried trailing echoes behind them, as if the house was empty.

"Baba?" she called out suddenly, like a frightened child. And there was something strange, she knew at once, in her calling out to him that way. She had never done it, not even when she was a child. Perhaps she had known even then that he was feeble. No, worse than that, that he was a nonentity and didn't matter. And yet, he once had battled on her behalf.

He came now in response to her cry. Looking at him, she knew why and how he looked different. He was happy. There had been an air of tranquillity about him that she had just glimpsed when he had opened the door to her, though it had vanished the moment he recognized her. Now it was back. Maybe he had adjusted himself to her presence.

She struggled to a sitting position, her body waking up to an awareness of new pains, of new areas of soreness, which came from sleeping on the hard ground. Blessedly clean pains.

Not like the others. I am a dark, damp, smelly hole, she often thought when the pains of the night came back to her in the day, shaming her as if they were evidence of *her* wrongdoing. I am like a house full of unclean things, never cleaned, never opened. Sometimes I don't know how I can bear myself.

"Have I slept long?"

"Almost two hours. Your bath water is ready. So is lunch. Madhav is home from college. Have your bath and come to eat. We're waiting for you."

There was that appetising smell of seasoning oil and roasting *chappatis*. She felt voraciously hungry. She had eaten nothing since lunch at home the previous day.

"I'll be ready in two minutes," she promised, getting up. Smoothing back her dishevelled hair, she rolled up the straw mat on which she had slept and went for her bath.

They sat in the kitchen to eat, the three of them, Madhav at present just a nondescript looking boy, whose only curiosity for her was his scrupulous adherence to mealtime rituals. He had removed his shirt and sat down on the plank, legs crossed, sacred thread prominent on his chest. Before starting on his food, he did all the things she had almost forgotten. Water in the cupped palm, the drops around the plate, bits of rice on one side of it. He saw her staring at him and coloured, the red staining his fair skin in blotches.

"What is it?" Baba asked.

"I'd almost forgotten these things," she said.

"It's my mother . . . " the boy said and simultaneously Baba spoke too. "Of course, your Manohar is . . . isn't . . . " He left his sentence incomplete as well. And yet she felt there had been something fantastically brave about his words. To say her husband's name . . . Manohar . . . Her mother had called him "that man" as if his name would have soiled her lips.

"Madhav's father," Baba went on, "is a priest and a very learned man. He wanted Madhav to follow in his footsteps.

But Madhav," and now he smiled at the boy, "has his own plans." The smile he offered Madhav carried pure affection with it. It gave her a jolt. To her, he had always been a negative man, incapable of strong feelings. But if he could smile that way . . . ? It was like being a child again, humiliated by the discovery that an adult has been fooling you all the while. If it's not him, then it has to be me . . . Her complacency, and feeling of condescension towards her father wavered.

"And what are Madhav's plans?" she asked.

He was shy with her, not meeting her eyes or looking her in the face, though it was he who served the three of them. Her mother would never have allowed that. Serving at mealtimes had always been her exclusive duty. Saru had been allowed to serve the salt, pickles, chutneys . . . that was all.

"I'm thinking of accountancy."

"Why that?"

"I like figures and calculations. It's exact and . . . " he hesitated and brought out the word apologetically, "clean." And there, she thought, speaks the Brahmin in you. I never was a Brahmin in that sense. I hated all of it, the meaningless rituals, the rites, the customs. They seemed to stifle me. Was that why I got out? Or was it because I met Manu?

"Why not maths then?"

"Maths . . . " he shrugged and suddenly smiled. "Accountancy is more paying, isn't it?"

"He's a sensible boy," Baba said and smiled again. Just like a fond parent, she thought. And her eyes were bleak.

"And your father?"

"Oh, he's reconciled to the idea now. After all, I have three more brothers."

Now she laughed. "The blessings of a large family. The children carry lighter burdens." She did not notice her father's face as she said that. She was thinking . . . There were only the two of us. And when Dhruva died, there was only me. But if there were any burdens on me, I threw them off. And she died alone. Did she mind that? Was it not her failure too?

There was a curious air of ease about the three of them after that. And when, lunch over, her father said, "Saru, will you clear up?" it was as if she had been accepted. Saru . . . he had said her name for the first time.

As she collected the not-dirty* things first . . . the salt, the pickles, curds and ghee, her earlier training coming back to her . . . and then piled up the dirty vessels outside the back door, she could hear the two of them talking in the outside hall.

Disinherited . . . the word came into her mind. And then she laughed at herself, thinking of how easily she had left all this behind. But then, I had him and I had my anger, and I wanted nothing more. But now, when this shabby old house meant nothing to her, why did she have this feeling of being disinherited? Though she laughed at herself, the anger was real. She could not rid herself of it by ridiculing herself. Resolutely she walked out of the kitchen, butting into their conversation. The boy was talking loudly and easily about something that had happened at college, and it was as strange to her as if she had found them exchanging obscenities.

He never took any interest in my school or college. He left it all to her. And she never really cared. Not after Dhruva's death. I just didn't exist for her. I died long before I left home.

"Baba," she said, interrupting them, "I want to show you some photographs of my children. Would you like to see them?"

"Oh, have you brought their photographs? Yes, yes, I'd like to see them. Let me see."

There was something apologetic about his tone, as if he knew he had been remiss in not showing any curiosity about his grandchildren.

"I often wondered . . . " and again he left his sentence incomplete.

"Now?"

"Yes, yes, of course, now."

She knelt down in front of her suitcase, which, like a home-less refugee, still lay desolately in the hall . . . which is my room? I have none . . . and opening it, took the photographs out of the side flap. The open suitcase for some reason brought back her home vividly. She hastily closed it again. And even as she did so, she had a curious sensation of having done this thing before. Of having had such a conversation with Baba once, in some other time, with Madhav standing and listening to both of them, just as he was doing now. With the same air of patience, as if he knew for certain that she was only a fleet-ing interruption, that she would have to go away, leaving him and Baba to continue their conversation.

Madhav? But I didn't even know Madhav existed until today! And yet, how is it that I know for certain that it was this way, Madhav talking to Baba, until I went in and interrupted them? As she clicked the lock of her suitcase, it came to her. Not Madhav. It had been Dhruva. Sitting on Baba's lap and talking to him. And I had thought . . . I must show Baba some-thing, anything, to take his attention away from Dhruva sitting on his lap. I must make him listen to me, not to Dhruva. I must make him ignore Dhruva. But she had not succeeded. Or had she? The memory became hazy again.

This time, however, Baba turned away from Madhav to her. He gave her all his attention. Or rather he gave it to the photo-graphs, looking at them intently, as if searching for something. Trying to make up, maybe, for his earlier indifference. But no, his interest was genuine. He could not pretend. He had never exhib-ited what he didn't have . . . neither love, nor anger, nor dislike.

"This is Renu."

"Renu?" Madhav asked, looking her in the face for the first time. His eyes, she saw, were grey, like the sea in the monsoon. But without its turbulence.

"Renu ka, my daughter."

Her father gave her an odd look as she said the words. But the words were merely explanatory, not proud. And her face wore a puzzled look.

Renu. My daughter. She stares at me critically at times, a cold, shrewd, objective observer behind those little girl's eyes of hers. And I become nervous, unsure, uncertain of myself. She does not talk much. She reminds me of a room whose doors are closed. Nothing emerges, neither her joys nor her sorrows. And I sense a lack of feeling, of sensitivity in her. But when she sits down with a paper and pencil, it is as if she suddenly becomes articulate. One drawing of hers is for me unforgettable. Trees, tall and straight, towering almost, drawn in black crayons. Scarcely any gap between the trees. A feeling of brooding darkness. Of frightening confinement. And in the foreground a child. Smiling. Smirking, rather.

What is this, Renu?
A forest. A thick forest.
And this child . . . why is she laughing?
Because she feels like it. You see . . .

No more. Just a closed up face.

She had not slept that night. My child, my daughter, draws not sunny gardens, colourful flowers, cheerful sunrises and playing children, but frightful pictures like this.

"She has a look of Kaku about her," Madhav said, after staring at the photograph.

"Kaku?" she inquired in turn.

He seemed astonished by her not understanding.

It was Baba who explained. "Your mother."

"Oh!" And then, swiftly, vehemently, "Oh no, she's not like her. Not like her at all."

And yet she knew how often Renu reminded her of her

mother. Her quiet watchfulness. The feeling she gave you of being weighed up, criticised, possibly rejected.

"And this is Abhijit," she went on, almost snatching Renu's photograph from Madhav's grasp.

"How old is he?"

"Five. Nearly six."

It was now Baba's turn. "He looks like . . . " He began and left it at that.

"Yes, I know," she said hastily, as if to stop him from going on.

And so the two of them tiptoed past the body. Or maybe, after so many years, there was no body at all. Just a chalked outline showing where the body had once been. Resentment rose in her again. Why can't you accept my children as themselves? Why do you have to link them to the past, to others I have nothing to do with?

"Is he troublesome?" Baba smiled at her easily for the first time. As if in this role, as a mother, he could meet her without awkwardness. It was only as a daughter that she made him uncomfortable.

"Sometimes. He's stubborn."

And full of secrets. Yes, but a child is always like that. Full of secrets. Secret wishes. Secret fears. And yet the secrets of a child are as light as leaves. Blown away in the very second of opening the door. But Abhi . . . ? Abhi. I chose the name myself. And yet, so often the tongue slips and I call him Dhruva. And Renu , watchful and sharp, a woman despite her young age, never fails to ask . . . Who is Dhruva, mummy? Who is Dhruva?

Why do I never tell her . . . Dhruva was my kid brother who died when he was seven. He was drowned. I watched him drown. And my mother said . . . why didn't you die? Why are you alive and he dead?

"Sarutai," he used to call her. She had hated it. "Don't call me Sarutai," she would say angrily. "All right," he would reply equably. And call out the next minute, whether out of stupidity, forgetfulness or wicked perversity, even now she could not guess . . . "Sarutai, wait for me. I'm coming."

"Hurry up then. And don't call me Sarutai."

Just three years between them. But what immense advantages those three years gave her. She had ruled over him completely. No dictatorship could have been more absolute. And yet he had had his revenges. Moments of triumph. Of cruel gloating. Of the knowledge that he could do anything he wanted with their mother. That even Baba would come out of his shell for him.

But he had been loyal. Completely loyal. He had never given her away to their parents. Not once. Their bond, their pact, had been secure against treachery. It was she, on the contrary, who had so often been treacherous. Running away from him.

Avoiding him.

Wait for me, Sarutai, wait for me. I'm coming too.

It was over. They had looked at the photographs, smiled over them, commented on whom the children resembled. She had nothing more to offer. She put the photographs back in their flap. Baba picked up his newspaper and said, "Go and lie down for a while, Saru."

"Don't you remember, I slept nearly two hours in the morning. I can't sleep again."

"Just lie down anyway. Have a rest."

"By the way," she suddenly remembered, "who cleans the vessels?"

"Madhav." The boy had gone in to get his books. He had to go back to college. "He does it after coming home. We have water in the taps only after four anyway."

You cook and he cleans. It's a partnership, wordless,

uncomplaining and perfect. A tacit understanding. As all good partnerships should be.

How does it feel when your wife earns not only the butter but the bread as well?

The bitch. Why did she have to say that? It was that day that it began. Or did it? Damn that bloody bitch anyway . . .

She came out of her thoughts with a start. Private profanity often gave her a kind of release. It had been amusing once, a face and an inner language so much at variance. But nowadays it left a bitter aftertaste in her mouth.

"I'll wash up today," she said.

"You!" Madhav had come back into the hall with his books.

"No, you can't."

"Why not?"

"You're not used to such work," he said awkwardly.

"No, I'm not." Her smile made the boy uncomfortable. "I don't even have to fold my clothes or put them away."

"Who does it for you?"

Their eyes, the boy's and the man's, curiously alike now, were not envious. They held the simple wonder of a child: How do you live? I'd like to know, though I don't really care. It makes no difference, to me, to the way I live.

"My *bai**. Janakibai. She came to me when Abhi was born. She looks after all of us now. Look at my hands."

She held them out. White, soft and clean. Oddly, it was the boy who realised that there was self-contempt or vanity behind the gesture.

"But you're a doctor. You don't have to work with your hands," he said, kindly, as if reassuring and comforting a child.

"Lady doctor," she corrected him, and her tone was now frankly mocking. "Yes, I'm a lady doctor."

4.

It was such an unpropitious beginning, maybe I should have been warned. There were despairing moments, days of unbearable tension and anxiety. I had come away from my parents in a fever of excitement after the last battle. The die was cast, the decision taken, my boats burnt. There could be no turning back. Then, this ridiculous anticlimax. To defy your parents and family, to resolve to get married in spite of them, and then to be obstructed by the lack of a home!

It was Manu who had been adamant about that. "I'm not going to have us live apart," he said. "I refuse to continue this way, meeting an hour or so each evening. We must have a place of our own, even if it's just a room."

And that was all we had finally. That too had seemed a miracle. His face, when he came to me in the canteen that day, told me the news before he did.

"I've got it," he said. Dragging the chair closer to me, he sat straddling it, staring at me as he spoke, as if to watch every expression of mine. "But promise me you won't refuse it."

"What's the catch?"

"It's just one room. In a *chawl**. You have to share the toilet. Want to back out? Wait, Saru, don't look like that, think it over. And this too. We may not get a place for months, maybe years, with the little I can afford to pay. You know I've been doing nothing but house-hunting for the last few months. This is the only possibility. You know Shridhar, don't you? No, you don't. It's his place. His wife is pregnant, she's going home to

her parents for her confinement. And he's being sent somewhere for training for a year. Which means that the place is
ours for the whole of next year. Fully furnished, down to the
pots and pans, brooms and brushes. We can move in next
month. What do you say?" He looked at me across the dirty
table littered with cigarette butts and brown teacup stains.
And at the look in his eyes, I suddenly panicked. I was eleven
again and trapped in that strange room with those strange men
and that friend of mine.

What was her name? I just can't remember. But she was
three years older than me and ours was one of those condescending (on her part), adoring, worshipping (on my part),
friendships that blossom so suddenly and unexpectedly
between girls. As our friendship progressed, she let me in on
some of her secrets. One of which was boys who gave her
things, a box of face powder, a hanky, a bottle of nail polish, a
pair of shiny earrings. These boys lived in a hostel a short distance away from our school and she sneaked in, she told me,
during the long break.

She took me with her once. We sat on a bed in an untidy
room smelling of sweaty clothes and hair oil. And the boys,
three of them, men to me at that age, sat in their vests and trousers and said things to her that made her giggle and shake her
head and behave in what, I secretly thought, was a very silly
manner. Most of the talk went over my head, and finally, after
she had ignored my numerous hints, I got up to go, bored, and
also uncomfortable somehow about the atmosphere in the
room. As I reached the door, one of the boys went swiftly past
me and stood barring my way. I can still remember his face
smiling at me, his body immensely huge, blotting out everything else, his odour crowding out other sensations. I can
remember too my heart pounding in my chest, and my fear . . .
child though I was, I ceased to be one for the moment . . . I
vaguely knew that my fear had something to do with the fact

that he was a male and I a female. He bent down, bringing his face closer to mine, terrifying me. At the same time his arms came away from the door frame. Suddenly I ducked under his arms and got away. Once away from his physical presence, it was as if I had been released from the fear and the strangeness in myself. I was a child again.

"I'm going," I shouted, and yes, now I remember, her name was Vijaya. "I'm going, Vijaya." I yelled.

And the boy's face changed too. He seemed to realise that I was nothing but a child.

"Go, baby," he said. "Your Vijaya will come later."

But I was no girl of eleven now. Why did I feel trapped when he spoke of our marriage? Was this not Manu whom I loved and who loved me?

"When we're together, it's Heaven wherever we are," he said.

It was silly, it was absurd, it was ridiculous, I thought. I felt humble, sometimes a fraud. It was impossible that I could mean so much to any human being. It was impossible that such things could happen to me. They happened only to girls in movies and books, not to girls like me. And yet, I could not doubt his love. He cared for my feelings as no one ever had.

"It's going to be painful for you," he said to me one day, looking at me with what seemed like compassion.

"What?"

"Cutting yourself off from your parents."

"No." My response was instant and brusque, like that of a rude child. "Never painful."

"That's not possible, Saru. I know you must be suffering. I only hope I can make up for it."

Suffering? Painful? I was impatient with the words because they meant nothing to me. After my last confrontation with my parents, I had already detached myself from them. For me, they were already the past and meant nothing.

"Shall I tell you something?"

My hand was on the table between us. He held it and gently turned it over so that the palm faced upwards. And, with the wrong end of his pen, he gently wrote something on it, something I presently realised was my name, Saru, over and over again.

"Tell," he smiled at me.

"Have you seen a baby being born? Do you know, Manu how easy it is to cut the umbilical cord and separate the baby from the mother? Ligate, cut, and it's done. There's scarcely any bleeding either. It's as if nature knows the child must be detached from the parent. No, Manu, for me there will be no trauma, no bleeding."

"So long as you aren't hurt . . . "

Yes, he loved me. Why then this fear, this trapped feeling?

Clinically, rationally, I analysed my own feelings. It was not sex, not fear of sex. I was after all, I told myself, a medical student, who knew all there is to know of male and female and what goes on between them. True, we had been so far, considering our opportunities, almost impossibly innocent in our relationship, never going beyond holding hands. Not even on the beach where we found ourselves surrounded by huddled shapes, soft whispers, sounds of suggestive laughter and kisses. Once or twice we passed another couple wordlessly, passionately locked together. And yet we stayed physically apart. It's my painful middle class inhibitions, I told myself, making marriage the open sesame of all enjoyment for me.

But when we got married it was like nothing I had ever imagined. After the first moment of apprehension . . . a purely physical response, or lack of it, rather . . . there was never any withholding in me. I became in an instant a physically aroused woman, with an infinite capacity for loving and giving, with a passionate desire to be absorbed by the man I loved. All the clichés, I discovered, were true, kisses were soft and unbearably sweet, embraces hard and passionate, hands caressing and tender, and loving, as well as being loved, was an intense joy. It was as if little nerve ends of pleasure had sprung up all over my body.

"Who said about some place . . . 'if there is a heaven on earth it is this' . . . or something like that?"

"Ignorant little medico," he said, tickling me with the ends of my hair, "that was Shah Jehan. It's written in the Red Fort."

"I'd like to put up a plaque here with those words."

"Here? You mean on the staircase, so beautifully stained by *paan?* Or near the toilets smelling of all the perfumes of Arabia?"

"You know what I mean. Oh, Manu, don't!"

"Don't what?"

"Don't stop."

I was insatiable, not for sex, but for love. Each act of sex was a triumphant assertion of our love. Of *my* being loved. Of *my* being wanted. If I ever had any doubts, I had only to turn to him and ask him to prove his love for me. And he would . . . again and again and again.

It was Heaven, in spite of the corridors smelling of urine, the rooms with their dank sealed-in odours, women with inquisitive, unfriendly eyes, men with lascivious stares. And we were happy.

But why is happiness always so unreal? Why does it always seem an illusion? It is grief that has a bulk, a weight, a substance and stays real even after years. Happiness is so evanescent, nothing is left of it. Sensations and feelings. So that all that I can remember of that time is the way days unfolded themselves. More leisurely. That life became more vivid, painted in deeper colours. And in contrast, the outside world became vaguer, inhabited by grey ghosts who passed us by soundlessly, invisible. And if they did not exist for us, we did not exist for them either. No one ever spoke to us. We were left severely alone.

And then, one day, things changed. It was the day there was an explosion in a factory. Burnt mutilated bodies poured in, in a horror so vast that it seemed meaningless. Feelings were blunted by the very immensity of the catastrophe. There was no time, anyway, either to think or feel. The world consisted of bodies from which I drew blood, bodies into which I transfused blood, bodies on which I did venesections, bodies to be dressed, bodies in agony, bodies blessedly, quietly dead.

At last it was done and we were free to go home. A friend gave me a lift in her car. Thankfully I got in, too tired even to take off my bloodstained coat. I got out of the car and walked through the refuse-lined avenue, unaware even of the stink. One or two people, I vaguely noticed, smiled at me. It was unusual, for there had been no overt friendly gesture till now. I smiled back, not really caring, wanting nothing but to lie down and go off to sleep. I passed a group of women and they stopped their talk and stared at me. As I closed the door of our room, I heard the words, "lady doctor, lady doctor."s

The next evening, I had scarcely got home when there was a knock at the door. Manu opened it. I heard him ask, "Yes?" A woman's voice replied, "Is the doctor at home?" There was a pause, and Manu called out, "Saru, someone wants you." It was a woman whose child had diarrhoea. I examined the child and wrote out a prescription. The next day it happened again. "Is the doctor at home?" And the day after. And the day after that.

And there came a day when, hearing a knock at the door, Manu said, "Open it, Saru, it must be for you."

I could not see his face, I was washing up the tea things then, but his tone was certainly odd. An affected indifference . . . yes, now I know that is what was in his tone then. But I did not stop at that time to ponder it. I was too busy, I was too tired, I was too exhilarated by the dignity and importance that my status as a doctor seemed to have given me. I was young and callow, and so unused to my profession , that to have real patients come to me gave me a thrill I could scarcely hide. And so I listened to them, and examined and advised and prescribed with enthusiasm.

And now, when we walked out of our room, there were nods and smiles, murmured greetings and namastes. But they were all for me, only for me. There was nothing for him. He was almost totally ignored.

I did not notice this then. Nor, if I had, would I have known that he minded. For he revealed nothing. But I can remember how he said, "I'm sick of this place. Let's get out of here soon." And how it was that, more and more often, I found myself shrinking from his lovemaking. I thought then that the fault was mine. It was because I was tired, always too tired after my long day at the hospital. *He* was the same. Still so eager to love me, so disappointed when I refused him, that I rarely had the heart to do so. And if there were times when he was rough and abrupt with me, I put it down to the ardour of his love.

In any case, these occasions were rare enough. So rare that I could easily forget them. But now I know that it was there it began . . . this terrible thing that has destroyed our marriage. I know this, too . . . that the human personality has an infinite capacity for growth. And so the esteem with which I was surrounded made me inches taller. But perhaps, the same thing that made me inches taller made him inches shorter. He had been the young man and I his bride. Now I was the lady doctor and he was my husband.

$A + b$ they told us in mathematics is equal to $b + a$. But here $a + b$ was not, definitely not, equal to $b + a$. It became a monstrously unbalanced equation, lopsided, unequal, impossible. But is that the only reason, or would it have happened in any case, what happened to us later, he being what he is and I being what I am? I have a feeling I will never know the answer.

5.

There was no more curiosity left. She knew now how her father lived. She had imagined her parents to be symbiotic, but here he was, almost the same as before, silent, reserved and withdrawn. And yet she knew that he was in some way content, and that to him his life was, in spite of its semblance of emptiness, full. Her coming home, she now realised, had made no difference to him. He had soon gotten over his initial awkwardness and embarrassment. His lack of curiosity about her motive for coming home, or about the length of her stay was, she felt, the result of his indifference to her presence. It was Madhav, who, without speaking, showed some curiosity. She often felt that he was on the brink of asking her . . . why have you come?

The loving daughter rushing home to comfort the afflicted father, Manu had mocked, laughing, his facetiousness barely concealing the underlying bitterness. She could admit it to herself now that she knew she had failed. It was not to comfort her father that she had come. It was for herself. But what had she hoped to find?

The urge to confide in someone, to talk to someone, was growing in her. Often she had found herself staring at people, sizing them up, thinking . . . are you on my side? Are you? And, even more often, waking up at night with a start, thinking . . . I am alone. Knowing, with a kind of cold hopelessness, that it was not a dream, but real. That she was awake, not dreaming, and was truly alone. That there was no one who could comfort her. That, perhaps, there never would be anyone.

For her, there was not even god. At one time she had feverishly clutched the thought of god to herself. She had gone in for *pujas,* fasts, rituals and mumbled prayers. But there was no comfort in it at all. Just the feeling of being a fraud, an actress acting out a role she didn't believe in.

Yet in the daytime, when the terrors which came with the dark disappeared, there was always the hope. There would be someone. One could never be so totally deserted, after all. And yet, she had the dismal feeling that she had frozen herself into an isolated, lonely suffering she could never break out of. When she came home, she had thought . . . I will break out of it. I will talk to Baba.

But it was already too late to talk to Baba. The moment when she could have spoken had already passed. May be she could have spoken on the very day of her arrival. Now, when conversation between them meant . . . Saru, have your bath. Why hasn't Madhav come home as yet? Is this today's paper? how could she break into this with . . . Baba, I'm unhappy. Help me, Baba, I'm in trouble. Tell me what to do.

It was impossible. Worse, it seemed indecent. Like removing your clothes in public. And there was something more. The fear that by speaking she would be unlocking the door of a dark room in which someone had been murdered. That by opening that door, she would be revealing to the world the pathetic, lifeless body of the victim, grotesque in an enforced death. And, her greatest fear was that they would all know the dead body to be his, her husband's. They would know too what she herself did . . . that it was she who was the murderer.

No, she would say nothing to her father. But oddly, at moments, she had wild thoughts of confiding in Madhav. Of telling him everything and asking him for his advice. With Madhav, her relationship had advanced much more than she could have imagined on the first day when he had evaded looking her in the face. He had been shy, wary and reserved. Fascinated too, as his quick, furtive glances had shown. But his self-possession, remarkable for his age, soon came back. He called her "Sarutai" now. She liked it, wondering why she had so resented it once.

Don't call me Sarutai.
Ai says I must call you that.
I don't care what Ai says. Don't call me Sarutai.

Perhaps it was their talk of flowers that broke through the last of Madhav's reserve. It was Madhav who had planted the hollyhocks. She knew it when she saw him digging, with painful grunts, another small plot next to the hollyhocks.

"So it's you who's the gardener," she said, going out to him. "I should have guessed. But why these flowers?"

He smiled at her, pleased by her interest in what he was doing. "Somebody gave me these seeds. I didn't even know what they were. What are they called?"

"Hollyhocks in English."

"Hollyhocks," he repeated, as if memorising the name. And she knew he would never forget.

"Look," he pulled a grubby envelope out of his pocket, "I've got some more seeds. What are these? Do you know?"

She peered at the small dark seeds, almost as pathetic as newborns, with microscopic bits of fluff on them. How could she guess? They were stubbornly discreet, hiding their identity from her.

"I don't know." She had suddenly lost interest. "I don't know much about gardening. Plant them and see. "That's the only way."

Then she asked him, "But why only flowers, Madhav?"

"I don't know. At home we have a small plot. This much,

maybe. My father grows things. Rather, he makes us children grow them. Chillies, coriander, leafy vegetables, things like that. Things you can use in cooking. I always wanted to plant flowers. He never let me." The sunlight fell full on his face, making the fair skin almost transparent. She could not avoid the pang of envy that shot through her.

Don't go out in the sun. You'll get even darker.
Who cares?
We have to care if you don't. We have to get you married.
I don't want to get married.
Will you live with us all your life?
Why not?
You can't.
And Dhruva?
He's different. He's a boy.

Madhav had suddenly stopped digging, and wiping his face, said awkwardly, but decisively, as if he had forced himself to get over his reluctance to say whatever he was going to say.

"Sarutai, has Kaka told you we have early dinner tonight?"

"No, he hasn't. Why?"

"He and I . . . we play *carrom** on Saturday nights."

She took the hint. "Well, I better go in and start the cooking then."

The day seemed to stretch into infinity here, with nothing but mealtimes to break it up into bearable fragments. Even the old grandfather clock seemed to take a rest between two dongs, dragging out not only the minutes and hours but the sounding and knowing of them as well. And yet, she did not find it dull. Instead she wondered how she had endured the hectic pace of her life for so long.

She had had no desire to do anything at first. Not even to participate in the household chores which the two men seemed to manage so competently. She had now begun cooking the evening meal. Nothing much . . . just rice, dal and one vegetable. Even that was an ordeal in what now seemed a primitive kitchen, with its Primus stove that hissed like a demon and yet took endlessly long to cook anything. The tap was in one corner, so low that you had to crouch to wash up anything, the cement floor below it cracked and black. There was no cooking platform. She had to squat on the ground to do the cooking. She marvelled now at the way her mother had produced meal after meal from that place. She had been, she remembered dispassionately, a good cook.

After dinner Madhav dragged out the *carrom* board. It was, it seemed, a ritual that the two men approached with utmost seriousness. Before starting their play, they asked her, awkwardly, like tutored, polite children, "Want to join?" Hoping, undoubtedly, that she wouldn't. She shook her head. "I'll just sit and watch." She sat and watched, noticing that Baba was like a child when he played, collecting the coins he had successfully put into the pockets with an eagerness that reminded her of Abhi. But he was not a particularly good player. His fingers quivered as he took aim, for what seemed an unconscionably long time. And then, he missed. Madhav, on the other hand, played well, winning with a ruthlessness that filled her with envy.

I had it too once, this desire to win, to excel, to be better than the others. When did I lose it?

The clickety clackety of the coins on the wooden board in that normally silent house was like a little tinkle in a vast emptiness. A parody of gaiety that was somehow pathetic. When the game was over, silence engulfed them once more. And now, for some reason, it filled her with a nagging discomfort.

She remembered a wedding she had gone to with a friend. It was the friend's sister who was to get married, and she had fought fiercely, passionately, to go, to stay with her friend for two days. She remembered the bliss when she had won. And the painful realisation later of how little her victory meant. For her friend, the only one she knew there, treacherously deserted her for others, cousins and closer friends. She had been scrupulously excluded from the tight intimate little groups that seemed to her so happy and purposeful. She alone, it seemed, had nothing to do, no one to talk to. Alone, desolate, humiliated by her isolation, she had attached herself to one group or another, hoping to be taken for one of them. Hoping passionately that she looked as if she belonged. But it never worked. The only time she did belong to a group was when they all gathered together for a meal, a ritual. And then, when it was over, the crowd dissolved into people who had nothing to do with her, shattering the semblance of belonging, of togetherness.

It was the same now when the game ended. Baba went back to his room, his book, his radio; Madhav, after tidily putting away the board, to his studies. And she was left alone. Reluctantly she was moving towards her bed, when Madhav called out, "Sarutai . . . " Thankfully she turned round. "I want to show you something. I wanted to do it in the evening, then I forgot. Look," he held a magazine in his hands which he opened out to a page of photographs, "isn't this your . . . your husband?" She peered at the photograph he was pointing at, and exclaimed, "Why, yes, its Manu!"

The boy flushed and she wondered why until she realised that it was perhaps the fact that she had said her husband's name. To him it was, maybe, like a revelation of some intimacy of marriage. She knew that in his home, his mother would never call his father by name. It would be . . . "your father."

Maybe it's safer to keep a man in that one place . . . as the father of your children. But will he consent to stay there forever? In the daytime, yes; but at night?

She shuddered violently and then, with determination, forced herself to listen to the boy. He had conquered his embarrassment and was saying. "I found this today . . . " But her attention had wandered again. She knew now what it was that had nagged at her since she saw Madhav. Why she had found his face faintly familiar.

"He looks a bit like you, doesn't he?"

"Like me?"

The boy's astonishment was so ludicrous she laughed.

"No, I don't mean that way. Not physically. He's much taller than you. He's five foot nine." she said, her preciseness mocking the very fact she was stating.

And he used to be slim. Very slim. Not any more. He has put on weight. And that has, somehow, not made him more of what he was, but less. As if that extra flesh has blotted out something else. He no longer has that keen looking-into-you gaze he once had. Actually, he's still as good looking as he used to be. But why is it that he no longer seems an attractive man? I'm not the only one to think that way. I rarely see any woman giving him a second look. And it isn't just because his chin is no longer sharp, but rounded, or that his hair is perceptibly thinning on top. No, it's something more than that. Something missing in the eyes, in the face, in the man himself. And, oh god, maybe I'm the one who's taken it away from him!

"No, I don't mean a physical resemblance. You couldn't be more unlike."

It's something else. A look about you that he once had as well. The same desire to get out of your background. To break away into something else. You grow flowers because your father never did. And Manu will never let me buy a bike for the kids because his father once kept a cycle shop.

"He was . . ." why the past tense? Was he dead? " . . . a poet, wasn't be?"

"Yes, he was."

She emphasised the past tense herself, knowing she was being cruel, but unable to help herself. And then, very deliberately, she changed the subject.

"What magazine is that?"

"It's an old issue of the college magazine. I found a pile of them lying in the library the other day and was looking through them when I found this."

His explanation was as glib as if he'd rehearsed it to himself earlier. Noticing that she was incurious about his actions and motives, he went on more confidently: "I found his photo in one or two other issues too."

"Oh yes, he was in it pretty often. After all, he was editor of the magazine for two years."

And she smiled. The boy wondered at the quality of her smile. It was, though he did not know that, like a crack in her air of deliberate composure, her poise, both of which seemed brittle. As if they would shatter at any moment.

6

He has, how odd it seems to think of it now, one of those students who are set apart from the others, with an aura of distinction about them. He was a postgraduate student when I entered college, and one of the Known Names by then. It wasn't just that he was a good student, academically I mean; he was also the secretary of the Literary Association, actively associated with the Debating Union and the life and soul of the Dramatic Society. And, in addition to all this, a budding writer and a poet of promise, with some poems already published in magazines.

My friend Smita was one of the many who had a girlish crush on him. It was Smita who dragged me that day to the inauguration of the Literary Society.

"Come on, I say, Saru. He'll be there, you know."

She called him "he" with a sickening coyness that made me laugh. "I'm not coming. You know I'm not interested in these things," I told her bluntly. And I wasn't. To me college meant lectures in the morning, practicals in the afternoon, exams every six months and medical college at the end of two years; if I worked hard enough and got a first class, that is.

"Can't you raise your head from your books once in a while?" Smita asked me irritably.

No, I couldn't. I had to work hard, to be a success, to show them . . . her . . . something. What? I didn't know. But I had to make myself secure so that no one would ever say to me again . . . why are you alive? Why was I alive? The answer, I then imagined, lay in hard work and success. How naive we can be when young! I could weep now with pity for the child that I was.

But, for some strange reason, I went with Smita that day. Sometimes I can almost believe those men and women who speak of fate and destiny and of something being "written on your forehead." Why else did I succumb to Smita that day?

The hall was crowded when we went in. It was because, Smita told me . . . and she was always *well* informed about such things . . . a fiction writer, popular among the magazine-reading public, had been invited to be the chief guest. But for me his face was . . . is . . . a blank. So was . . . is . . . the room, the speeches, the audience.

I can remember the table, though, with its white cover with a large tear in it which someone had tried to camouflage and failed miserably. But, this apart, he was the only person I saw that day. Yet, when I thought of him later, I could not remember the whole of him. It was as if the sight of him had been so overwhelming that I could not take all of it in. Instead, bits of his face clung to my mind like barnacles. As if they were sentences in my book I had underlined with a pencil, writing in the margin, v. i., very important. Straight dark thick eyebrows. A firm chin. (And whoever said that a receding chin is a sign of weakness?) Full lips, almost as full as a woman's. And that mannerism of his, of pushing the hair back from his forehead with one hand, showing off his slender, long fingers. Yes, they stayed with me, these things, though the significance of it did not come home to me then.

A few days later, Smita, giggling, pointed out something to me in a magazine she was reading.

"What is it?" I asked impatiently, making entries in my journal, "A poem? I don't read poems."

No, I never did. I had no time for poetry. And besides I found poetry foolish, artificial, unreal.

"But just look Saru, look who's written this one."

It was signed Manohar.

Smita giggled again. "It's him." I could almost see the adoring circles around the "him."

"And this 'Padmini' he writes about . . . you know who she is, don't you?"

"No, I don't. How will I know all these things? I know nothing except what you tell me."

"Okay, okay, don't get irritated. I won't keep you from your first class any longer. If you're not interested . . . "

"Oh, come on, tell. You know you're dying to tell me." And I was dying to know. But I wouldn't give myself away. It was as if I became, in one moment, devious and cunning, the female as she is supposed to be.

"It's that Jayanti in the Sr. B.A. Haven't you seen her? Walks with her nose in the air because she's good looking. If you ask me, what has she got but a light complexion? Just because she's fair . . . "

Smita's complexion was a sore point with her. I laughed. "All right, so it's that not-so-good-looking Jayanti."

"But he's crazy about her. That's what everyone says. Now I can believe it. Read this . . . "

I read it. It was a love poem. Unabashedly a love poem. It created a ripple of excitement throughout the college. Everyone knew who had written it and who the inspiration for it was. Smita pointed her out to me in the ladies' room a few days later, with sly pinches, nudges and whispers. She was, I noticed, very fair, tall, slim, self-consciously aware of her looks and disgustingly coquettish, her earrings dancing with the constant movement of her neck.

That evening I went home and tried to imitate the way she had done her hair. And failed miserably. In a fury, I oiled my hair, and slicked it into one tight plait. And went to college, knowing how unattractive I looked, with my plump high cheeks, my oiled hair, my unpowdered face with its spattering of pimples. There was even, I remember, a kind of triumphant misery in knowing how awful I looked, how unlike, terribly unlike, his "Padmini." Yet what does it matter, I asked myself savagely, how I look? He will never see me, he will never know me, we shall never meet.

As if I had been tempting Fate by thinking that, we met just a short while later. Smita had managed, by her usual unsubtle policy of pushing herself ruthlessly forward, to get a minor role in the play being produced for College Day. He was directing it and Smita took me with her one day to watch a rehearsal. He opened the door for us himself. He had just recovered from some illness . . . infective hepatitis, I learnt later . . . and looked gaunt and ravaged. A scarf wrapped round his throat gave him an air, not of ill health, but of distinction accentuated by his long hair and pale pallor.

"What do you want?" he asked me rudely.

I gulped, while Smita rushed to explain.

"She's my friend. She wants to watch the rehearsal."

"You know I don't like idle spectators. They spoil the mood."

"Oh, please, let her come in and sit down. She won't disturb us, I promise. She won't say a word. Please!" Suddenly he smiled. "looks as if she's dumb, anyway. Okay, come on in. But absolutely quiet. One word and" he whistled, "you're out."

I nodded, as if I had become truly aphonic, and tried to make myself as inconspicuous as possible. I needn't have bothered. Nobody looked at me, except Smita once or twice. They were so whole-heartedly absorbed in what they were doing that they infused the bare room, the scarred benches and dingy walls, with an atmosphere of gaiety and enjoyment. Once again, the others were . . . are . . . faceless, nameless non-entities to me. He was the only person I saw. His effortless control over the others, his anger at their mistakes, his smiles that came and went in a flash . . . these were the things I memorised this time. And once, I remember this even today, he began to recite some poetry, falling into it easily, unselfconsciously, some lines that were appropriate to what he had been saying to the heroine earlier. When he finished, there was mock-serious applause, and cries of "*Wah wah*." I was silent, neither laughing nor applauding; but something inside me responded to the gesture, the words with a loud cry of ecstasy. I went home in a daze.

As a child my fantasies, my dreams, had no relevance to the fact that I was a girl. The fact had not meant to me then what it would later. But as I grew up, they became the dreams of a total female. I was all female and dreamt of being adored and chosen by a superior, superhuman male. That was glory enough . . . to be chosen by that wonderful man. I saw myself humbly adoring, worshipping and being given the father-lover kind of love that was protective, condescending, yet all-encompassing and satisfying. There was no "I" then, craving recognition, satisfaction. The craving, which when it eventually came, was always to be accompanied by a feeling of guilt if the "I" dared to overreach a male, as if I was doing something that took away shreds of my femininity. That came later.

After that day, he was the figure I fantasised about, the person round whom I wove my foolish dreams. No, not dreams; just one dream really. Always the age-old feminine dream of a superior conquering male. Sometimes he was a great writer, a poet, and there were throngs around him, offering him gifts, praise, adulation. He saw me among the many, our eyes met, his carrying a secret message to mine. So that I met him alone later and offered him my small, foolish gift. And he said . . . this is more precious to me than anything else in the whole world.

Sometimes I worked with him, for him, subordinating myself so completely to him that I was nothing without him. And yet he could do nothing without me, either. At times he was imperious, at times tender, at times, even, to my own shame, passionate, though my dreams did not go beyond a kiss. Those other dreams, when my own body became at once my delight and my torment, came later. At this time a kiss was daring enough, shameful enough.

But the fantasies, the dreams, paled into ghosts before long. He was too far removed from me for my dreams to coalesce into something harder. It was like having a crush on a movie star. It was not part of my real life.

Reality was different and I never let it go, not for a moment. And that was my approaching exams, my studies, likely questions . . . the reproductive system of a frog . . . and what if I did not get a first class, after all?

7

Madhav had clearly, with a patient cunning, waited for the right moment to ask her this. Her first reaction was panic; then outrage. How dare he ask her this! It was not for this that she had come home. But Madhav's face, as he spoke, showed that he was not thinking of her at all. Only of Baba. Which was why he had waited until Baba went out and only the two of them were at home. For a moment his complete disregard of her and her feelings gave her a feeling of not existing.

"Kaka's left everything as it was," Madhav went on. "I know he's not comfortable with it, but he doesn't like to go into her room. She lay sick in that room for nearly a year. And she was in a terrible state just before they left for Bombay. She could eat nothing. Her arms were this size."

He made a small circle with thumb and forefinger.

Carcinoma stomach. People die inch by inch, bit by bit, the agony stretched out until the very last moment. But perhaps it helps, the pain. So that in the end there is nothing but pain. No dead sons, unforgiven daughters and feeble husbands. Only pain and the desire for death.

"When I look into that room I remember her suffering. How does he feel? I'd have cleared up the room myself, but since you're here now . . . "

At last her silence seemed to penetrate. His voice trailed away and he appeared confused. But now she was in control of herself.

"Why not?" she said wryly, amused at the thought of this strange boy pleading on her father's behalf.

When she spoke of it to Baba that night, he gave Madhav a sharp look as if he knew the boy was behind it. Madhav's face was bland and disinterested. And Baba turned back to her saying, "Why not? I should have done it long back, but somehow . . . It's all in order, actually. She made me clear it up before we left for Bombay. She could do nothing herself then, but she told me what to do and I did it."

His matter of fact tone astonished her. And she wondered whether his unusual volubility spoke of relief. As if he could now admit to himself that she was dead. As if he had been drifting all these days, putting off thinking about what had happened, living in a world where she was neither alive nor dead.

"Do it tomorrow," he said. "Do it tomorrow."

And lifting up the edge of his dhoti, he blew a loud honk into it, like putting a full stop to be subject.

He went out unusually early the next morning. Cap on head, stick and bag in hands, he came to her saying, "I'm going out. Everything has been done. There's only the rice. Will you . . . ?"

"I'll do it," she said. The morning meal was his job. He must have got up earlier than usual to get it over with. She knew he didn't want to be at home when she did what she had to do.

As she entered the room and opened the large almirah, she had a vague sense of being a child again. She remembered how she had, when she wanted to take something out of the almirah without her mother's knowledge, quietly, stealthily pushed down the large handle, praying her mother wouldn't hear the squeak it gave out. But she always did. And even now, as it squeaked, she expected to hear her mother's voice calling out, "Saru! What are you doing in my cupboard? Leave it alone and get out of there. At once!"

And later, as a growing girl, she had come to look at herself in the full-length mirror on the door of the almirah, willing herself, almost passionately, to be pretty. She could remember saying to herself in the mirror, "I'm ugly, I'm ugly." Hoping the mirror would contradict her, tell her she was not ugly, she was pretty. For if she wasn't, how could it happen to her, the fairy-tale ending that had to happen . . . of a man falling in love with her and marrying her?

As she opened the almirah, there was that peculiar smell of mothballs, attar and rose water. And there were all those things that had seemed such splendid treasures to her as a child. No jewellery, though. What had he done with it? The silverware was there, however, tarnished and black from long disuse. A few glasses and one water container. Small bowls. The *attar* tray. The rose water sprinkler. These had been regularly brought out each year for the *haldi-kumkums** held at home. The one time when she became more important than Dhruva. The daughter of the house who could apply attar with tiny swabs of cotton to the backs of women's hand. Sprinkle rose water over them and distribute the flowers.

And Dhruva crying . . . Let me. I want to. Ai, look, she won't let me.

Sssh, Dhruva, let that alone. It's not for you. That's for girls. So there!

Putting out her tongue, making a face at him. Triumphant. Exultant.

So there! Not for you. Only for girls.

And here, in this bundle, tied up in an old soft cotton, was the sari her mother had worn for *haldi-kumkums.* This *Benaras** however, had been worn only for weddings and thread ceremonies. It was too heavy, all the brocade weighing it down. She had longed for a *Chanderi**.

"They're light. I'll buy one when Dhruva has his thread ceremony*."

It had never happened, neither the thread ceremony nor her *Chanderi* sari. With Dhruva's death it had all come to an end. There had been no more *pujas,* no more going for or holding *haldi-kumkums,* attending weddings or thread ceremonies.

There was another bundle here. Squares of cotton and silk, just enough for a *choli*.* Traditional auspicious token gifts to be given to married women on ceremonial occasions. She remembered being invited by a friend to a ceremony held in the eighth month of her pregnancy. The mother had done all the prescribed rituals for the pregnant daughter, ending up with the gifts of sari and blouse piece, given to the girl along with a coconut, *paan-supari** and grains of rice, all of which the girl had held awkwardly in the end of her sari against the bulge of her body. Suddenly at the sight of the two, the mother and daughter, she had had tears in her eyes. I never had this. So many deprivations, she wondered now why that one had hurt so much?

A packet full of photographs. One of the two of them, her parents, obviously taken in a studio soon after marriage. She sitting stiff, unsmiling in a chair, he on the arm of it, equally stiff, the two of them a pair of puppets, posing there because they had been told to. And how strange, they were like this even when I left home and went away . . . a pair of strangers posing together because they had been told to do so. There were one or two photographs of Baba when he was in college. He looked strange and unfamiliar in trousers and shirt that left his neck open and somehow vulnerable, the very tilt of his head proclaiming a different man. The photographer's name embossed in one corner was loud and blatant, while all the figures in the photographs seemed to have faded and aged. There were no photographs of herself, she noticed without emotion.

As if she had indeed been annihilated. No, here was one. She must have been reluctant to throw this one out because Dhruva was in this photograph too.

It had been Dhruva's birthday . . . the day came back to her with an astonishing clarity. And they had gone to the studio to be photographed. Here was one of Dhruva alone, smiling, self-consciously pleased with himself in his new clothes, a *churidar**, Nehru shirt and jacket, cap on head. But in the photograph of the two of them, he looked solemn, something lost and bewildered in the eyes. And she, skinny, smiling in a painful attempt to please the photographer, showing gaps in her teeth, one hand on Dhruva's shoulder.

Put one hand on your brother's shoulder, baby. That's right. Smile now, both of you. Like that. No, no, don't push her hand away. Let it be. Now, smile again.

Perhaps she had pinched Dhruva, or squeezed his shoulder or something . . . she couldn't remember now . . . but she must have done something which accounted for the hurt look on his face.

She was smiling at the thought, still staring at the photograph, when Madhav came in.

"Have you finished, Sarutai?"

"No," Hastily she put away the photograph. "I've been sitting and staring. And look, what does one do with all these clothes of hers? Her saris, I mean."

"You could take them"

"No." Her negative was sudden and sharp. "What would I do with them, anyway. I can't wear them, they're nine yards."

"Maybe for your daughter. Just to remember her grandmother."

For Renu? To remember her grandmother?

My grandmother, mummy? I never knew I had a grandmother. Why didn't you tell me I had a grandmother? Why did I never meet her, mummy? Why did she never come here?

"A grandmother she never saw. Who she didn't know existed until a few days back. A grandmother who never cared for the child's existence. Why pretend, Madhav? I don't have any good memories of my mother. I want nothing of hers."

"She was good to me," the boy said simply. And then he saw that the words had, for some reason, angered her. She had been putting the saris away, wrapping them back in the old piece of cotton, making a dhobi's bundle of it. Now she tightened the knot of the bundle with a violent jerk. The gesture made the boy uneasy, as if he had seen something he wasn't supposed to. And then pushing away the bundle, she suddenly looked up into his face and said, "Does your mother wear nine-yard saris, Madhav?"

"Yes, she does. She's very old-fashioned."

And he smiled. The smile astonished her. *Will Abhi smile like that one day when he talks about me? Will he say with such affection . . . my mother is old-fashioned?*

But I'm not. I'm not old-fashioned. I take great care not to be left behind. My legs are weary, my heart is numb, my mind a blank, but I keep marching on. I have even cut my hair, though with that I feel I have lost one means of expressing myself. My hair had its fluctuating moods, as regularly variable as my hormonal cycle. But I cut it because I have to conform, to be like the others. Or else . . . ? Or else, . . . ?

"Then why don't you take these saris for her?"

"My mother?" He was shocked. Feebly he offered, "What will Kaka say?"

"I don't know. You ought to know. But I imagine he won't mind. He'll be glad, I suppose."

"He doesn't seem right, somehow."

Yet his eyes lingered wistfully on the saris. His mother had none like these. There never was any money for clothes; and she came last, in any case. Besides, his father despised people who took (too) much interest in clothes.

"Take them the next time you go home. I'll tell Baba about it if you're feeling shy."

It was all done. There was great relief. She had done it. She closed the almirah with a loud clang, with a feeling that she was locking in the skeleton in the cupboard. But I was the skeleton in her cupboard. And now she's dead and I'm outside. No more the skeleton in the cupboard. Or maybe, she thought confusedly, I'm now the skeleton in my own cupboard.

"The keys, Sarutai," Madhav reminded her.

The keys that her mother had clung to with such passion, never letting anyone have them. Now she could do anything she wanted with them.

And for the first time since she had heard the words . . . do you know your mother is dead? . . . the finality of it pierced her. Her mother was dead. But the realisation brought not grief but anger. A childish rage filled her. It was no use now. She would never "show her" as she had so often told herself she would.

I'll show her. I'll make her realise.

But her mother had not waited for the reply. She had gone, leaving the battle unfinished, taking victory away with herself. All her postures now crumbled into dust, into nothingness. She had been posing, making gestures of defiance at a person who wasn't there at all. She felt foolish and ridiculous.

"Look," Madhav stooped to pick up something, "here's something you forgot to put back."

It was the photograph of the two of them, Dhruva and she.

"Is this you?" He looked at it, at her, then back to the photograph again, "You've changed a lot, haven't you?"

8

I was an ugly girl. At least, my mother told me so. I can remember her eyeing me dispassionately, saying . . . you will never be good-looking. You are too dark for that.

I am ugly. I stood in front of the mirror and mouthed the words to myself. And as I stood there, she came up to me, saying . . . how many times must I call you? Looking at yourself in the mirror! I'll give you a certificate to say that you're beautiful. Will that satisfy you?

But there was hope, always the hope of a miracle. That one day I would grow up and be beautiful. The two became almost synonymous to me. Once I grew up, I would be beautiful. I would be like . . . Yes, there was the girl who came to our school for a few months, looking like an exotic bird in the midst of us ordinary sparrows. I can remember her face still. She was all bones, and beautiful. High cheekbones, a straight high nose, and eyes that looked nonchalantly at the world out of this beautiful face. I fell in love with her the instant I saw her.

Today everything has a sexual nuance, and when a girl says she loves another, it can mean only one thing. But lesbianism was an unknown word and an unknown concept to me then. And for long after. That love . . . the feeling I had for her . . . should lead to something else was also an unknown idea. It was enough to love, to gaze upon her face, to thrill in ecstasy at the sight of her. I wanted nothing more than that. To possess meant nothing. I just loved her deeply and all the more because she knew nothing about it. And then she left school and went away and it came to an end. But it was perfect while it lasted. And all because she was beautiful and I was not.

And then suddenly, some time after Dhruva died, I began to change. I had been a skinny girl, with large knees darkened by the scars of myriad falls and prominent elbows that nothing, it seemed, could soften. Now I began to put on weight. My figure began to burgeon. A softness here, a tenderness there, a strangeness all over.

"You're growing up," she would say. And there was something unpleasant in the way she looked at me, so that I longed to run away, to hide whatever part of me she was staring at. "You should be careful now about how you behave. Don't come out in your petticoat like that. Not even when it's only your father who's around."

And it became something shameful, this growing up, so that you had to be ashamed of yourself, even in the presence of your own father.

Soon after, my period began. It was strange sensation. I knew something had happened to me; and yet it was too fantastic, too frightful to be revealed to anyone, especially her. But I had no choice. I had to tell her. And then she told me what had happened and that I would bleed like this for years and years and years.

I knew about it, of course. Older girls casually dropped hints, and there were women who, looking covertly, curiously at me, asked my mother . . . has she begun? Yes, I knew it was something that happened to all girls. But not to me! It was like death. You knew it was there, you knew it happened to others, but surely it couldn't happen to you! I can remember closing my eyes and praying . . . oh god, let it not happen to me. Just this once and no more. Let there be a miracle and let me be the one female to whom it doesn't happen.

But there were no miracles. It was torture. Not just the

three days* when I couldn't enter the kitchen or the *puja* room. Not just the sleeping on a straw mat covered with a thin sheet. Not just the feeling of being a pariah, with my special cup and plate by my side in which I was served from a distance, for my touch was, it seemed, pollution. No, it was something quite different, much worse. A kind of shame that engulfed me, making me want to rage, to scream against the fact that put me in the same class as my mother.

You're a woman now, she said.

If you're a woman, I don't want to be one, I thought resentfully, watching her body. The cleft that ran down her back, a deep furrow, dividing her body sharply in two. The two buttocks sharply outlined by the kind of sari she wore, tucked in between her legs. The way her hips moved as she walked. I can remember walking as stiffly as possible, holding my pelvis rigid, willing it not to move, so that I would be as unlike her as possible.

If you're a woman, I don't want to be one.

It was only when I began to study anatomy and physiology in my first year of medicine, that I was suddenly released from a prison of fears and shames. Things fell, with a miraculous exactness, into place. I was a female. I had been born that way, that was the way my body had to be, those were the things that had to happen to me. And that was that!

After that I changed once again. If I had been a skinny child, I had become an over-plump adolescent. I can still see myself as I was when I entered medical college. Too plump, those hideous skirts that hesitated midway between the knees and my lumpy calves. Two pigtails on two sides of a round face. A religiously straight centre parting.

And then I shed all that extra weight. Maybe it was all the work, maybe it was the hostel food I never learnt to relish after my mother's cooking. But I became slim. My breasts, which had caused me agonies of self-consciousness earlier, making me feel everyone was staring at them, so that I longed to wear some kind of armour that would hide them from the world . . . now they became something to be proud of. I learnt how to dress, to accept the curve of my hips, the slimness of my waist. To take in male stares and admiration with outward equanimity and secret pride.

He didn't recognise me at first. There was a kind of triumph in that.

"Do you remember me?" I asked him in the college canteen that day. "I'm Smita's friend."

And you are Smita's Manu, I wanted to say. That was how I had thought of him. But, seeing him here, away from the old place, he became just Manu; though I didn't call him that until long after.

It was not the first time I had seen him in the canteen. I had noticed him a few times earlier. He was in the company of some senior students and interns, and though I had recognised him, I had not dared to go and speak to him. That day he was alone, waiting, apparently, for his friends to arrive. He was smoking and as we got up to go, my friends and I, he stubbed out the cigarette firmly in the overflowing ashtray. He seemed so aloof, so untouched by all the dirt and din of a college canteen, and I knew I had to speak to him. "You go ahead," I told my friends. "I'll catch up with you in a moment. There's someone I want to say hullo to."

I walked briskly to him . . . if I didn't do it now I never would . . . trying to ignore my accelerated heartbeats, my clammy hands and dry mouth. Just extra adrenalin, I told myself.

"Do you remember me? I'm Smita's friend."

He looked blank. I could not give up now, though my heart seemed to have dropped from my throat into my abdomen.

"She was acting in the play you were directing. And I came with her for a rehearsal one day. You nearly threw me out."

His eyes, which had narrowed as he stared at me with a frankness that was somehow not displeasing, now opened wide. His chair, which he had tilted up, came down, he put both his palms flat down on the table and said, "Of course! The girl who couldn't talk. And Smita pleaded for you."

I felt ridiculously happy. "And that's why you relented and let me stay."

"No, not that's why. It was to stop Smita talking."

He grinned and I grinned back, enchanted at being allowed to share a laugh with him, uncaring that poor Smita was its butt. And now, like a good child who has tried to please teacher, I had my reward.

"And because of you. The way you looked like a kid begging for a treat. But I must say . . ." The eyes changed and now he was a young man, and I a young woman, and, his eyes told me, an attractive young woman, . . . "I must say, I wouldn't have known you. You've changed."

"Have I?" I could not hide my pleasure. "But you haven't. I knew you immediately."

It was not true. I mean, I had recognised him, but he was not unchanged, though I could not pinpoint the change then. It only came to me later when I saw the same eyes, faintly puzzled and bewildered, look at me out of the face of a movie actor who had, at one time, been at the top, and then had unaccountably slid down. The face of a man who couldn't understand what had happened to him and why.

That was how Manu looked. He had been the man who was to take the literary world by storm, the man on the brink of doing so. And now, he was just another man clinging to a job.

But I didn't know all that then. Only that my recognition and my undisguised admiration pleased him immensely. The old look imperceptibly came back. And soon, he could have been the same man I had seen that day, standing in front of the mike, confident, assured, holding everyone's attention, one hand with the long slim fingers pushing hair back from the forehead. For me, he was that man. As if that image had been riveted into me that day and nothing could displace it.

He walked back with me to hostel. When we parted nothing was said about our meeting again. Yet, I knew that he knew we would meet again. When I went to my room, I peeled off my coat, unwound my sari and lay down on the bed in my petticoat. "Manohar," I said the name to myself. Then again, "Manu." And through my left nipple, which was pressed against the bed, I could feel the beating of my heart, strong and regular.

He was there, outside the hostel, when I came down the next morning on my way to college. I was not surprised to see him. I left my friends and went to him. He walked with me to the lecture hall. "What time are you free in the evening?" he asked me as we parted. I told him I was. He was there to meet me. And then again the next morning. And the evening. And the morning after. And the evening.

It seemed incredible to me that I could evoke an emotion so strong in anyone. That anyone could care for me in that way and to that extent.

"I wake up to thoughts of you," he told me, "and I know why I was born and why I'm alive." I thought they were the most beautiful words anyone had ever said.

"The most beautiful?" he said with a gentle scorn when I told him so. "Listen, I'll tell you the most beautiful lines ever said by a lover."

And he quoted, bringing back to my mind the young man who had recited poetry that day, holding all of us enthralled.

"I long to believe in immortality. If I am destined to be happy with you here . . . how short is the longest life."

"Who said that?"

"Keats . . . to his beloved Fanny Brawne."

I marvelled, not at Keats, but at him for knowing so much, for remembering such lines, for saying them to me. He wrote me a poem. My whole being exulted. Padmini . . . I had defeated her after all. And yet there was always a gnawing disbelief . . . how could I be anyone's beloved? I was the redundant, the unwanted, an appendage one could do without. It was impossible for anyone to want me, love me, need me.

And that he, a man set apart from the others, above the others . . . how callow they seemed now, the boys in my class ·. . . should love me seemed even more incredible. The fisherman's daughter couldn't have been more surprised when the king asked her to marry him. But the fisherman's daughter was wiser. She sent the king to her father and the father it was who bargained with him*. While I . . . I gave myself up unconditionally, unreservedly to him. To love him and to be loved.

And still the fear was there; the secret fear that, behind each loving word, each kiss, lay the enemy, the snake, the monster of rejection. Some time, some day, I thought, the truth will come out and I will know I was never loved.

But these were the dark thoughts of dismal moments and I could forget them most of the time. I met him each morning and each evening. And he told me he loved me and I told him I loved him, too. And no one, I thought, has felt this way before. Not with this intensity, anyway. Surely we were unique?

PART TWO

I wake up and I am in my own room at home. I have to orient myself. Yes, I am at home, in my own room. The huge wooden wardrobe is in front of me. And the dressing table, with its mirror that sways too far back unless propped up by a piece of paper. I have to be surer, more certain. I walk out of the house, out of the gate, and on to the road. Turn to the right now, and there it is, the crossroad. And the signboard painted yellow, with words and figures in black. Here I hesitate. Somehow I feel, I know, that I have to turn right again and take the road leading to . . . the road which will take me to . . . that road . . .

This time she truly woke up. It was only a dream. Such a senseless, pointless dream at that. But why the hell, she thought with a touch of petulance, couldn't the dream have gone on a little longer? For now it will stay with me always, a feeling of regret that I do not know where that road would have led me to; that I did not even think of reading the yellow signboard to find out what lies in that direction. And therefore, just because I do not know, will never know, the dream and the road will always have a significance for me, an importance they do not really merit.

But perhaps, she thought, hopefully, all that the dream meant was that I chose to come back here to this house, an unknown factor when I decided to do it. And even now I don't know why I continue to stay on here, as if my children, my home, my practice, my patients, count for nothing. As she framed the thought in words, she knew she had left her husband out of the reckoning. Recklessly she said the words to herself . . . I don't want him. And the relief of admitting it, even to herself, was enormous.

I know all these 'love marriages.' It's love for a few days, then quarrels all the time. Don't come crying to us then.
To you? God, that's the one thing I'll never do. Never!

No, theirs was not a case of love dying, or even of conflicts. Instead, it was as if a kind of disease had attacked their marriage. A disease like syphilis or leprosy, something that could not be admitted to others. This very concealment made it even more gruesomely disgusting, so that she was dirty and so was he and so was their marriage. She wanted no more of it, but there were the children, and she was still hung on to the past, enough to make the word divorce a frightening one.

Don't come back and tell us . . .
That's the one thing I won't do . . .

Yet she knew she could not go on, either. If only she had belonged to another time, where a woman had no choice but to go on! Human nature may not change, but isn't there such a thing as a frame of mind, a way of thinking, which is shaped by the age you live in? It was so much easier for women in those days to accept, not to struggle, because they believed, they knew, there was nothing else for them. And they called that Fate.

She thought of her grandmother who had been deserted by her husband only a few years after marriage, leaving her, a young woman, with two little daughters, one of whom had been her mother. He had disappeared, no one knew where, though there was a family legend that he had taken *sanyas*. Her grandmother's father had taken the deserted woman and her daughters into his house, looked after them, got the girls married. But there had been, obviously, the burden of being unwanted, of being a dependent. Yet her grandmother had never, so she had heard, complained. It's my luck, she said. My Fate. It was written on my forehead.

If only I could say that. My luck. My Fate. Written on my forehead. Will that help me to accept, to passively endure?

No, it could not. How could it when she knew it was a lie? This wasn't something that had just happened to her! It was something she had helped to happen. If not for the children . . .

There were letters from them. Two separate ones from the two of them. They had written the address themselves. She smiled at Abhi's scrawl.

Noticing the smile, Baba asked, "From the children?"

"Yes, Baba."

Then he said what he hadn't said so far: "Aren't they missing you? How do they manage without you?"

And at once he knew he had been unwise to ask her that question. He wouldn't have, really. It was only that she had seemed for a moment, as she smiled, more approachable. As if she had let her defences down. But obviously they hadn't been let down for him.

An irritated frown creased her forehead. Manage! What a weak, what an ineffectual word! A word like you. I want to be needed, to know that they will find existence impossible, insupportable without me. And you say . . . can they manage? I suppose that's what the two of you did when I left. You managed without me.

With an effort she fought down her irritation. "They're used to being without me. I'm out most of the day, anyway. And I told you about my Janakibai. As long as she's with them, I don't have to worry."

But Abhi refuses to go to bed until I cover him with his blanket. He will never let his father or Janakibai do that for him. If I'm late going home, I find him asleep, curled up in the middle of his bed, the blanket folded into a perfect square at the foot of it, staring at me accusingly. And Renu . . . who will not go to school unless I am at the door at the moment of her leaving. I ask her . . . do you have everything? Your hanky? Water bottle? Your crayons? You have art today, don't you? Yes, mummy, she says impatiently, brusquely, as if she finds the sameness of my questions irritating. And yet, Janakibai tells me, if I'm not there, she lingers, looking back again and again.

"No, I don't have to worry about them," she repeated. And then with an abrupt change of subject that would not even have deceived a child, she said, "Look, Baba, this is Renu's drawing."

She showed him a slip of paper Renu had enclosed with her letter. For the first time she saw a look on his face that associated him with her children. It was an expression she had seen fond grandparents wear, a look of fatuous pride and affection. She had deprived her children of that. She had come to terms with the guilt that overcame her at the thought of leaving them and going out to work. But this . . . ? Suddenly she felt helplessly confused, floundering, all her confident grasp of her own life lost to her. And I don't know any more what's important, what matters, how I am to go on.

Baba, who had solemnly examined the drawing through his glasses, gave it back to her without comment. Only now she looked at it herself. It was the beach and the sea, with a few dotted figures dwarfed by the huge waves. In the background was the sun . . . the usual circle with spokes for rays. Yet, why did it seem menacing, like a fearful doom hanging over the world?

Hastily she went back to her letter.

"We went to the beach yesterday. Papa took us. He bought us ice cream. Abhi wanted one more. Papa said no. Abhi cried like a baby. I didn't cry. I had fun."

Sibling jealousy. It always frightened her. Most parents

smile at it. When she visited a newborn, they told her with smiles what the older child had said or done. They said . . . isn't it cute? She could never smile back. When Abhi was born, Renu retreated into silence. She never referred to the baby herself and ignored all references to him. The day they were to take Abhi to the doctor for his vaccination, when she saw them preparing him and themselves, she had suddenly skipped to her mother, a child again, not a grave, withdrawn person, and said, "Oh, are we going to return him now?" looking as if happiness was once again within her reach. It had scared her.

Dhruva and I . . . Dhruva and I . . . Did I push him? The question sprang at her out of nothing, again and again . . . Did I? Did I?

There was a letter from Manu too. He showed concern, anxiety, as if she had gone home to recuperate from some long illness. It angered her. What right had he to blithely assume that all was well between them, that her feelings for him were unchanged, that whatever was wrong had nothing to do with him? The ego of the male, she thought wryly, unwilling to believe that he had lost the art of pleasing, assuming that marriage, possession, gave him a lifelong right to affection, love and respect.

Love . . . how she scorned the word now. There was no such thing between man and woman. There was only a need which both fought against, futilely, the very futility turning into the thing they called "love." It's only a word, she thought. Take away the word, the idea, and the concept will wither away.

The children's letters left her with a lingering unease. When Madhav came to her saying, "There's someone who wants to see you," she welcomed the distraction.

Surprise followed almost immediately.

"Me? Who is it?"

"Our next door neighbours. I think you know them. The Dixits."

"The Dixits? Yes, of course. There was Vidya and . . . yes, Asha, and two or three boys."

"This is S.D. Dixit."

"Oh, Sudhir."

"His child is unwell. He wants you to go and have a look at him.

For some reason it outraged her. It was like being caught in the bathroom with her clothes off.

"How do they know I'm here? And what I am?"

There was panic now. A feeling of being trapped. The house had been a fortress. Here, now, was the first breach. She shrank from her professional role. Wasn't it to escape that that she had come here? But Madhav was laughing at her. Her affronted look amused him.

"How do they know? Why, everyone knows everything here. You know that. This isn't Bombay, Sarutai. He's waiting for you outside."

As she still hesitated, he added casually, "He seems very worried. You could just meet him for a moment."

"All right," she said, feeling as if she was putting her head in the noose again. And she went. She moved her hands and shoulders, the boy thought, as if she was putting on a coat.

"I don't even have a stethoscope with me," she murmured. She repeated this in a louder tone when she went out. He smiled at her, a short, paunchy man, wearing the black coat of a lawyer. It was an ingratiating smile. Had he guessed her reluctance?

"I don't know, really, what I can do to help you. Don't you have your own doctor?"

"He's gone out of town. Otherwise . . ." the smile on his face faded away. "Just come and have a look. He's been having very high temperature for the last three days. He's worse today."

Now he was a familiar person, not the Dixit's Sudhir, but an anxious parent, looking at her with hopeful eyes.

"Let's go," she said brusquely.

They walked in silence to his house. It seemed strange to go out of one gate and enter through another. Her usual way had been over the wall. The wall was now crumbling, toeholds having become footholds and footholds large cavities.

She went in to the child and it was like entering a familiar world. The mother sat by him, large-eyed and anxious. Dressed up she had, perhaps, a kind of small-town smartness. Now, there was no vestige of it in her. But Sudhir, she saw, put a chubby hand reassuringly on her shoulder.

She had prepared herself for a cursory examination, for the advice, if necessary, to call in another doctor. Luckily it was a simple matter. The child had measles. As she pronounced her diagnosis, she became the dominant figure. They looked at her in dumb obedience, while she wrote out the prescription, gave instructions, reassured the mother and comforted the child.

And then it was over. They went back to being what they were. Sudhir . . . the Dixit's boy, his wife, whom he called Prema, and Saru . . . Kamalatai's Saru. At that she remembered.

"Where is Mavshi?" she asked.

Mavshi . . . Sudhir's mother. The motherly type with an overflow of motherliness from her own five children for Saru.

Come here, Saru, let me plait your hair for you.

Who's plaited your hair? That woman? Why do you let her do it? Open out those plaits and let me do it properly.

No one could comb her hair like her mother did. She would comb with a kind of passion, going on and on, merciless to knots, tangles and the scalp alike, until the comb whistled cleanly through soft untangled hair. But she had preferred Mavshi. Mavshi who plaited her hair so tight that the skin on her forehead was stretched back until it ached. But Mavshi chatted as she combed, asking her all the while, "Is it all right, Saru? Tell me if it isn't."

It was Mavshi who had taken her home after Dhruva's death. She had stayed there for a few days. When the time had come for her to go back home, she had held back saying, "I don't want to go. Not today."

"You have to go, Saru. Your mother says you must."

"I want to play with . . . Asha."

Asha, the colourless, sickly child with whom she never knew what to talk about. None of her poor subterfuges had worked. She had had to go back.

What had Mavshi guessed and said to her mother? She must have said something because all visiting had stopped after that. If ever she tried to climb the wall, her mother would call our "Saru, where are you going?"

"To Mavshi's house. To play with Asha and Vidya."

"You are not to go there. Come back."

"But why?"

"Because I say so. And, remember, if I catch you sneaking away there . . ."

"Ai?" Sudhir made a face. "She's in her room. Want to meet her? She's aged a lot. And not keeping very well, either. She has diabetes and she's supposed to diet. When we remind her of it she gets furious. She tells everyone we're . . . Prema is trying to starve her. It's difficult. I don't know how to manage her. Old people are a problem."

Suddenly Baba's figure took on a stature and dignity she had never invested it with. He was no "problem!" But perhaps if Manu's parents had lived with them . . .

She remembered how painful even their brief visits had been. They had been two glaring incongruities in their son's home. The mother, rustic looking with her sari covering her head, green tattoo marks on chin and forehead, and feet that looked clumsily unaccustomed to the slippers she wore. And the father, with *paan*-stained teeth and lips, his coarse speech and thickset body so much at odds with his features, which had a strange delicacy. The visits had been total failures. She had never been the cruel daughter-in-law. On the contrary, she had been too gracious, too patronising and had felt their resentment and disapproval. And over it all had hung Manu's shame. But when his father died, Manu had put up his photograph on their bedroom wall.

Now she thought . . . shall I put up one of my mother as well? Filial devotion . . . like murder, it will out some time. And then she was choked by laughter at the thought of his father and her mother hanging side by side on their bedroom wall, the same incense sticks burning for both.

"Ai grumbles all the time. She's never satisfied whatever we do. She's always nagging at Prema. Well . . ." he sighed heavily, thinking of his griefs.

"And your father?"

"He's dead. He passed away eight years ago. I took over his practice. Come on, I'll take you to Ai. I have to go back to the courts after getting Bal's medicines . . . "

The woman looked completely unfamiliar without her *kumkum* and black beads. They had been such an integral part of her that without those symbols of her wifehood, she seemed a colourless ghost. She had been a plump woman . . . this, along with her placidity, had been a part of the motherliness which had so attracted Saru. Now she was frankly mountainous. Her eyes had sunk into dull apathetic slits, lost in the folds of her cheeks.

"Saru, is it?"

There was nothing in her tone, neither surprise, curiosity nor welcome.

"When did you come? You look just the same."

The eyes hadn't even looked at her.

"Sudhir tells me you're a doctor now. He called you to have

a look at the child, did he? All that fuss for a little fever. It's her fault, really, taking the child out when he had a cold. And giving him a bath, too. I told her not to do it, but who listens to me? I'm just a stupid old woman who knows nothing. I never brought up five children of my own. And who looked after her husband when he was so ill with typhoid that even the doctor said he would die?"

Where had it all gone, the old affection, the concern, the interest, the curiosity? There was nothing left. She lived in her own world of querulous complaints, carrying on a perennial warfare against her son and daughter-in-law, seeing the world in black and white, she, the wronged, the others, the wrong-doers. And suddenly Saru hated her, the smell of old age and fat that eminated from her, her complaints, her indifference to everything but her own concerns, the loss of everything that had made her a warm and sensible human being.

It was only when she was leaving that the old woman came to life.

"Your mother was a lucky woman, Saru."

"My mother? Lucky?"

"Yes. She died."

And then an enormous pity filled her. A feeling of cama-raderie as well. So, you're one of them, too. In which case, I am on your side. I am on the side of the weak, the lonely, the defeated, the forsaken, the unhappy . . . for I know what it is to be all of these.

"Yes, Mavshi, she's dead. But you're alive. And you have to go on living until it's time for you to go."

Nonsensical, threadbare morality. What comfort can there be in such words?

She remembered her sense of outrage when she had first heard the parable of the Buddha—who told the grieving mother of a dead child, seeking his help . . . get me a handful of mus-tard seeds from a house that has not known death. And the mother, after a vain search, realised there was no such house. There, said the Buddha. Learn the truth and be comforted. Death is an inescapable human condition. And so the woman was comforted. How can that be possible, she had thought when she had heard this story. Does the suffering of multitudes mitigate mine?

"You're telling me nothing new, Saru. I know all of it. But tell me, you're a doctor and know all about dying and living . . . "

All about living and dying? She almost laughed aloud.

" . . . and so tell me this, Saru. Why am I, a fat, old, unwanted woman left alive when he, so useful, so much wanted was taken away? Why am I alive when he is dead?"

It got her right in the stomach. She felt sick and stared at the old woman in stupefaction.

"Why am I alive when he is dead?" . . . she repeated the words and miraculously the woman caught at her meaning immediately.

"Did your mother say that to you when Dhruva died?"

"Yes."

"Poor girl."

There it was, the pity she thirsted for, the sympathy she craved for. But the old woman's eyes were even then withdrawn and she knew she was already thinking of something else. Of her food probably. The hands which stroked her back were perfunctory, forgetting what they were doing and why, the action purely mechanical and meaningless.

"I must go," she said, getting up, knowing she did not want to meet the old woman again.

As she walked through the hall, the younger woman came to her, and asked her with an overt anxiety, "You will come again?"

"If I'm really needed."

"Please come. You must, "she pleaded.

And she knew she would. There was no escape.

2.

It had evaporated long since, my pride in my professional status. There was only the work left. And that was now sheer necessity, the only thing that held me together. But if it was my anodyne, it seemed to be the cause of my disease as well; and the temptation was frequent and strong to let go. The reasoning was simple, clear and remorseless. It is because I am something more than his wife that he has become what he is. If I can go back to being nothing but his wife . . . and yet was I ever that? . . . he may no longer resent me. And then . . .

But no, the answer was . . . we will be happy together ever after. However often I calculated, however many methods I used, that result evaded me. At best it was . . . he may leave me alone. But even that was enough for me. To obtain such a respite, an interlude of peace, I would give up much. Even my work? Yes, even that.

The trouble was . . . how would I say it to him, what excuse would I offer? Often I rehearsed the words to myself, even the manner of saying them. I would be . . . What? I debated with myself. Whimsical, perhaps? Or firm and emphatic? Reasonable, prepared to discuss?

But when the moment came, all my ruses deserted me and I blurted out the words, startling myself as much as him. I came home late that night. There had been an unforeseen visit to a newly admitted patient, an emergency only I could deal with. Telling Nirmala to ring up home, I went directly from my consulting room to the nursing home. When I came home I found him sitting with a brooding expression on his face that made my heart give painful, quivering little jumps. What is it now? Oh god, what is it now? What have I done? What has someone said?

"Did Nirmala ring you up?"

Perhaps it was that. Maybe she had forgotten and he had been waiting for too long. I should have rung up myself. Why hadn't I?

"Yes."

It wasn't that then. What else?

"Renu? Abhi? Are they in bed?"

That was obvious, but I had to talk, to go on proving my penitence, my contrition.

"Yes."

"Have they eaten?"

"Yes."

"And you?"

"No."

"You should have. You shouldn't have waited for me. I'm sorry I was so delayed. I won't be long now. Just five minutes while I have my bath and change."

Janakibai had, as usual, kept clean clothes ready for me. I poured water over myself as if it was some kind of a ritual. After wiping myself dry, I powdered myself lavishly in a frenzy of wanting to be clean, sweet-smelling. Then in to Abhi, to cover him up. To Renu, to put away the book she had been reading, to switch off her light. Nothing left now. I could procrastinate no longer.

"Janakibai," I called out from the dining room. "Get the food on the table."

He joined me only after I had served both of us.

"Did the children eat well?"

"I don't know."

Pretend there's nothing wrong. Pretend this is normal. Talk to him. Keep talking.

But it was no use. When Janakibai went out, there was silence. And I knew it was no use. Terror waited for me in our room. I could not escape it.

"I want to give up working." Was it I who had said that? We stared at each other in equal astonishment. And silence again. But now I knew my lines. They came to me, the words I had rehearsed to myself. "Manu, I want to stop working. I want to give it all up . . . my practice, the hospital, everything."

"You what?"

I saw that the glaze that had come over his eyes had lifted infinitesimally. Was this the right method of appeasement then? If only I knew the right way . . .

I thought of the devotees I had seen in a famous temple, showing their devotion, their penitence, their whatever-it-was, in a multitude of agonising ways. In horrified astonishment I had watched one man, bare except for a grimy towel round his loins, mortifying himself by rolling over and over on the hard, stony ground, arms stretched straight over his head, palms rigidly joined together. Why do you do it? I had wondered. Now I knew the answer.

"I said I want to stop working."

"You're joking."

Do I look as if I am? Do I look as if I could?

"No I'm not. I'm serious."

"But why? There has to be some reason. Has something gone wrong somewhere?"

Tell him. Tell him now. Tell him what he does. Tell him you can't stand it any longer. Tell him you're prepared to sacrifice everything as long as he leaves you alone. To sleep alone in a room, to be by myself on a bed, to be untouched, unhandled . . . only then can I be clean again.

"But why, Saru? Come on, I know you're joking."

It was like a reflex action. My body, which had been tense and rigid with fear, relaxed to the sound of my name. The danger was over, had receded, at least for the present. He had said my name.

"What is the matter, Saru?"

"I'm tired," I said, and I knew to my chagrin I sounded like a sulky child.

"Tired of what? Your work?"

"Everything. I just want to give it all up."

"And do what?"

"Janakibai, where are the curds? And get me a spoon. Why don't you see that everything is on the table?"

Poor Janakibai, made the scapegoat, the whipping boy for the sins of others.

"I asked you, Saru . . . give it up and do what?"

"I don't know. Live like the others do, I suppose. Stay at home and look after the children. Cook and clean. What else?"

I saw myself, the end of my sari tucked into my waist, hair tied into a neat knot, smiling at them all as I served them. And all of them smiled back at me. A mother in an ad, in a movie, dressed in crisply starched, ironed sari. Wife and mother, loving and beloved. A picture of grace, harmony and happiness. Could I not achieve that?

"And how will we live?"

His voice rasped against my visions so that the images were distorted by fine scratches. And now we were no longer smiling at one another but snarling.

"Why, on . . ."

I could not go on. I could not say it. He said it, instead, and to my amazement he was smiling as he said it.

"On my salary? Come on, Saru, don't be silly. You know how much I earn. You think we can live this way on that? Janakibai, get me another bottle of cold water."

"We don't need all this, do we?"

His Adam's apple moved up and down as he drank straight out of the bottle. I looked away. Janakibai began to clear up.

"You mean that?"

"Of course, I do. I'm telling you I'm serious. We did without all this once, didn't we?" I went on doggedly and hopelessly.

"Yes, we did. But now? Can you bear to send the children to a third rate school? To buy them the cheapest clothes, the cheapest of everything? To save and scrape and still have nothing after the first few days of the month? No, Saru, there can be no going back. We have to go on." He pushed away his chair and stood up. Then he saw me still sitting there, doodling with one finger in my plate, and said, "But I really don't understand why you've suddenly raised this problem."

"I'm tired," I repeated going on with my circles. One circle in another, one circle in another. And now he came to me on his way to washing his hands. With his left hand he rumpled my hair, oblivious of Janakibai's presence.

"Poor girl. You really are tired, it seems. Come on, wash your hands and let's go to bed. Relax now. Why don't you take the day off tomorrow? Forget about the hospital, forget about your patients. Stay at home. Maybe we'll go for a movie in the evening, just the two of us. What do you say?"

What could I say? I said nothing and sat there drawing my entwined circles . . . no, they could never be disentangled . . . until Janakibai came and took away my plate. Then I got up and washed my hands.

That night he behaved like a young man with a girl he loves. He was tender, teasing and infinitely protective. And when his hands began to caress me, gently, and I said . . . no, not today, I'm tired . . . were there no other words in the world? He ceased at once, not importuning me further. He tucked me into bed instead like I did Abhi, and saying "Good night, Saru," went off to sleep. While I lay staring into the darkness thinking of his words . . . we can't go back, we have to go on.

Go on where? But the darkness yielded no answers.

3

The nights had lost their quality of fearfulness. She could go to bed without fear and wake up, not fragmented and torn, but whole. The aches, the bruises, had disappeared. So had the desire to talk to someone. Had there been a woman who had agonised over it once? She felt cut off from that self by a chasm so great, an abyss so deep, that there was no going back.

But if the new tortures had ceased, the old ones had come back. As if she had exchanged one pair of pinching, torturing shoes for another. The childish grief of being unwanted swamped her unreasonably again and again, and looking at Baba and Madhav together, she felt stricken anew. There was something in Madhav, a kind of breeding or training maybe, which made it effortless and natural for him to look after the older man. Little things she would never have thought of, never have done. And how easily I deserted them, she thought, never thinking of the fact that they might need me some day, some time. But how can you desert a person who doesn't need you?

"Nobody likes me. Nobody cares for me. Nobody wants me . . ." she had written these words in a notebook once. And she had written them, not in English, which she scarcely knew then, but in Marathi. So that it had come out as, "I am not liked by anyone. I am not cared for by anyone. I am not wanted by anyone." With the stress on the "I." Which was how it was then, the whole world related to the "I." But surely it should be different now?

And yet, this was nothing. This she could endure with a shrug, even with a smile. It was the other thing. The other fear that began when the lights went out.

It was a power failure, so common in those days. And even now, as Baba's and Madhav's unhurried, obviously-done-often-before actions showed.

"Madhav, have you filled the lamp with oil?"

"Yes, Kaka. You wait there. I'll light it and get it."

"Get the other lamp too. Wait, here are the matches."

No, they were unperturbed. It was she who sat terrified, her skin prickling with a deadly, secret fear. Someone was in the room with her. Not just someone, but a someone who carried a fear within him so great that it rose up and choked her like a deadly fog.

Dhruva . . . he had been terrified of the dark. It was one of the secrets they had shared together, something he had never told their mother. She had not revealed it, either, though she had said it a hundred, a thousand times . . . wait, I'll tell Ai.

It was their mother who had insisted, when Dhruva was four, that he should sleep all alone by himself in a room. Their mother had been invariably stern with Dhruva; but, child though she was, she had known even then that the sternness was only a crust: that to her mother, compared to Dhruva, she herself was nothing. She wondered now why her mother had insisted on Dhruva's sleeping alone in a room. Perhaps she had imagined herself to be Jijabai, the heroic mother who moulded the brave son Shivaji*. Had that been her dream? If so, that magnificent dream had ended in a slimy pond scarcely five feet deep.

Dhruva himself had never openly demurred at his mother's fiat. Instead he had, with infinite patience and cunning, waited until Ai was asleep and then crawled into her bed, waking her up. She would be cross.

Sssh, don't disturb me, I'm dreaming.
Of what?

There was nothing, but how could she blunt her own weapon?

I won't tell you. You won't understand.

Said with a withering scorn. But Dhruva, as long as he could get away from being alone in the dark, refused to be withered by anything.

Tell me, Sarutai.
Don't call me Sarutai. And I won't tell you. Now, shut up. Or get out. You've got to lie down absolutely quiet. Don't kick me. And no giggling. No, don't move at all.

He would lie still, motionless as a corpse, willing to do anything she said. Even then, she would be painfully aware of his presence. The touch of his skin was, for some reason, distasteful to her. Once, her hand moving in the dark, brushed against his lips, wet and baby soft. She drew her hand back in disgust.

Cchi, you're a dirty boy.
But what am I doing?
Go away to your own bed. Why do you trouble me? I was sleeping and having such nice dreams and you spoilt everything. You always spoil everything.
And you're always scolding. Wait, I'll tell Ai.
Go on and tell. And I'll tell her you're scared of the dark and come to my bed. No don't, Sarutai. Don't tell. I promise I won't say anything to Ai. I'll keep quiet. I'll do anything you say.

Poor little scared boy, who never grew up to know that the dark holds no terrors. That the terrors are inside us all the time. We carry them within us, and like traitors they spring out, when we least expect them, to scratch and maul. It happened to her when she was watching a movie. It had been Satyajit Ray's *Pather Panchali.* She had been prepared for the right responses a Satyajit Ray movie called for . . . a well-bred enthusiasm, a discreet admiration. She was totally unprepared for what happened. Suddenly it appeared on the screen like a scene from her own past . . . the sister Durga holding her brother Apu's face by the chin while she combed his hair for him. In that instant she got up from her seat, scarcely knowing what she was doing, moving blindly towards the exit, fumbling among the heavy dust-smelling curtains. Getting into the lobby at last, sitting there on the plush seat bent over in agony as if she had cramps. That was how Manu found her. He had followed her and asked, "What is it, Saru?"

"Nothing," she said. "Just some pain."

Thinking . . . oh my god, some pain? All the pains, every pain. Not just his death but what I did to him when he was alive.

Perhaps there is something in the male, she now thought, that is whittled down and ultimately destroyed by female domination. It is not so with a female. She can be dominated and she can submit and yet hold something of herself in reserve. As if there is something in her that prevents erosion and self-destruction. (If not, she would have been destroyed too easily. But then have I not been destroyed?)

Does the sword of domination become lethal only when a woman holds it over a man? Dhruva had been dominated by two females, making him a creature full of terrors. And Baba . . . even then a cipher, a man who didn't count, because she so emphatically did. Even his mistakes and omissions were unimportant because they could never affect anyone else.

When she got married she had sworn . . . I will never domi-nate. I will never make my husband nothing as she did. And yet it had happened to them. It puzzled her, and sometimes it frightened her, giving her a feeling that there was something outside her self, driving her on; that her own will counted for nothing. Can one never control one's life? Do we walk on lines chalked by others?

She remembered the first time. She had been reading in bed when he turned to her, pulling the book savagely out of her hands.

"That's enough. Come to me now."

And he began what was then for them a peculiar kind of lovemaking, with something in it that set it apart from all their other times together. It was not just that he was more intense, with nibbling little kisses interspersed with long devouring ones so that she could scarcely breathe. It was the feeling that he was whipping himself on, trying to arouse himself to some pitch of excitement that remained beyond him. For, when she felt him against her, she knew there was nothing. It was a sham. And something about it sickened her.

"No. No. Please, no."

He drew back and looked her in the face . . . the table lamp was still on and the two of them were in the dim penumbra of its light . . . and his eyes, even in that half-shade, looked pathetically appealing.

"Saru," speaking with an intensity that fell just short of beg-ging . . . "don't refuse me now. Don't."

She didn't. But it was no use. For the first time in their years together, he couldn't go on. At last he gave up and fell back in his place. She lay rigid, rampant with anger. How dare he? How dare he? Then she got up and matter-of-factly washed herself. She combed her hair and even lightly powdered her face. When she came back to bed, he was still in the same posi-tion, with a rigid stillness that told her he was awake. But she avoided looking at him, his body ugly now to her with its aura of failure.

No, don't. Talk to him now. Say something. Comfort him. Soothe him. Tell him it isn't important. That it doesn't matter.

She turned over on to her side, away from him, and picked up the book he had snatched out of her hands. She read. going back easily to the point at which she had left off, until she felt sleepy. Then she switched off the light and prepared for sleep which she knew would come.

Now, as she thought of it, for some inexplicable reason, a conversation she had heard between her mother and a neighbour came to her mind. The neighbour had been telling her mother about a woman who had been apparently ill treated by her in-laws in a grotesque manner. She had been tied to a peg in the cattle shed for ten years and fed on scraps like a dog. And then, after ten years of this life, she had at last died.

"Poor woman," the neighbour had ended. And her mother had said, "But how do we know what she had done to be treated that way? Maybe she deserved what she got!"

And there had been something so hard, so cruel, so merciless in that judgement that she had shuddered and hated her mother for it.

And yet that night, she had slept peacefully and well. And when she woke up, she had been in the same mood, angry, triumphant, remorseless. It was his failure. It had nothing to do with her. Nothing at all. She had fiercely rejected the idea that his failure was in any way related to her words to him that evening.

We don't have to worry about a loan any more.
Why?

His face both puzzled and relieved.

Booze's giving me the money.
All of it?
Yes, all of it.

Why? The word, the question seemed to hang in the air between them. It remained there. He didn't ask her that question then. In fact, he never did.

4.

We called him Boozie. The name came out of his initials, which were, oddly enough, B.O.Z. But there was something more to it than that, something satisfyingly irreverent about that nickname. It was a matter of prestige with us, as it is with students anywhere, not to admire the staff. We took immense pleasure in criticising them, ridiculing them. But it was difficult to ridicule this man. He was perilously close to a women's-magazine hero . . . dark, rugged, handsome and masterful. Everything about him . . . his language, his accent, his stride, his pipe, his swift progress through the wards, his banter with his patients, the caustic humour with which he flayed his staff and students, the faint masculine perfume that hung in the air around in with him, his very clothes he wore, and has thatch of slightly greying hair contributed to the aura that surrounded him. They were all props, I decided later, to help create and maintain the necessary image. For by then I had learnt it, too, to create an image of myself for the world, to live within it, hiding my real self so resolutely that at times I forgot myself it was just a facade.

But then I learnt not just this but so many other things from him: all the veneer of good living. It surprised me when I discovered later that he came from a mediocre middle class family. He looked as if he had been born to all the things that surrounded him when I saw him. The best of everything. Yes, girls, too. It was part of his reputation, his fondness for pretty girls. Before he began with a batch of new students, there were guesses made and bets laid . . . who would it be this time? The final choice was very predictable. It was not enough for a girl to be merely pretty. She had to have an air about her, a chic, and intelligence as well.

I never was one of his favourites. Not at first. As an under-graduate, moreover, I had little to do with him. It was only when I was doing my first house post that I came into close contact with him.

The beginning was dreadfully unpromising. Once again like a woman's magazine story where the hero and heroine begin with a dramatic misunderstanding, which it takes so many pages, so many instalments, to clear up. But I was no heroine, certainly not at that moment. Just a scared girl, caught in a wrongdoing, humiliated and shattered by a public rebuke, feeling worse because I knew I deserved it.

It was Jatin, his Registrar, who faced the first muttered rum-blings that soon turned thunderous. He had been flicking over the reports, taking them in with a quick, scarcely-a-seconds' flickering glance when he stopped.

"CSF bloodstained. Traumatic tap. No opinion can be given," he read out, menace in the very monotony of his tone. And then, like an explosion . . .

"Who's the damn fool, the congenital idiot, who did the lumbar puncture?"

I could not hide myself any more. Not in fairness to Jatin. While Jatin mumbled something indistinct, I stammered, the sweat suddenly breaking out on my forehead, my upper lip, "It was I . . . "

His eyes met mine for an infinitesimal moment. My heart was thudding wildly within me. I could feel its savage irregular rhythm tearing at me.

"You!" It made a worm of me, a cockroach, something base, crawling and repelling. "And why couldn't you do it? What have you learnt in your five years here? Nothing, it seems. I don't want incompetent, clumsy uninterested females cluttering up this place. Go home and play with your rolling pins and knitting needles instead. Even a moron could have done this simple thing. Why do you come here when you aren't interested?"

Not fair, not fair. It was like having my clothes torn off me in public, like having an ugly nakedness displayed to the world. My throat hurt with the effort of holding back my sobs, my eyes pricked with unshed tears. I would not, could not, cry now. That would be one more thing against me. I would become, not just an incompetent, disinterested female, but a weepy one as well.

And then, there was this other hurt too. The feeling of being betrayed. I had imagined, I had thought, that here, in this place, I was accepted for what I was. Instead, it seemed I had been admitted on sufferance, tolerated as long as I hid my essential female qualities.

Now suddenly, dramatically, his voice dropped to its normal pitch. "And now, thanks to you, I can do nothing for this child. I have to sit and watch him."

He turned away from all of us to the child, and there was no more anger, but despair. A wonderful actor. But I didn't think of that then. I was too stricken to think at all. There was only shame now, shame at my cowardly self. A revulsion against my self. I was worrying about my own petty self when a child's life hung in the balance.

But the worst was over as far as I was concerned. A small smile showed at the corner of Jatin's mouth, as if he knew the all-clear had sounded. Everyone knew, though I didn't, not then, that his tempers, which blazed in a moment into a fierce conflagration, died just as suddenly in a downpour of goodwill. Now it was pure dramatics. "Why should the surgeons alone have their drama?" he had said once in an unguarded moment. He certainly gave the wards their fair share of colour and drama.

He now began giving instructions to Jatin. Whispered instructions, very obviously excluding me. I didn't mind. I was still in a state of shock. I had been unprofessional when a human being depended on my being skilled and professional. I had rushed through the job, thinking of Manu waiting for me at home. Now I scourged myself with all violence and savagery of a young and active conscience. And I prayed that the child should not die.

I was still praying when they wheeled in the child for a lumbar puncture the next day. He was to do it himself.

"Come in, Madam," he said to me, not jovial as his words implied. but unspeakably, rigidly grim. "Come in and see how a thing should be done."

It was not just bravura, not just bragging, though there was enough of that too in him. He was, I saw, quick, gentle, meticulous and skilled, doing the job with a marvellous dexterity. When I saw him I knew I would never pray any more for a patient. I would learn this instead, this skill, this proficiency, this perfection. I knew he was a good teacher. Well, I would learn from him. Everything that he could teach me. I would learn.

It was a bit of luck that he began to show an interest in me at about the same time. It was so much, once again, like a magazine story, that if I had been outside it, I would have been amused. But I wasn't. I was very much in it, unable to think, just reacting from moment to moment. From the day he stopped his car at the bus stop where I stood and took me out for a cup of coffee, saying. "The day I have no time to take a pretty girl out to tea, I'll cut my throat."

It took me a long time to realise that his interest was in me as a woman not as a student. It was not innocence that deluded me but my feeling that because I was married, I was out of bounds for all males. I thought no male would take *that* kind of an interest in me. Yet, here was one. That was soon obvious, even to me. It was only the "why" that remained a mystery.

Perhaps it was, when I analyse it now, the fact that I belonged to another man. I remember his wry . . . "in a hurry to go home and taste married bliss? Hasn't the sweetness begun to cloy?"

Perhaps it was the Pygmalion-Galatea story all over again. I was the raw material to be shaped, moulded, chiselled into something more polished, nearer perfection. Confronted by his urbane sophistication I felt crude, graceless, terribly young and unformed. But I picked up. God, how fast I learnt things, apart from Paediatrics I mean, from him. It was he who taught me to dress with elegance and simplicity, he who taught me how to speak good English, he who improved my accent, he who taught me how to enjoy good food, how to read and what . . . oh everything! All the small graces of living that so transform a person.

And Manu? I told myself my relationship with this man couldn't, wouldn't hurt Manu. It was just a teacher-student relationship. If he put his hand on my shoulder, slapped me on my back, held my hand or hugged me . . . that was just his mannerism and meant nothing. It had nothing to do with Manu and me.

On the contrary, I told myself, I was helping Manu. It had already penetrated then, that all of Manu's literary talent and ambition had reached a dead end. "Shelley", Prof. Kulkarni had called him. "And you are his Harriet," he had said to me once with a small smile.

"Who's Harriet?" I had asked.

"You little ignoramus," Manu had said. "She was Shelley's runaway bride."

Much later, out of a morbid curiosity, I read more about this Harriet. I learnt of her dreadful end, a bloated corpse in a river, with another man's child inside her. But that was much later. Then it was exciting to be Shelley's Harriet, whoever she was. Yet, soon enough, I knew he was no Shelley. I knew also that it was I and not Manu who would get us out of the morass we were in.

It is a marvel how we managed to live. Manu's salary, never very much, barely covered our expenses. And for two years I was earning nothing. At first it didn't matter that I was out of all the things that were so much a part of student life—the parties, the eating out, the movies, casual trips. Manu, my work, my home and my studies were enough for me. And things, we told each other, would change once I had my degree.

But they didn't. An M.B.B.S. degree was no open sesame to prosperity. If I had to amount to anything at all, I had to go on and specialise.

"Can we afford it?"

"We must," I said angrily.

I had begun to wonder at his acceptance of our shabby way of living. For me, things now began to hurt . . . a frayed sari I could not replace, a movie I could not see, an outing I could not join in. I knew now that without money life became petty and dreary. The thought of going on this way became unbearable.

Meanwhile it was growing in me . . . a conception of the kind of life I wanted. I would not stay in a dingy two-room flat in a far off drab suburb all my life. I would not bring up any child to a life of deprivations. I wanted it soon . . . that finale of a middle class dream . . . a house of our own. Furnished with all the geegaws that are an indispensable part of the dream.

And here he was, the fairy godfather who could, with a wave of his magic wand, make things easier, miraculously, wonderfully, easier for me . . . if only I could please him. I knew I could if tried. I did. Within a few months he gave me work in a research scheme that brought in some badly needed extra money every month. (And kept me for longer hours from Manu. He sulked and I was either impatient with him or ignored him.) A year later I was his Registrar. In less than two years I passed my M.D. Four years later I was an Assistant

Honorary at a suburban hospital. With a consulting room of
my own in the midst of other well known busy consultants.

"I've got the money."

"How?"

"Boozie gave it to me."

He could have asked me then . . . why? And I would have
told him . . . What would I have said? But the occasion didn't
arise because he never asked me. And there was, perversely, no
relief in me, but contempt that he didn't.

But we were together, husband and wife, host and hostess
the day I had the formal opening of my consulting rooms. It was
the auspicious day of *Dasara** and the room was hot and damp
with Bombay's sultry October heat. My clothes felt moist, my
body prickly, but I could not keep down the jubilation, the glee
within me, from breaking out into a smile. As I moved among
the guests, accepting congratulations with a put-on air of indifference, my mind sang out loud . . . a song of exultation. I did
it. I did it. And there was Manu coming to me, saying,

"He's here."

"Who?"

No need to ask, really. No need for him to reply. There he
was, smiling genially at everyone, filling the room with himself,
his personality, so that all eyes were turned to the door in
which he stood.

"Invite him in. And look after him."

I knew there was plenty of talk about him and me. I knew
what they said about my rapid climb since the day I met him.
I could feel, even here, in spite of the assumed well-bred airs,
the sniggers, the ugly meaningful looks as Manu greeted him.
If Manu noticed the looks and smiles, he ignored them. He
behaved like a host with any guest. And I thought of the day I
had said . . . I've got the money. Boozie is giving it to me. And
he had, a little later, tried to possess me and failed. And I had
turned my back on him.

I did it again. I turned my back on both of them and bus-
ied myself with other guests. Later, he came to me, purposefully striding across the room, leaving Manu stranded on the
other side.

"What is this, Saru? No time to greet your old teacher?
Why are you avoiding me?"

"Perhaps I'm worried about my reputation."

"Your reputation?"

And he laughed. The attractive laugh that came from deep
within him. "Tell me, have I really harmed your reputation?
Have I?"

He put his two hands on my shoulders and shook me gently, seemingly affectionate. I could feel the stares. Everyone's
except Manu's. Who would not look at us. And I should have
hated him then . . . not Manu, for he had done nothing then
for which I could hate him, but this attractive, ravishingly masculine man who was doing this deliberately. Attracting attention to the two of us. But, funnily enough, it was not him I
hated. It was Manu for doing nothing.

This man . . . No, I could not hate him, knowing what I did
about him. That behind the facade of aggressive, virile
masculinity there was nothing at all.

I never revealed that to anyone. Not even to Manu for he
asked me nothing. And they began then . . . the silences that
grew between us. Just grew and grew like Jack's beanstalk.

5

S ilence was an essential part of the life they lived together now, Baba, Madhav and she. It had come upon the house after Dhruva's death. But that had been an ugly brooding silence, full of anger. The anger that, so much more than the grief, had filled the house. Or, was it that the anger had touched her and the grief passed her by?

Now, there was neither grief nor anger. Emotions, like the sounds of domestic tasks that came to her as she lay in bed in the mornings, were muted. She woke up late, in spite of the fact that she went to bed ridiculously early, leaving Madhav at his books and Baba waiting for the nine o'clock news. In the mornings, she listened to the sounds as if she had never heard them before, with a feeling of being swaddled in some kind of a soft cocoon. The hiss of the Primus. The clink and clatter of cups, saucers and spoons. The clang of the bucket and the slap of wet clothes against the stone. Soft swishes as Madhav swept the house. The low hum of devotional songs from the radio. Rarely, a conversation between Baba and Madhav, Madhav's sing song tones interspersed at regular intervals by Baba's "hum hum." The sound of water splashing as one of them had a bath. Only then she would get up, wash her face, brush her teeth at the tap in the backyard and go into the kitchen to make a cup of tea for herself.

The very monotony of the sounds and happenings, the feelings they aroused in her that nothing had happened, nothing had changed, made the thought of the day to come bearable.

There had been a time when this very monotony had wearied her unbearably. But now, it was not this existence that seemed claustrophobic; it was the other. Here she felt a measure of freedom that had eluded her in the other. But freedom to do what? To be what?

Freedom at last, she had exulted when she had left home and entered medical college. It had been not just relief but a kind of rebirth to get away from home to the hostel, so different with its cheerful feminine jangle. She had never known the kind of effortless, casual intimacy that living in the hostel allowed. At first it had shocked her orthodox middle class self, the kind of talk that went on.

Oh, damn. I must change again. It's like a tap, that's what it is. O god, look at me. I must clean my underarm.

For long, she had unconsciously used her mother's standards, judging others by her mother's standards. Until she went home for her first vacation and realised how much she hated the atmosphere at home, with its rigidly regulated way of living. When she returned to the hostel, she left behind all that her eighteen years at home had taught her. And so . . . I was ripe for Manu.

What caste is he?
I don't know.
A Brahmin?
Of course not.
Then, cruelly . . . his father keeps a cycle shop.
Oh, so they are low caste people, are they?

The word her mother had used, with the disgust, hatred and prejudices of centuries had so enraged her that she had replied . . . I hope so.

If you hadn't fought me so bitterly, if you hadn't been so against him, perhaps I would never have married him. And I would not have been here, cringing from the sight of letters, fighting with terror at the sight of his handwriting, hating him and yet pitying him too. For he is groping in the dark, as much as I am.

It was part of the same pattern that had mystified her from the day it began, . . . his cheerfulness the next morning, his air of being as usual, the complete, total normality. She had almost given up trying to put the two men together, the fearful stranger of the night, and the rather pathetic Manu of other times. But it never ceased to frighten her, this dichotomy.

I should have spoken about it the very first day. But I didn't. And each time it happens and I don't speak, I put another brick on the wall of silence between us. Maybe one day I will be walled alive within it and die a slow, painful death. Perhaps the process has already begun and what I am is a creature only half alive. And it seems I can do nothing to save myself.

But she had tried. Once, twice, she had been on the brink of speaking out. Not to him. No, not that. She had said the words to herself at first, tasting them, savouring their texture, their flavour on her tongue . . .

My husband is a sadist.

She had tried to say it to Prof. Kulkarni that day.
How is Manohar?
Your Manohar? He's a wreck, a ruin, a sadist.
She had thought of saying it to a lawyer, any lawyer, chosen at random, when once, in a moment of desperation. she had walked up and down on a road, reading the names of lawyers on ancient boards. Nerving herself to enter, to say . . .

Can I divorce my husband?

Any reasons?
He's cruel.
How? Will you be specific. Please give details.

At that point the dialogue . . . unreal maybe, in any case, for surely no lawyer talked like that . . . came to an end. There was no more she could say. Bed, the one she shared with her husband, was to her an intensely private place. She could not, would not, draw aside the curtain that hid it from the world. Renu and Abhi, if they come to know, . . . and they will eventually, I cannot hide it from them forever . . . I will never be able to look them in the face again.

If only someone would tell her what to do, she would do it at once, without a second thought. It was strange that after all these years of having been in full control of her life, she now had this great desire to let go. To put herself in another's hands. And yet, how few they were, the people who could shoulder any burdens at all, even their own.

For some reason she had thought of Boozie one day and on an impulse gone to him. When he opened the door, she smelt the drink on his breath. Boozie boozing . . . she had stifled a schoolgirlish giggle at the thought. But he had swamped her with his welcome.

"Saru, by all that's wonderful! How long is it since you came to see me, girl? I think of you every day. Every single day. Come in, come in."

He had pulled her in and given her a hug. As always, his masculinity overwhelmed her. And as always, the astonishment that behind it all was nothing.

And for her, too, she soon realised with an emotion close to despair, he had nothing. Why had she imagined he could help her? Worse, she had seen hairline cracks in the image he had built and presented to the world all these years. It horrified her, like the deterioration in a work of art.

His breath . . . had he really begun drinking when alone? And that was not all of it. From the gentle insistence with which he ushered her into the tiny gallery outside the drawing room, she knew there was someone inside. The way he looked—an uneasy face. an unwilling smile, a wilting, strained joviality—made it more obvious. He wanted her to go away. The person, whoever it was, annoyed at being left alone. How could she have hoped that he would provide her with the answers . . . he was floundering himself. He looked as if he had lost grip on his personal life. He had always been so immensely discreet, never a look, never a glance at the male students. The drama of interest in pretty girls. The facade of an affair with one of them. Yes, she had been one of those pawns too. When had she realised that she, as a woman, left him cold? But she didn't care. Not by then. For if she was a pawn in his game, so was he in hers.

In a short while he went in and sounds of an altercation came to her. He came out, like a sheepish husband forced by his wife to do something he didn't really want to do, with a young . . . young? not really, only comparatively . . . man in tow. Nothing effeminate about him in the way he dressed, moved or spoke. It was something else . . . a nebulous aura of femininity about him, faked, spurious and, therefore, all the more assertive.

She got up to go and she knew he was relieved. We have that in common, she thought as she smiled at him in farewell. Cowards, both of us.

You won't be happy with him. I know you won't. A man of a different caste, different community . . . what will you two have in common?

How little her mother knew! We belong to the same caste really. Both of us despise ourselves. What he does to me, he does it not so much because he hates me, but because he hates himself. And I . . . I hate myself more for letting him do it to me than I hate him for doing it to me.

Oh yes, she could be reasonable and rational enough now, at this distance from him and their life together. She could dispassionately analyse his motives, her motives, her reactions. And try to find out why what happened to their marriage had happened. But at home, sitting in the same room as him, watching the familiar glaze come into his eyes, the mask-like rigidity come over his face; at night, waiting for the terror to strike, she became a terrified animal. Thinking of how she could do nothing against his maniac strength. Of her panic that made her incapable of resisting. Of the children in the next room who pinioned her to a terrified silence. And when it was over thinking . . . I can't, I won't endure this any more. I'd rather die. I can't go on.

Recently, as if she had become psychic, she knew, hours earlier, when it would be one of those days. Nights, rather. Psychic? No, perhaps it was something infinitely more prosaic. Signs and portents she had become adept at understanding. His silence. A heavy, dull, brooding silence, immediately following a spurt of gaiety. And the children, catching something from the atmosphere, silent, too.

But they knew nothing. That was her only comfort. That the children knew nothing.

(What about that guarded watchful look in Renu's eyes as she looks at us? What about Abhi's hostility to me recently?)

When the silence became so unbearable that she felt she would do anything to shatter it, she would say . . .

Why aren't you speaking?

What can I say?

And she thinking . . . If only I could get away. Get out. But where?

And then the next morning . . . I will do it now. This moment. I'll talk to him. Tell him I can't go on.

And there he would be in the balcony outside, having his tea. One leg stretched in front of him on a stool. Newspaper in hand. looking up from it to smile at her. Saying . . . "Oh, there you are. Janakibai, your *tai** is up. Get her a cup of tea. Look at this, Saru. Exams put off again. God, what are we heading for? Do you want the first page? Here."

His eyes dear and unclouded. Nothing in them. Was it possible for a man to dissemble so much? The violent stranger of the night . . . and now, this. Am I crazy or is he? Can a man be so divided in himself?

6

We went to that temple every Friday, my mother and I. I longed to carry the brass tray that held flowers, coconut and the *haldi* and *kumkum* containers. But she would never let me. You'll drop it, she would say, as confidently as if she had seen me doing it. It was no use insisting. Dropping the Devi's* offerings would be not only a heinous crime and sacrilege, but a catastrophe as well. You could be cursed with so many awful things by her. She looked a dreadful cursing kind of Devi, anyway. The women sometimes called her "Mother!" Imagine, I thought, having a mother like that, with a brass head and staring, frightful brassy eyes as well. No wonder all the women were scared of displeasing her.

As for me, I was uneasily fascinated. She gave me a cold feeling in the pit of my stomach. Those staring eyes seemed to follow me everywhere. I couldn't get away from them, even when we went to the back of the temple where the water that trickled after the *puja* through a tiny drain had left a green mark along the wall. But in spite of my uneasiness about the Devi, I never missed a Friday. I went there each week.

There were compensations. Putting the money, our offering, in the deep wooden box with brass railings and slanted sides. Ringing the deep-toned bell, listening to the sound that trailed away in the small, stone building into fascinating echoes. The smell of oil, camphor and flowers. The cheerful babble of female talk that made me feel warm and secure. There was, I now realise, a kind of comradeship among the women, as if they were soldiers fighting in the same war. In this place they had a momentary respite, a brief instant of getting away from battle, comparing strategies, discussing plans.

To me there was something comforting in the sameness of their talk, their attitudes, their responses. They were safely predictable.

But everything, it seemed, was deceptive. I never felt the same about the women after I saw what happened to one of them that day.

She was a middle-aged woman, like so many others, plump, large-hipped, with seven-pearl earrings in her ears and black beads round her neck. Her hair, like that of the others, parted in the centre and tied into a tight bun just above the nape of her neck. One moment she was all this, just one more woman worshipping the Devi, holding her tray of offerings in one hand, the other stretched out to apply *kumkum* to the Devi's large, brassy forehead. The next moment there was a loud clatter as her tray fell out of her hands. My heart jumped into my mouth. What would happen to her now? What would the Devi do to her? And then, when I saw her face, I forgot all about the Devi. It was as if the woman had gone away leaving a dreadful changeling in her place. A creature with a frightening mask-like face and popping eyes that stared fixedly at the Devi.

And then she was alone as the women moved away, leaving her isolated there in front of the Devi. The woman began to gyrate, turning round in a slow, peculiar motion I would have giggled at any other time. But now the taut silence petrified me. In that silence her deep gasping breaths could be heard loud and clear. Then faster and faster, both body and breath, the face a grotesque travesty of what it had been before. It scared me. I moved closer to my mother, clutching the end of her sari tightly in my fist. Meanwhile the woman continued, feet thumping, hands flailing, sari coming loose, hair flying round that awful face with those frightful eyes. And the open mouth out of which the breath came loud and rasping. The breathing was now a grunt and a pant, grunt and a pant. It was horrifying, for some reason obscene, something I just could not understand. Only now, as a grown woman, I realise how much the whole thing resembled the crescendo of excitement during intercourse.

The reactions of the other women were even more inexplicable. One of them now moved forwards, not timorously as I would have imagined, but confidently, and applied *kumkum* to the rotating woman's forehead. Even as she applied it, the face moved on in its perpetual motion and the finger left a smear of the red powder across the forehead. Another woman repeated the action, then another, my mother too, shaking off my tightly clutching hand. The whole face became an ugly bloody red, *kumkum* and sweat mixing together to form a ghastly mask. Until at last, with a long drawn out shudder and sigh, the body making convulsive, febrile movements, she began to slow down.

As if this released me from the vice of stillness that had held me in spite of my fears till then, I fled. Anywhere, away from those women staring at that other woman who had become as terribly inhuman as the Devi herself. I ran out into the open courtyard, up some steps and into the covered hall where, later in the evenings, the women would gather to listen to the man in the red shawl recite the *puranas* in a singsong tone, the rich deep voice moving with scarcely a jerk into tuneful song. Now there was no one there. Only the black stone bull in the centre, looking blissfully disassociated from the feverish atmosphere I had left behind. Coldly detached from any unnatural excitement. I sat by him and touched the tiny stone bells round his neck. People had applied *kumkum* to him, too, and there were offerings of flowers placed between his dainty feet. Even these, however, could not make him anything but what he was . . . a dear little bull carved out of black stone.

Some time later, my mother came out looking for me, a worried-angry expression on her face. I saw her before she saw me, but waited until she called out for me. Then I jumped down to where she stood.

"Let's go home," she said.

"My *prasad**?" I suddenly remembered.

She put her hand into the cloth bag she carried with her and gave me my handful of roasted gram. I had just begun eating them, holding some in my hand, feeling their warmth, their prickliness, when I saw her. The woman. She sat leaning against a pillar, her legs stretched out in front of her, face relaxed and empty, the *kumkum* on her forehead wiped away except for the usual mark between the brows.

When she saw us, she smiled. I stopped, my hands dropping to my sides, my jaws suddenly still, the saliva and the half-chewed gram mixing together to form a paste that nauseated me.

"Got your *prasad*?" she asked me. "Here's something for you."

I held back. I didn't want to go to her, but with my mother pushing me relentlessly forwards I had to, my arms still held rigidly to my sides. She gently took my right hand, the one without the gram, and opening the closed fist, put a lump of rock sugar in it.

"There. Eat that."

Her smile was pleasant, her face gentle. But I could not eat the rock sugar she gave me. I held it in my hand for some time, then, stealthily, eyes fixed on my mother's face, let it drop out. And only the stickiness remained. Feverishly I scrubbed my hands when I reached home to get rid of that.

And only then I asked my mother, "Is she mad?"

"Who?"

"That woman who gave me the rock sugar."

"Mad? What do you mean?"

"Why was she dancing like that? She looked crazy."

I got a smart slap on my cheek. Her gold bangles flicked the skin, leaving behind a stinging pain. But there was something in the action that hurt more than that.

"Don't talk like that about things you don't understand. Mad? What a stupid thing to say. The Devi entered into her, understand?"

I didn't. I didn't understand how a woman who could smile and look so pleasant, could also fling herself about with an ugly wild abandon like that. I just could not put the two women together. Perhaps, I thought, they were two women after all, not just one. Only then did it makse sense. That a person could be so divided in herself, into two entirely different beings, was something unknown to me then.

7

It had not been there when she had left home. Now it occupied a place of honour in the hall. It intrigued her, this tray, a large one of stainless steel, with a brazen good luck wish emblazoned on it in a garish green. It was the kind of thing you saw in so-called "novelties" shops; and she wondered what they had bought it for and why.

The mystery was solved when she saw Baba sitting down and polishing it with all the solemnity that attended the performance of a ritual. "It's mine," he said in answer to her question. "The Bank gave it to me when I retired. This, and a time piece."

He handed it to her with a certain child-like complacency. She turned it over. There was his name, the date, and an inscription . . . "a devoted and a sincere worker."

I suppose he was, she thought now, remembering how he had gone to work each morning, punctual as the proverbial time piece, his brown cap, shiny with age, on head, trousers encircled by the clips he wore when cycling. With trousers narrowed below the knees by these clips he had a false air of jauntiness as he went to work. I never thought of him as anything but Baba, but he had a life of his own there. She wondered now whether it had been more satisfying than the life he led here and if he had an importance there he had never achieved at home.

She had seen him in the Bank only once. She had gone with some friends there on one of the school's sporadic fund-raisers.

She could still remember the girls standing near the door and giggling, prodding her, saying, "Where's your father? Go ask him, Saru. Go on."

"I don't know where he is," she had lied. The sight of him sitting in a cage while the others sat in the open had, for some reason, shamed her. She had pretended she hadn't seen him. He had not glanced at her, either. Nor had he referred to the matter when he came home in the evening.

We rarely spoke to each other, even then. Dhruva, yes, they had conversation together. And he took him out on the bike with him, Dhruva perched in front of him on the small seat specially fixed on the handle bars. The reserve was perhaps part of an old-fashioned attitude that daughters are their mothers' business. But my mother had nothing for me, either. Whose business was I then?

She wished she could talk to him now. The unchanging bleakness of their relationship saddened her. Perhaps we are fated to be strangers, she thought. And then, angrily rejected the thought. She would not believe in Fate.

"Baba," she began resolutely, determined to say something, anything, not to let the moment go, when he took the tray back from her.

"Your mother," he said, not noticing that she had spoken, carefully, almost reverently, putting the tray away in its place, "she hated this."

Suddenly she felt as if he had taken a step towards her, wearing the three-league boots she read of in her children's story books.

"'Is that all?' she used to say, 'Is that all for thirty-five years of work . . . a painted tray?'"

Is that all? A painted tray. An empty house. One child dead. Another alienated. And then the final reward . . . pain, suffering and death. She could have wept, but her mother's suffering was for her, only an idea still. She could not believe in it entirely.

It was Mai-kaki who brought her mother's illness home to her. That was one of the strangest things about her stay, the women who came to visit her. As if the Dixits' Bal had been the first breach in her wall of isolation, she suddenly found herself being visited by neighbours, old friends of hers and her mother's.

Bal was better, though irritable and fretful. But for his parents, Sudhir and Prema, it was miracle enough. They escorted her to and from their house as if she was royalty. More, they infected all those they met with their belief in her, so that the attitude of the women who came to see her was both deferential and admiring. An attitude that was, despite everything, immensely satisfying. It was then she realised that there had been something lacking in her life before. They had not seen her success, those who had known her as a child in unbuttoned frocks and bare feet. Now, to confront these people with what she was, to see them take it in, gave her a brief, an infinitesimally brief spurt of gladness. And then it was gone. If they knew . . . She could imagine the gossip, the remarks, the wagging heads and clicking tongues. She shivered at the thought, feeling as if she had been pushed out of the warm hole into which she had retreated, and now stood outside, open to all the winds.

It had become routine now, the knock on the door, the voice asking Baba, "Is Saru in?" and Baba's, "Go in, go in, she's in there." The visits were invariably in the afternoon, the only time, she knew, when the women could call their own. She would be lying down on the straw mat in the small room which she had made her own. She would not be sleeping, but reading one of the Marathi magazines Madhav brought for her from the circulating library. At the sound of voices she would get up, trying to smooth her dishevelled hair, pulling her sari into place, saying, "Come in, come in." Trying to remember sometimes . . . which one is this. Indutai or Saralatai? Hema or Lata?

After a few minutes she would make the customary offer of a cup of tea. Polite refusals, which were a part of the game, were ignored, and with an odd feeling of "I've done this before" she would go into the kitchen, the woman following her, still demurring at the trouble. She would pump up the Primus back to life, setting on it the long-handled brass vessel always used for making tea, water being measured out first with the cup that had lost an ear. The gestures, the actions, the very words that accompanied them were, though she did not realise it, her mother's. As if she was unconsciously mimicking the mother she had never admired, never endeavoured to imitate. But there was in her, as she made the tea, a curious confusion. I've done this before. No, not I, but my mother. This is what she did when there were visitors. And she went on jumbling herself with the dead woman, sometimes feeling she was acting out a role, sometime feeling she was her mother herself. And somewhere was that unloved, resentful, neglected child, Saru.

The visits, the intimate familiar talk, the curious probing, took on for her an inexplicable charm contrasted to the kind of socialising they did in Bombay. There was something soothing in the conversation about trivialities, about the predictable responses. Something comforting in the lack of pretence of interest in anything but known people and their doings. Curiosity, envy, and disapproval were rarely veiled.

With the women to whom she was Kamalatai's Saru, the talk would be personal. "How many children?" they would ask, and the photographs would be passed round. There would be questions about her children, exclamations about their resemblance to her or her parents. They rarely mentioned her husband, nor did she ever refer to him. But she would be conscious of the eyes probing curiously, subjecting her to a kind of unspoken . . . third degree, wasn't it what the Americans called it? They would make good inquisitors, she thought, these women, making you feel guilty for god-knows-what.

There were others to whom she was not Saru, but a "lady doctor." Artlessly, they would turn the talk to some complaint of theirs. In a few days she knew the whole range of them. The myriad complaints, the varying symptoms. She thought, if put together, they would provide a world of data for a treatise on the condition of women. Backache, headache, leucorrhea, menorrhagea, dysmenorrhea, loss of appetite, burning feet, an itch "there" . . . all the indignities of a woman's life, borne silently and as long as possible, because "how do you tell anyone about these things?" Everything kept secret, their very womanhood a source of deep shame to them. Stupid, silly martyrs, she thought; idiotic heroines. Going on with their tasks, and destroying themselves in the bargain, for nothing but a meaningless modesty. Their unconscious, unmeaning heroism, born out of the myth of the martyred woman, did not arouse her pity or her admiration. It made her angry. "Why didn't you do something about it earlier?" she often asked. But they had schooled themselves to remain silent.

Her earlier resentment at their imposition upon her had worn off. She now advised, suggested, and prescribed with almost the same enthusiasm she had had as a fresh graduate. Perhaps, she thought, I should come and stay here, where I can be of so much use. And then she laughed at herself. Such pat solutions existed only in books and movies . . . the hero or heroine ending up as a do-gooder in a village, beloved by all. She could not change the course of her life to that extent, not unless some impetus from outside forced her to it. She remembered having read somewhere, in a magazine maybe, of Betty Friedan saying that it was easier for her to start the women's lib movement than to change her own personal life. That was how it was. Slippery paths they may be, but you know the risks, the dangers, the treacherous points well . . . or so you think . . . and you would rather go on than turn to other paths.

Mai-kaki came to her for no other reason than that she was Saru. She had been one of the few women with whom her mother had been intimate. Listening to Mai-kaki she wondered whether it was indeed her mother of whom she spoke. Mai-kaki called her a brave woman, a woman of courage who never complained.

"She never told anyone about what was happening to her. The amount she ate . . . I tell you, a sparrow would have eaten more. Your father never noticed because she never ate with him."

Always the drama, the pretence of submission, she thought with anger. But she never fooled me, though.

"But I saw it and I was anxious for her. 'I'm all right,' she said to me. 'I don't have much of an appetite, that's all.' And then she began vomiting. It was like a pregnant woman vomiting, but I knew it was not life she carried inside her, but death. Her face was grey, like the ash on a burnt coal. 'Go and see a doctor,' I told her, not once but many times. 'I'll come with you,' I said. But she would never agree. You know how she was."

Mai-kaki paused, looking at her expectantly, and she nodded impatiently, the gesture asking the other woman to go on.

"She was immensely strong. There aren't many women like her now. For the smallest pain, they rush off squealing to doctors. Tonics and injections and whatnot. But not your mother. She lost so much weight, her *cholis* were hanging off her. And her bangles came up to here." Mai-kaki pointed to her own plump forearm near the elbow.

"At last I spoke to your father myself. He tried to persuade her to go to a doctor. 'No doctor for me,' she said. 'I don't want to see their faces.'"

How much she must have hated me!

"It was Madhav who finally got her to agree to see a doctor. But by then it was too late. They asked her to go to Tata Hospital . . . it's Tata, isn't it? And she went to Bombay only to die. She never came back."

But why then this strange feeling that her mother was still there, still hating her?

"I told her . . . 'go to Saru. She's your daughter, after all. Where else should you go at such a time?' But she . . . " Mai-kaki shook her head. There had been a kind of hard glitter in her eyes, the shine of unshed tears. Now, she wiped them with the end of her sari and said, "That was the one point on which I could never agree with her. Her refusal to be reconciled to you. Even then, when she was dying, she said the same thing, when I asked her to go to you. 'What daughter? I have no daughter.'"

And now the small room grew full of the smouldering anger of the dead woman. The thought of that anger was like a cloud, blotting out everything else. Even the happiness of her early married life vanished as if it had never been.

I hate her, sapping me of happiness, of everything. She's always done it to me . . . taken happiness away from me. She does it even now when she's dead.

8

It was actually our first holiday. Earlier there had been no money; and later, as I found myself increasingly occupied with the children and my work, there was no time. Now it seemed we could afford to get away for a few days. How I looked forward to it! I should have known better. The very intensity of my expectations should have warned me. For, hadn't it been there with me now for so many years . . . a fear of happiness? In earlier years it had been just a shadow, skimming over me, touching me, very lightly, if at all. Then it became definite, an instinct, neither foreboding nor supersticious, but a certainty, a knowledge garnered through years of experience. That it's always there, waiting round the corner, disaster, catastrophe, grief. The cartoon of a man walking briskly, a merry whistle on his lips, while round the corner a man on a ladder is on the point of overturning a tin of paint . . . it isn't just a joke. To me it carries message . . . expect happiness and you've had it.

The first time this came to me I was but a child. I could not put it together then to form a cogent thought. It was just a confusing, unpleasant experience, no more; sharp, like all the experiences of childhood, brief as they always are.

We had had a skipping contest during the break, a test of endurance to see who could go on the longest. To everyone's surprise, I, the youngest of the group, had survived after all the others had given up. I had been petted, made much of by the older girls. I went back to class suffused in a glow of happiness, almost literally walking on air. And then I discovered that the bell had rung long back and I was late. The other girls were at their places. I had no excuse for coming in late and I was punished. As I stood on the bench among the virtuously working girls, who gave me quick looks and just as quickly averted their glances, I plumbed the depths of humiliation. And there it was, success and humiliation inextricably linked together.

Now, here it was again, the paint waiting to drench me as I went along whistling, dreaming of my holiday. When we met them, that couple, it seemed just one of those casual meetings that mean nothing. But they were really, though I did not know it then, the man-on-the-ladder, from whom I would receive a disastrous drenching of wet paint.

We had gone out shopping, Manu and I, for a suitcase and a few other things we needed when we met a colleague of Manu's and his wife. We stopped and confronted each other with smiles.

It's like a ballet, I often think, or a Bharat Natyam dance, these meetings between couples, between families; not with the beauty and rhythm of the dance, but with all its rigidity. It's as if we move on chalked lines, no deviations allowed at all. The men slap each other on the back, feigning a greater intimacy than there really is. The females smile and simper, talk of children and servants, and, if the children are there, coo at them. And then, saying to one another with equal insincerity . . . do visit us, you must come . . . we part, the smiles falling off our faces with remarkable rapidity, the women slipping smoothly into criticism and invective. Stupid, idiotic drama. But essentially harmless. Not that time, however.

"Going somewhere?" the man asked, looking down at the suitcase.

"Yes, we're having a small holiday."

"Where?"

"Down South. Ooty for a few days, Bangalore and Mysore on the way."

"Oh!" The face lost its grip on the smile for a moment. Then with an effort, held on to it again like a tired swimmer clutching at a plank he had lost hold of for a moment.

"Lucky fellow. We've been dreaming of Matheran for years. Can't afford even that."

"If you had married a doctor," the wife said tartly, "you'd have gone to Ooty too."

"Ooty? I'd go further . . . London, Paris, Rome, Geneva."

"We aren't in that class as yet."

The man laughed, his wife laughed and the two of us laughed as well. And no mirth in any of us.

We drove back in silence. I thought he was, maybe, tired. In the evening when I returned home after my consulting hours, he seemed his usual self, telling me about the children, about a student who was being troublesome. We went to bed. He was still reading when I dropped off to sleep.

I woke up to darkness and an awareness of fear. Panic. Then pain. There it was, for the second time, what I had just lulled myself into believing was just a nightmare. The hurting hands, the savage teeth, the monstrous assault of a horribly familiar body. And above me, a face I could not recognise. Total incomprehension and complete bewilderment paralysed me for a while. Then I began to struggle. But my body, hurt and painful, could do nothing against the fearful strength which overwhelmed me. My mind, fluttering, threw itself despairingly on the walls of unbelief and came back staggering, bruised and spent. And then, mercifully, the end, the face still hovering over mine, changing as the body relaxed, becoming the familiar, known one of my husband. The face and body both moving away to become a familiar huddled shape by my side.

The same face smiling at me the next, morning, saying, "Morning, Saru. Slept well?"

"I'm glad we came here," he said in Ooty. "You look very tired and strained. You need to take things easy, relax. Look, I'll take the children off your hands. And no more dark circles under your eyes, okay?"

A sham, a farce, a ghastly pretence? Or was it I who was dreaming, going through a terrible nightmare that left behind this horrible aftertaste of fear? But what about my bruises then? I was still groping in the dark, hands outstretched, fingers held out to touch, to feel. But once again . . . nothing.

Yes, I was just tired, that was all. That was my excuse once again when he took the children out that day, Renu on a little pony, Abhi with his father, the children too excited even to speak. And he too, looking gay and young again, saying to me, "I wish you were coming with us, Saru."

"Me too. But I'd rather relax. Have a nice time."

I went back into the hotel, to the reading room with its British-era solid teak furniture and huge glass windows through which you could see the view on three sides. And as I looked I could see them, my husband and children, Abhi bidden by his father, Renu looking tiny by his side. Sitting there in that bright, glass-enclosed room, watching them move away, I felt a deadly fear. As if I was isolated from everyone, from the whole world, by what was happening to me; I was doomed to sit and watch happiness, watch it recede from me; doomed never to participate in it, never experience it myself.

The figures dwindled and it seemed that there was more than just a sheet of glass between them and me. And I was a child again . . .

How old was I? Four or five? Or perhaps a little older. I was sitting cross-legged in front of my mother who was combing my hair. She did it as precisely as she did anything else, making two neat parts, the point of the comb hurting my scalp as it ran over, marking the lines. And now I had to sit sideways so that she could plait the left half of my hair, which she held in one determined fist. I would have turned when I saw through the window, in the open space of land that lay on one side of our house then, a pony. The pony was jumping, running, with all the awkward energy of over-enthusiasm. Clumsy and awkward though it seemed to be, its movements and the gently sloping green ground harmonised into a beautiful whole that somehow enchanted me.

"Turn this side."

"Wait, mother."

With an angry jerk at my hair that pulled my whole head painfully with it, she said again, "Come on, hurry up. Turn round."

"Oh, wait mother."

Now the pony was galloping, the four legs flashing together, then moving apart in an effortlessly beautiful flow of joy and energy that somehow came across to me through the window.

"Turn." Another angry jerk that sent a sharp pain through my head. "I have other work to do. I have no time to waste like you have. 'Wait, mother'! What should I wait for?"

And with her hand she turned my whole body away from the window. I neither protested nor cried. I knew I was powerless. But the pony . . . Large tears rolled down my cheeks, tickling my nose, my ears, making my lips tingle, until I put out my tongue to lick them away. I tasted salt and mulled the taste and flavour over in my mind. And there was the end of that grief!

Now it came back, as if it had been waiting patiently all these years for the right moment to return to me. To my horror I began to sob. A man sitting in a large armchair and reading a magazine gave me a sharp look, then went back to what he was reading. But I could no longer control myself. It was beyond me. The sobs tore through me, harsh and ugly. Dimly I realised that the man had got out of his chair and walked out of the room.

At last, with an effort greater than I had ever made in my life, I managed to control myself. I had wiped my face dry by the time the man returned with a glass of water in his hands, as if that was a panacea for grief. He looked relieved to see me calmer, but I, who had hoped that he had gone away, cringed with shame at the sight of him. And yet there was comfort in the thought that he had not gone away. Perhaps one would never be totally deserted after all.

I drank the water and then we began to talk. I can't remember what it was we talked about. Something, I suppose. Anything to forget what had happened. So that we became, after a while, just two strangers talking polite trivialities in a hotel room.

PART THREE

1.

It was a reunion. The three of them had formed a close unit in school and had been inevitably nicknamed the Three Musketeers. When they went to college, their paths diverged. Saru and Smita had gone in for Science and Nalu had taken up Arts. Nevertheless they had kept in touch and stayed friends.

"Isn't it funny," Smita said now, "to think of us meeting after so many years?"

Only Smita, Saru thought, could have used the word "funny" to describe their meeting. As if Nalu felt the same way, she retorted, "Funny? It isn't funny at all. It's tragic. How easily we give up things. You could have met me any time if you had tried," she said accusingly to Smita.

"You come here almost each year."

"But, how could I?" Smita complained. "I rarely stay here more than a few days, and when 'he's' with me . . ."

"Ah! There it is! 'He'! There's always time to do all the things 'he' wants to do, but never any time for doing the things you want to do. You just tag on to him and drift, a small boat towed by a larger ship . . ."

"Small?" Saru asked, eyebrows raised.

Smita had been a slim, rather frail-looking girl, with large, vulnerable eyes. Now she seemed armoured all over with fat and hideously invulnerable. Her fat looked not only ugly to Saru, but obscene, remembering the quality of delicacy there had been about her. But Nalu didn't pause, not even to smile.

She went on fiercely, ignoring the interruption, "Do you have to surrender so easily?"

"Surrender? What have I given up?" Smita protested.

"Your name for one thing," Saru said wryly.

When they had exchanged addresses, Saru had stared down, frowning, at the paper on which Smita had written hers.

"Geetanjali?" she said questioningly.

"Oh, that's my name now. Of course, you didn't know. He chose it himself when we got married."

Smita's conversation was littered with 'he's . . . her own 'he' distinguished from the others by a scarcely noticeable something . . . a kind of coy emphasis.

"He used to read Tagore in those days."

Well, why not? Don't we burden our children with names that mean nothing to them, if so much to us? But that's different. This drastic change of identity, changing both the names that identified you for so many years . . . how then do you know yourself, and who you are?

"And he hates anyone calling me Smita now. He gets very annoyed if anyone does that. He calls me Anju himself," Smita ended with what came close to a simper.

"Well, I refuse to call you Anju or Geetanjali or whatever. To me you are Smita and will always be Smita." Nalu spoke as if she was asserting something, a viewpoint maybe, or an attitude.

Yes, we could very well be symbols of three totally different attitudes, she mused. Nalu, the spinster, dedicated to her job. Smita, wholly wife, mother and housekeeper. And Saru, who combined a career and a family so well.

It's all a question of adjustment, really. If you want to make it work, you can always do it.

Who said that? Why, Saru herself, in that inane interview she had granted to a woman's magazine. No, better not think of that now, neither the interview, nor the girl who had done it, nor what followed after.

Yes, they had changed, all three of them. It was inevitable. Human beings are in a continuous process of change. The idea that you can pick up life, or any relationship, she thought, where you left it earlier is incredibly simple. Not only that, it's impossible. With Nalu and Smita, she thought, the attitudes had so hardened that they seemed like two opposing ends of a stick.

But sometimes it seemed that the attitudes were just shells, thin shells that cracked at the tap of a finger. Like Smita, the happy wife and mother, who wanted nothing else in life, suddenly asking Saru, brashly, though her eyes were anxious and the expression faintly shame-faced . . . "Saru, can you lend me some money?" She was serious. The conciliating look on her face was proof enough.

"How much?"

"Can you give me a hundred? You know I came here for my nephew's thread ceremony. 'He' gave me just enough to buy a small gift for the boy. But I had to buy a sari for my sister-in-law as well. It would have looked very mean if I hadn't. All the others did it. And four of us, the children and I, staying here for nearly a month. 'He' doesn't understand these things. 'He' takes it for granted I'm welcome here. Now if I tell him I've bought a sari as a gift, he'll be furious. So I thought, if you lend me a hundred . . . I haven't paid the shop for it as yet . . . I can return the money to you later . . ."

"Oh, that's all right. You don't have to worry about that."

"I must." Smita's face lost its pleading look. She appeared more comfortable now as if the assertion of her desire to return the money restored her to an equality with her friend. "I'll send it to you as soon as I can. I manage to save a bit from what he gives me for the household expenses. Last time I made some dresses for the girls and he never realised it."

Smita looked triumphant, but Saru felt sick. "He calls me Anju." Oh my god!

"That's all right," she said again. "Take your own time. Shall I give you the money right now?"

"If you don't mind." As Smita held the money in her hand, she said, "You don't know how lucky you are not to have to ask anyone for money. If you knew my problems . . ."

Nalu would say that it was marriage and men that had degraded Smita. But Smita had done it even in those days, lying at home about where she went and what she did, getting money from her mother for books and splashing it in the canteen. So perhaps it was really Smita after all. Perhaps it meant that one never really changed, which in turn meant that there was no hope for the future.

It was impossible not to envy Smita her amazing resilience. Now, the money in her hands, she forgot her bitterness and went back to her normal manner. Since they last met, she had graduated, married, given birth to three children, doubled her size, lost her father. But through it all her habit of nudging, pinching giggling, and clutching had stayed with her. Worse, what had been just a hint, a nuance, was now exaggerated into a full-blown fact, so that her capacity to inbue every remark with lewd implication had turned to a general gross vulgarity,

"I must go back home next week," she told Saru. "'He' writes and says he can't be without me any longer." A nudge and a pinch, opening up vistas of sexual hunger on the husband's part, and a coy if passionate response on Smita's. How do they do it, she wondered dispassionately, looking at Smita's shapeless body? And, thank god, that's the one thing that's so difficult to imagine about others! If we could see on the faces of certain men and women what goes on between . . .

She pushed her secret back into its place, trying to enter into Smita's mood of exchanging confidences. She had thought she was succeeding remarkably well, when her complacency was shattered by Smita's plaintive, "Honestly, Saru, you've changed terribly. Don't tell me he's influenced you so much."

"Who?"

"Who else? Your Manu. And does he still write poetry? I never get a chance to read anything these days. There's house-work and the children the whole day, and if I try to read at night, 'he' won't let me."

Another pinch and a giggle. Obviously an insatiable hus-band.

"I say, Saru, do you remember that poem he wrote in a mag-azine? Padmini or something. You remember the girl about whom he wrote that? What was her name now? Goodness, I've forgotten everything. Bet you give him hell now, don't you, if he writes poetry for other females, eh Saru?"

A roguish slap. I'll be black and blue by the time she leaves. Both physically and mentally. I hate being touched. Maybe that's why I'm comfortable here with Baba and Madhav. There is no touching, physical or emotional. Each one of us is intact, a separate whole.

"No, he doesn't write much poetry these days."

Why did he stop? I don't know. It has nothing to do with me. Have I ever prevented him from doing what he wanted to do? On the contrary, I left him free, making no demands, giv-ing him opportunities he would never have had otherwise. And Professor Kulkarni saying that day . . . He was one of my best students. As if he was accusing me. Am I always to be the guilty one?

"What does he do, then?"

There was something comforting in Smita's unconscious cruelty.

"He teaches. He's been teaching in a college for the last ten years."

He could have achieved something there, but he didn't. Same college, same lectures, same notes.

"I bet the girls are after him, eh, Saru? My! I remember how my heart used to go pit-a-pat, pit-a-pat, whenever I saw him. Is he still the same?"

The same? No, better turned out. So many expensive clothes, always in the latest modes. And recently, a beard as well. To be in the trend? To hide something? To add something? To her, it screamed the lack of the very thing he tried to assert.

She could have broken down and wept on Smita's capacious bosom. But Smita was, in spite of her three children, a child herself. So she changed the topic and made tea for Smita. And Smita chattered and giggled and nudged and pinched.

With Nalu it was entirely different. Nalu, if she had altered at all physically, had improved. She dressed well, simply, with no fuss and had acquired an air of dignity that suited her. There was more confidence, too, but with it a conviction of her own rightness that made her seem overbearing and dogmatic. There was a whole world of bitterness within her, ready to spring to the surface at any moment. She complained about her brother and his family with whom she lived, her students and colleagues, the administration of the college—she taught in their old college—politicians, the government, everything. Remembering the Nalu of old with her endearing enthusiasms, she wondered at the bitterness. It's easy to generalise, she thought, and say she is bitter because she never married, never bore a child. But that would be as stupid as calling me fulfilled because I got married and I have borne two children. I could talk to Nalu about my problems and maybe she would understand better than most people would. But to her, I would be a warned woman, my problems those of a warned woman. But this is mine, Saru's, and has as much to do with what I am, apart from my being a woman. It's not only I, it's Manu and I, and how we react against each other.

And so once again, silence was the only answer.

"Has your friend gone?" Madhav peered in to ask.

"Yes, it's all clear. Come in, I'm sorry if you're disturbed by these people."

"Oh, I don't mind. And I think Kaka likes it. I have a feeling he used to be rather lonely, alone at home the whole day. When you go away, he'll find it difficult getting used to the loneliness all over again."

When you go away . . . she shied away from the words.

"You had a letter from home today, didn't you?"

"Yes, from my mother. Its rare to get a letter from her. She did some schooling . . . till the fourth standard, I think . . . but now she says she's forgotten all that she had learnt and finds even letter writing difficult. But she wrote this time because she's terribly worried about my younger brother."

"Which one? Satish?"

She had learnt all their names now.

"Yes, Satish, He's crazy about films and sneaks off to the next town to see one whenever he gets a chance. My father knows nothing about it. My mother knows, but she'll never tell him. My father wants him to learn Sanskrit like himself and give up his schooling. Satish detests the idea. He's threatening to run away. To Bombay."

Madhav smiled, an incredibly adult smile. As if he knew that the idea of escape was ridiculous, impossible.

"He acts mild and obedient when father is around, but he's terribly wild, really. And mother is scared he'll really run away. I'm wondering whether I should go home for a day or two . . . and try to get some sense into that kid's head. But what's the use? Father will scold me for wasting money on bus fare, Satish won't listen, and I can't talk to father, either. None of us can talk to him."

The boy looked so dejected, she felt sorry for him. And angry with the mother who burdened him with her problems.

"And the others?" she asked. "How are they?"

"Oh, they're all right." He smiled again. "As long as they're fed and they can play, nothing matters to them. Its only we older ones . . . There's Mrinal. She's between me and Satish. She's unhappy too. She hates our village and the kind of life she's leading. Going on and on with the same things day after day. Get the water, look after the kids, help Mother . . . oh, she's fed up, she says. She wants to get away too. 'I don't care how,' she says. She's prepared to marry anyone who'll take her away from there. Father is looking out for a bridegroom for her, but he'll never think of consulting her or asking her what she would like. And if it's someone living in a village, she says she'll drown herself. "

"Oh, poor girl," she exclaimed, taken out of herself for the first time.

"Poor girl! She's a silly girl," he said scornfully, secure in the fortress of his own male reasonableness. "She reads stories in magazines and books and dreams of love and all that nonsense. She thinks it will happen to her, too, and that she will escape that way."

"Does she?"

And the girl and her romantic dreams seemed something distant, unimaginable, like a home abandoned in childhood and almost totally forgotten.

"Are all girls that silly?" he asked, and now he seemed only a boy complaining about his sister.

"Yes, all of them," she said.

I, too, once. Man and woman, male and female, how exciting that game had seemed! And that she could play that game well had seemed even more incredibly exciting. "You're a woman now," they had told her when she began menstruating. But she did not feel then that it made her any different. She was the same Saru, with the burden of that curse added on to her like an appendage each month. To be shed as soon as it was over and forgotten. But the thought . . . *I am a woman* . . . had come to her when she had first felt a male look at her, when she had felt an unwilling response within her to that look.

And now? It was as if she had lost awareness of her own femininity. Since coming home she had almost ceased to think of herself as a woman; a woman, that is, with the attributes of attracting a man. She had stopped using make-up. Her lips had, for the first few days, felt chapped and dry without lipstick, almost as if she was parched by a perpetual thirst. Now, the dry flaky skin had fallen off and her lips felt soft and somehow sweet-tasting.

For long she had religiously followed the fashions, all the meaningless innovations, revivals and rejections. Now the thought aroused a vague surprise in her. Why had she done it and who was it all for? The answer, though, was easy. From her childhood, when she had heard her mother say . . . don't go out in the sun, you'll get dark . . . to her girlhood, when every look in the mirror had been a vague search for reassurance . . . do I look nice? . . . it had been a furious attempt to please someone else. At first, everyone, then a generality of males, then a nebulous "right man," who would some day miraculously fall in love with her, thinking her beautiful.

And at last it had been Manu. Her deference to his tastes had seemed wholly natural at first. Now, for the first time, she found herself, waveringly, hesitantly, making her way back to her real self. I, as I would like myself to be. But hunting for that real self had become rather like a dog scrabbling for a long-buried bone. Piles of earth flew up, but where the hell was the bone? Or, had there never been a bone to begin with?

And yet it was not that loss which filled her with such grief now. It was the other thing . . . the thing she knew she had lost forever . . . the eternal female dream of finding happiness through a man. It would never come alive for her again. Too soon, I lost it too soon, she thought. And it was like a silent mourning wail inside her.

2.

We met outside Akbarally's*. I had gone in to buy a few things for the children . . . Abhi's birthday was only a week away . . . and, coming out, was adjusting my glasses against the glare, looking out for a taxi, when I heard him call out, "Sarita."

I identified the voice even before I saw him.

"Hello, Padma," I greeted him when he came up to me. He looked hurt. "I say, don't call me Padma. Call me Rao." I laughed. That was the way he had introduced himself to everyone in our first few days of college. "Call me Rao" he would say. His insistence on that, making his first name a very obvious secret, naturally drove the boys to ferreting it out. It was, they discovered, Padmakar. And, of course, after that, he was Padma to everyone. But he never got used to it.

"I say," he would urge earnestly, "don't call me Padma. Call me Rao."

He became immediately the butt of our batch. But he was one of the few boys with whom I felt comfortable, as if the feminine name Padma deprived him of his maleness.

The distinction between boys and girls had been very sharply observed in college. The girls, often infuriatingly called "ladies," retreated between lectures and practicals to the "ladies room," which carried an aura of a zenana, with its ceiling-high wooden partition and its separate staircase. I can still remember the smell of that room; the talcum, which some girls dabbed on themselves, feeling no doubt incredibly sophisticated, and the stink of the urine that forced its way out of what was euphemistically called the cloak-room. The stench followed us as we walked to the classrooms, wafting indelicately along the corridors.

Here in medical college, I had realised with some qualms, boys and girls mingled together easily. It took me long to get used to it, and I was initially, never comfortable with any male except Padma, who was my partner.

"You know, Sarita," he said to me, when we went back into Akbarally's for a cup of coffee, "when I first found out you were to be my partner, I was disappointed."

"Why?"

My mind was on the time, hoping I could get away as soon as possible, so that I could spend an hour with the children before going on to my rooms. And on the cake I had brought on the spur of the moment, wondering whether Abhi would like it. Or would he sulk, saying, "Why brown icing, mummy? I want white icing."

"But this is chocolate, Abhi."

"I don't like it. I don't want brown icing. I want white."

"I like it," Renu would be sure to say. "I love brown icing. Is it really chocolate, mummy?"

And she would lick her lips in gusto, theatrically feigning greed. "I love chocolate icing. People who don't like it are fools."

"Why were you disappointed?"

"Oh, you looked so . . ." he made a disparaging gesture that was more uncomplimentary than words could have been. Poor Padma, always so tactless, so unerringly hitting on the wrong thing to say, so that within a month he was the most unpopular student in the batch; specially among the girls, whom he regarded with an ingenuous, critical curiosity. His remarks on their clothes, their walk, their ways of talking made him an immediate enemy. And yet he never seemed to realise that he had done anything wrong. "I say, what have I done?" he would ask in frank surprise.

Yet sometimes he made a remark that seemed incredibly shrewd for so foolish a person as he seemed to be, and we wondered whether his moronic behaviour was one big pretence, and whether he was, perhaps, laughing at us for being taken in. This didn't make him any more popular. His trick of saying the wrong thing helped him to twice flunk in his viva and practicals, despite the fact that he was fairly intelligent and enormously sincere. There was a story about him . . . it later became a legend . . . that he had once tactlessly blurted out to an examiner, who went on and on about his, the examiner's, favourite subject . . . "I say, how long are we going to discuss this?"

"I didn't know much about girls," he went on, "and I was hoping for a glamorous creature . . . somebody like Marilyn Monroe maybe," he gave me his disarming grin, "as a partner. Instead I had you, in that ridiculous skirt and blouse, those two tight plaits, and stiff expression on your face, as if you were disapproving of everyone, specially me."

"Well," I said with chagrin, "you were no Clark Gable, either, were you?"

"And I haven't changed much since then, have I?"

Oddly, he hadn't. He still had the awkward gangliness of an adolescent, fidgeting as if he didn't know what to do with his hands and feet.

"I say, I haven't offended you, have I? What I was trying to say is . . . you've changed beyond all recognition. By god, Sarita, you have!"

His admiration was as obvious as his earlier disparagement had been. His eyes beamed praise, his lips were pursed as if to whistle admiration, I felt strangely pleased, almost exhilarated by his reaction to me.

"And what are you doing now?"

He had always lacked something, a hardness maybe, or a will to compete and succeed. Nevertheless, when he told me he was a G.P., I was surprised. He had been the kind of bookish, theoretically sound person who's fated to ending up an academic.

"Does it make me such a pariah, my being a G.P.?" he asked, noticing the expression on my face.

"It's not that, Padma. I thought you had done your M.D."

"I didn't. I did register for it, but I didn't go on." He said no more and I left it at that, sensing an old hurt. As we came out, he asked me, "Can we meet again somewhere?"

"Why don't you come home?"

He made a face, looking a boy as he stood there, jingling coins in his pocket. It was hot and intensely humid and I could feel the sweat trickling down my thighs, tickling me as it trailed down.

"I'm not much of a one for polite, formal visits. You know me. But I say, you go to the hospital, don't you?"

"Yes, five times a week."

"I go there myself. Six times a week." He grinned, and answering the question in my eyes, said, "Something of my own. I need some research done, and I use the library, too. I'll see you there sometime."

He must have made a special effort to meet me. Why had we never met before? He was sitting on the low wall of the car park, sloppy, uncaring how he looked. I envied him for that.

"Give me a lift?" he asked.

"Where's your car?"

"Never had one, never will have one. Cars frighten me. They confound you with your own ignorance. I hop either into a bus or a taxi, depending on how much of a hurry I am in. A taxi if I have enough time, a bus if I haven't."

I laughed. His candour, which had been a bore then, was refreshingly welcome now.

"Have lunch with me?" he asked.

"I have to go home."

"Oh, home! You go home every day. Come on, I know a place where you get wonderful biryani."

"So South Indian Brahmins have become carnivore, too!" I teased. "But some other time. Not now. Just a cup of tea, maybe."

It became a habit with us. A cup of tea or coffee. Once or twice, his "wonderful biryani," which was, in fact, atrocious, stale rice warmed over, yesterday's smell and taste about it, mixed with huge hunks of bone. He ate it with unbelievable relish, though. We went to the college canteen once and he behaved as if we were still fledgling students, conscious and proud of our gleaming stethoscopes and white coats. Sometimes we met in the library. He would be sitting absorbed in a book or journal, but so aware of me that he would look up the moment I entered, however noiselessly I did it.

And we talked. He spoke to me of his work. He had his practice in the heart of one of Bombay's worst slums.

"And if you think you can't make money in those places you're quite wrong. You can earn more than in any posh place. For one thing, you don't have to put up a show. You can keep expenses down to a minimum. And, for another, even if they live in the slums, those people have money. The whole family goes out to work. And a doctor is one of the things they're prepared to pay for. They can't afford to be sick. Oh yes, I know you people in big hospitals can give them specialist services which I can't. But they lose days when they go to you . . . waiting in queues for every damned thing. They'd rather pay me and get well fast. And what I do is right. They haven't read the Reader's Digest and Science magazines which tell them all about diseases and their cures. So they don't argue with me."

I laughed. I know all about that.

But doctor, too many antibiotics aren't good, are they?
I'm sure, doctor, it is an allergy . . .
Are you sure, doctor? I read the other day . . .

How long would we have gone on this way? Forever, perhaps, if it had been left to me. But, it wasn't. He snatched the
reins out of my hands with an abruptness that shocked me to
an awareness of what I was doing. I hadn't seen him for nearly
a week or more when one day I found him waiting for me near
my car, leaning against it in his usual spineless way, his knuck-
les tapping an impatient tattoo onto the glass.

"I've been waiting for you for ages," he said in an aggrieved
tone, as if we had made an appointment for which I was late.

"Well, how was I to know that?" I asked reasonably.

"Come on, move aside. Let me open this door."

"You've got to lunch with me today," he said as soon as we
were in the car, his eyes gleaming oddly behind his glasses.
"Anything you want today. Anywhere you'd like to go, even
the Taj*."

"What's the occasion? Your birthday? Or, have you won a
lottery?"

And then it burst out of him. "Now I know how those pros-
pectors felt when they found gold. I've struck gold today,
Sarita. "

I had turned the key in the ignition. Now, I switched it off
and sat back.

"You better explain," I said, knowing he was dying to do so.

And then he told me, surrendering his reticence on the subject for the first time, why he had been haunting the hospital
laboratories and library all these days. In his practice, he had
been coming across a number of cases of diarrhoea which
refused to respond to the usual line of treatment. His curiosity
aroused, he had taken the help of an old friend and had some
investigations done. And now, he told me, they were almost

sure they had isolated a cholera-like vibrio which was responsible for the illness.

He was bubbling with excitement and I listened patiently until he was calmer.

"What about lunch then? This is better than any birthday, isn't it?"

"Well yes, but . . ." I looked at my watch. "Sorry, Padma, no time for lunch today."

"But Sarita . . ." His jaw sagged, the eyes behind the glasses were those of a hurt puppy, "you've got to come. I mean, I've been waiting here for so long. I never imagined you'd say no. You can't refuse."

It was getting out of hand. I tried to hold on to my business-like composure.

"Look at the time, Padma," I said trying to sound reasonable. "I've got two more visits to get through before I go home."

He was suddenly quiet now, all his effervescence evanescing, as if it had never been.

"You mean it? You'll walk out on me now?"

"Oh, don't be silly and dramatic, Padma. There's no question of walking out. It's just that I've no time today. Some other day, perhaps . . ."

But he was not listening to me. He was tugging at the handle of the door, trying to get out. He opened it after a moment's fumbling, and banging the door behind him, walked away without a backward look at me.

I sat where I was, rigidly still for a moment while rage filled me, and the world faded away into a blur. Then it came back. I started the car and drove away in a fury. And I knew my anger was not so much at Padma as at myself. It was my fault. I had listened to him as, perhaps, no one ever had. I had talked to him, smiled at him, given him that which was most precious to me . . . my time. What had I done it for?

I had refused to think about it, but I knew I had been drifting and let him become a habit, not realising that nothing is
more fatal than a habit, more difficult to get rid of. Anyway, it
was over now, I told myself, sickened at the same time by my
complacency.

And then one day, there he was, stepping out of the queue
at a bus stop, standing there in front of me, thumb down like
a hitchhiker. I had to stop. He got in. "A cup of coffee?" he
asked as if it was just another time. "No," I said, feeling
trapped, hating the panic that overcame me. "I'll drop you
anywhere you want."

"Sarita," he said, and the way he said it scared me even
more. There was still that little girl, scared of men and rape
inside my sophisticated exterior, panicking at the thought of a
man being interested in me.

"Just ten minutes," he said more calmly and I gave in. For
the first time, there was an awkward silence between us.

"It's a week since I saw you," he said.

"Yes, a week," I replied.

His fingers traced circles on the table between us and I
remembered that we had been partners for dissection. I had,
that first day, felt sick at the sight of the body that lay on the
table before us; but he, I had realised, was much worse. His
face averted, he had clutched Cunningham's Manual to him
like a drowning man holding desperately on to something. He
had been so obviously terrified, I had immediately felt bolder.
"I'll start," I had said in a fit of bravado, picking up the scalpel.
"You read out the instructions."

The next day we had followed the same pattern, until he
had suddenly pushed the manual at me, saying, "Here, you
take this. I'll do that."

And, picking up the scalpel, he had begun working freneti-
cally, as if he would dismember the body within seconds.

"I'm very sorry, Sarita, about my behaviour last time," he

said, reminding me of that moment. His apology was like that of a boy who has been coached by his mother.

"Oh, that's all right," I said with a false heartiness. "I can understand you were disappointed. What have you done, by the way, about your finding?"

He shrugged as if it meant nothing to him. "Nothing. I mean, the authorities aren't interested in knowing about it. Say the word 'cholera' and they clam up. Cholera? Impossible! 'Must be gastroenteritis,' they say."

"But, surely you can . . ."

"Oh, leave it, Sarita. I want to forget about that now. Let's talk about other things. "

And there was silence once again.

"Oh, what's the use, Padma," I said at last. "There's no point in our meeting this way. Neither of us has the time, really."

His face fell. He looked like a child who finds an adult breaking a promise.

"What do you mean, Sarita? No point? I enjoy meeting you, talking to you. Don't you?"

"Well, yes . . ." I said, making my hesitation obvious, but he wasn't interested in my reply.

"It gives me pleasure, Sarita. It's an innocent happiness after all, isn't it?"

I said nothing. He went on angrily as if I had rebutted his statement with my silence. "How does it harm anyone if we meet and talk? There's no one else I can talk to. Absolutely no one, I tell you."

"Your wife?" I asked.

We had never mentioned her so far. Neither his family nor mine. And I felt now as if I had begun dissecting, but this time there was no manual he could read to me from, telling me how to go on.

"My wife! She can't talk about anything but servants and the children. And prices. I earn enough, but she's perpetually trying to economise. She never has her food until I go home and have mine, she cooks just what I like, and she never calls me by my name."

I did not know it then, I learnt it later, that his parents had pressurised him into marriage soon after he graduated because his father had needed the dowry his wife had brought them for Padma's own sister's marriage. Padma's father-in-law had agreed to maintain the couple until he completed his postgraduate.

Padma had, on learning this, given up his idea of a M.D. in a fit of pique and gone into general practice.

"A good wife and mother." I said, still trying to keep it light. "And it means nothing to you. What can I give you she can't?"

I had met him, smiled at him, listened to him. And now I knew it had not been thoughtless on my part. I had done it deliberately, coolly, with calculation, because, foolishly perhaps, I had imagined it would give me an escape route, something that would lead me out of my loveless trap. Wasn't it always the solution for a woman who found no happiness with one man to try and find it with another?

But looking at Padma's face now, I knew I had miscalculated. He was like a child, able to see no other point of view but his own. Like an adamant child, wanting some thing, refusing to think of the consequences, angry when reminded of them.

And myself? Now I knew it was not just the consequences I feared and hated, but the thing itself. What had I imagined? Love? Romance? Both, I knew too well, were illusions, and not relevant to my life anyway. And the code word of our age is neither love nor romance, but sex. Fulfilment and happiness came, not through love alone, but sex. And for me, sex was now a dirty word.

Suddenly I felt cold as if I was left alone in the middle of nowhere, one more hideout discovered, one more illusion destroyed.

3

The past was receding and there was no future. There was only this woman who stayed at home, did some chores, talked, and then, when the day was over, slept. And she a normal, sane person, not that two-in-one woman who, in the day-time wore a white coat and an air of confidence and knowing, and at night became a terrified, trapped animal. Both these women had been left behind. At times she felt there was nothing of the old Saru left. She thought for some reason of the glass bowl one of the girls in the hostel had bought. She had claimed it was unbreakable. "Why don't you drop it and see?" they had urged her. Goaded to recklessness at last, she had flung it down and it had not just broken but shattered so completely that there was nothing left of it, not even bits and pieces, just some fine dust.

And yet there were inescapable links with the other woman. The patients to whose presence even here, in this life, she was now resigned. The letters, which, on the other hand, made her angry and resentful when they arrived. Why can't they leave me alone? Why do they pester me? The children, she could see, were already bored with letter-writing. The brevity and preciseness of their letters, as if someone had dictated to them, showed her that. She herself wrote composite letters to the three of them and each time it was the same. There was really nothing to say. But there were occasional spasms of longing for the children. The feel of Renu's soft cheek against her lips, Abhi's weight on her lap, the smell of him when he woke up in the morning, baby-sweet and fresh. There were so many nights when she woke up with the dreadful fear crushing that she had forfeited all rights to the children forever. It had been in her for some time now, a feeling that her unhappiness was a taint that would eventually stain them as well.

It had begun the day when the four of them had been watching a TV programme. Manu had been sitting with his feet up on a stool, and unconsciously she had stared at them . . . soft white, unmarked and flabby. Like his hands. And his laugh . . . it was rather silly. A kind of bray, almost. Why had she never noticed that before? And had he always picked at his ears that way, deftly, rather stealthily? She did not know how long she stared. It was like seeing a man she had never seen, never known. A man whom, now that she knew him, she rather despised. And then, suddenly, Renu had flung herself at her father, burying her head in his lap, and burst into tears, her body quivering with the violence of her sobs. What had the child seen on her mother's face? It had unnerved her, the way she had scared her own daughter. I wish, she had thought passionately, I had stayed what I was once . . . a blindly adoring female.

But the thought no longer appealed to her. Not since she had seen the metamorphosis in the woman who lived in the next street. As a child, on her way to school, she had often seen that woman. She would be on the doorstep, seeing her husband off. She had noticed them one day, smiling at each other, oblivious of everything else. It had fascinated her, a growing girl, who had seen nothing of this man-woman relationship in her own home. And once she had seen their hands touch, a contact so swiftly ended that it was like a passing shadow. But she had seen it and she never forgot.

This time, a few days back, she had seen the woman again. A widow now, with a bare forehead and drab sari. But her eyes, lost and empty, were the ghastliest signs of her widowhood.

They had frightened Saru. To put all of yourself into another and then be left alone . . . She shuddered. Better after all, perhaps, to be untouched. But I'm not that, either, she thought in an angry desperation. I'm just nothing.

Smita had left, but Nalu still visited her regularly. She welcomed her presence as the one person who never mentioned the children, never inquired after the "family." Nalu and she, they were two women who had gotten somewhere, women whom Smita envied because they never had to ask anyone for money to spend. Yet, when they met, she felt as if she was seeing a mirror image of her own despairing loneliness in Nalu. It was Nalu who brought her books to read, and for the first time in her life she read them and absorbed them into her. Something quickened in her at Virginia Woolf's mention of a woman's right to a "room of her own." She immediately related the phrase to her own life and thought . . . my mother had no room of her own. She retreated into the kitchen to dress up, she sat in this dingy room to comb her hair and apply her *kumkum,* she slept in her bed like an overnight guest in a strange place. And I have so much my mother lacked. But neither she nor I have that thing, a room of our own.

It was Nalu who sent the two girls to her one day. "Come and give a talk to my students," she had suggested. Saru had forgotten all about it when the girls came. They were, they announced with solemn pride, the President and Secretary of an Association the girls had formed, mainly on Nalu's encouragement.

"What shall I talk about?" she asked.

They had come prepared. They had the answer to that as well. "You can talk about Medicine as a profession for women," they suggested.

She smiled. The smile, more a twist of the lips than anything else, made her look ugly. But she agreed.

On the day she fussed over her appearance, regretting the

fact that she didn't have a good sari to wear, that she hadn't brought any of her makeup. She found some of her mother's pins in the old wooden box with the mirror in which her mother had kept her things, long black pins looking like the legs of some hideously large spider, and used them, putting up her hair in a roll. Her hair, she noticed, in faint satisfaction, had grown enough to let her do that. But when she looked at herself in the small square of the faded mirror in her mother's box, it was like seeing the face of a stranger.

In spite of her groomed, unruffled exterior, when she stood on the platform looking down at the faces that stared so intently at her, some of the girls, even, with pens poised over notebooks, ready, out of habit, to take down everything she said, she had a moment of panic. It was, once again, the fright that came upon her on entering a room full of people. The constriction in the throat, the tightening of muscles in the abdomen, even, shamefully, the feeling that she had to go to the toilet. There was something more too than just this fright . . . a feeling of being a fraud, a sham, an imposter. And, entwined with this, a queer feeling that she was not up here at the podium, but down there among the girls, staring at a young man whose long fingers periodically brushed his hair backwards in one fluid movement. She was not thinking about him, really, not dreaming either; just absorbing his presence, his looks, his gestures into her. And beside her was Smita, nudging her, breathing hard in suppressed excitement, saying . . .

That's Manu.

And then she was out of it. She began to speak. She had, at home, carefully prepared her talk, rehearsed to herself the words she would say.

Listen, girls, she would say, whatever you do, you won't be happy, not really, until you get married and have children. That's what they tell us. And we have to believe them because no one has proved it wrong till now. But if you want to be happily married, there's one thing you have to remember. Have you girls seen an old-fashioned couple walking together? Have you noticed that the wife always walks a few steps behind her husband? That's important, very important, because it's symbolic of the truth. A wife must always be a few feet behind her husband. If he's an M.A., you should be a B.A. If he's five foot four, you shouldn't be more than five three. If he's earning Rs 500, you should never earn more than Rs 499. That's the only rule to follow if you want a happy marriage. Don't ever try to reverse the doctor-nurse, executive-secretary, principal-teacher relationship. It can be traumatic, disastrous. And, I assure you, it isn't worth it. He'll suffer, you'll suffer and so will the children. Women's magazines will tell you that a marriage should be an equal partnership. That's nonsense. Rubbish. No partnership can ever be equal. It will always be unequal, but take care that it's unequal in favour of your husband. If the scales tilt in your favour, god help you, both of you.

And so you must pretend that you're not as smart as you really are, not as competent as you are, not as rational as you are, and not as strong either. You can nag, complain, henpeck, whine, moan, but you can never be strong. That's a wrong which will never be forgiven.

Don't struggle, don't swim against the tide. Go along with it; and if you drown nevertheless, well, that's an easier death after all. They will tell you about economic independence and an independent identity. Forget the words. If Draupadi* had been economically independent, if Sita* had had an independent identity, you think their stories would have been different? No, these are things that have been voluntarily surrendered, consciously abandoned, because that is the only way to survive. And what, in the long run, matters more than survival?

And it is your own teacher, this same Nalu, who told me once, indignantly, an episode in Kalidasa's "Shakuntala." Of how Shakuntala, when rejected by the King, was advised by the escorting ascetics to stay on nevertheless in the King's harem, or as his slave, because he was, after all, her husband. And when the girl, weeping, shamed, humiliated, tried in spite of this noble advice, to follow the ascetics back home, one of them turned round and thundered at her . . . what, wanton girl, do you desire independence?

And then she had finished. As she sat down, there was a spurt of applause, and she realised with an honest astonishment, that she had not made this speech after all. She had spoken instead of . . . what was it the girls had suggested? . . . yes, medicine as a career for women.

Once, during her brief tenure of music lessons, she had been asked to sing a small song for the school concert. Her master had trained her and she had thought she had performed fairly well. But when she went down and sat among the audience, Smita had asked her in amazement, "Why didn't you sing?"

"What do you mean?"

"You just recited it like poetry. You never sang." Others confirmed this and then she realised that, at the crucial moment, music had deserted her. And now, she had failed once again.

She sat down feeling as shamed as she had felt then. She had to get up immediately as one of the girls approached her with a fragrant garland of tuberoses. She had a moment of panic. I can't accept it. Then she submitted. The girl was taller than she was. She did not have to bend to let herself be garlanded. But the garland was too heavy.

The function was over. It was time to go home. Nalu came up to her and said, "Come on, I'll drop you home."

"You don't have to. I can go home by myself."

"Don't be silly. I have to pay for your conveyance, anyway. I might as well go along with you. You don't mind dropping me first, do you? I'll pay the man his fare, of course."

As though it mattered to her, a rupee or two. But she had learnt to hold her tongue, not to reveal how little money, the spending of it rather, meant to her. She remembered her hostel days when she would get off the bus two bus stops earlier to save some money. It has not been easy, living on the sum Baba sent her each month.

But then it had been a kind of miracle anyway, her joining medical college in spite of her mother. Standing up against her, asserting her will against hers . . . that had seemed impossible. But she had done it. I won that time. But I was not alone then. Baba was with me. He helped me. Without him, I would never have succeeded. Now I wonder whether his was a fight for me or against her. Whether he used me as a weapon against her? Whether that hurt her more than my own rebellion did? Is it waiting for me too, a taste of that bitterness? Will Renu turn mocking eyes on me one day? Will Abhi defy me? Will they betray me as I betrayed her? But that guilt is not mine alone. He has to share it with me, for he helped me, my father.

4.

I suppose she was someone's niece, or maybe grand-daughter, who had come to our place for a short visit. Looking back now it seems to me that she must have been quite young and had, possibly, only just passed. But to the child that I was then, she seemed a woman. A tall young woman, with a composed face and two very short plaits that looked odd on her height and yet added a strange elegance to her looks.

Yes, I remember her looks with an astonishing clarity; but even more distinct is the memory of her air of detachment; she was set apart in some way from the other women. (There were many women there that day. What was the occasion? I can't remember that. It's an absolute blank.) And I, who had always thought it some kind of a disgrace to be alone and silent in a crowd, envied her her detachment that day. I knew, instinctively, that she was somehow superior to all the other women there. Later, as the women talked, I learnt that she was a doctor. And so I put the two together. It was because she was a doctor that she was like that. I had seen other good-looking girls with that same air of superiority. That road, however, was barred to me forever. But I could be a doctor. Yes, that would be the key that would unlock the door out of this life, which even then seemed to me dreary and dull. To get married, and end up doing just what your mother did, seemed to me not only terrible but damnable.

Strangely, the ambition stayed with me through the years.

All my friends knew about it. My essays . . . "What would you like to be when you grow up?" proclaimed it to the world. But I never spoke of it at home. By the time my desire had hardened into an ambition, silence had settled down on our house. Dhruva was dead, I was alive and I could not speak. But I worked though, God, how I worked! I gave up all pleasure and concentrated on studies.

I got it at last—the passport to medical college—a first class in my Inter Science . . . but there was no room for jubilation in me. I had worked too hard and I was tired. Besides, there was one more ordeal waiting for me.

I went home and told her nothing but that I had obtained a first class. "Good," she said. No more. But that night there was something special for dinner, something fried, something sweet, and I knew she was pleased, though her face told me nothing. And there was no more talk than usual as we had our dinner, Baba and I. She never joined us. I cleared up after we had done, and then she ate, all by herself, in the kitchen.

I was nerving myself to speak, imagining myself saying it, framing a sentence in my mind, rejecting this word as no good, substituting it with another, when Baba forestalled me. And it was as if he was, unknowingly, helping me by giving me my cue.

"What subjects do you want to take up for your B.Sc., Saru?"

"I'm not going on for a B.Sc."

They stared at me. "You mean you don't want to . . ." he was beginning hesitantly, when I blurted it out. "I want to do medicine."

She had been serving us dal and as I spoke the spoon clanged noisily against the side of the vessel, as if her hand had let go too suddenly.

"You mean you want to become a doctor?"

I did not reply. I would not answer her. I stared at Baba instead, waiting for him to say something.

"Baba," I said, louder this time. "I said I want to go in for medicine. "

"Where's the college?"

Again I ignored her and spoke to him.

"Shall I send in my application, Baba?"

We were like the three points of a triangle, eternally linked, forever separate.

"I said, where's the college?"

"Baba," I spoke as if to a deaf man, my voice getting shrill as I tried to raise it. I felt prepared to shake him, beat him, pound him. Why did he not speak?

"I said . . . shall I send in my application?"

"I heard you."

"And I'm asking you . . . where's the college?"

"I have a first class. More than sixty-five per cent. I'll get admission, I'm almost sure about that."

"But you haven't answered your mother's question . . . where is the college for you?"

"Bombay," I said and a weight rolled off my mind. I had said it.

"Bombay! And where will you live?"

No, I would not talk to her, not even now, but when he asked me, "Will you live in a hostel?" I had to say, "Yes."

"No," she said.

I looked at him again, trying to appear composed, confident, trying not to show the appeal in my eyes.

"Shall I send in my application, Baba?"

"No, I said. Didn't you hear me? No. In a hostel? What do you think . . . your father's a millionaire?"

Now, for the first time I looked at her.

"I'm not talking to you. I'm not asking you for anything. I know what your answer will be. No, forever a 'no' to anything I want. You don't want me to have anything, you don't want me to do anything. You don't even want me to live."

I had sworn I would be cool and calm. But here I was instead, raging, crying loudly, noisily, fighting as vehemently as if I was eleven or twelve instead of eighteen. My voice was high and shrill, there was a pain in my chest, my throat ached intolerably, there was a buzzing in my ears, a blur in front of my eyes. I hated her. I wanted to hurt her, wound her, make her suffer. But I did not know how. I was no more that naive child who had once said, trying to wound her, "I dreamt you were dead."

Actually, it was Baba who I had dreamt was dead. I had seen his body burning on the funeral pyre and I had begun to sob wildly, loudly. My own sobs woke me up. My cheeks were wet. I heard my mother's voice call out, "Who is it? Saru? Dhruva?'"

And suddenly I know it was not Baba who was dead and burnt, but Dhruva who would never come to my bed any more to escape the dark. But why then was she calling out his name? I had held my breath, afraid she would come to me. But there was silence after that. I tried to settle back to sleep, taking care not to move, not to let my sheets rustle. She did not call out again. And then, just as I was dozing off, the silence was broken. It was my mother, moaning, making animal-like sounds that were terrifying. I stuffed my fingers into my ears trying to shut them out.

The next morning when I woke up, I found her making the tea, looking her normal self. I stared at her curiously, and as I moved away I jogged her elbow, spilling some of the tea she was straining. Suddenly fiercely angry, she slapped me. "Can't you be more careful?"

And I said, "Yesterday night I dreamt you died. I saw your body burning."

She looked at me for a moment, her face now impassive, then went back to straining the tea. "Call your Baba to come and have his tea," she said.

If I could not hurt her then with my crude attempt, how could I do so now? And anyway, it's a child's reaction . . . to hurt when you can't win. And this time I won. I wouldn't have but for Baba's help.

"Pusillanimous" . . . I had come across the word in my English text once, and I had dutifully underlined it, reminding myself to look up the meaning in the dictionary later. "Faint-hearted," the dictionary had informed me and I had written that in the margin. And then, on an impulse, I had written below it . . . like my father. I had looked at the words for a moment, smiling in satisfaction, and then just as suddenly, savagely scratched it out.

But this time he was with me. For the first time he ignored her as I had done and spoke to me, excluding her. Not purposefully, not intentionally, but as if he did not, could not see her at all.

"Are you sure you want to do it? Have you thought it over?"

"Yes, Baba."

"You can't change your mind later. This isn't something like taking singing lessons."

I flushed. Why remind me of that?

"I'm eighteen now. Not a child . . ."

"It isn't easy. You'll have to work enormously hard."

"I know that. I can work."

I was impatient with this catechism, but I forced myself into patience. It was necessary. It was as if he was acting out a charade for her sake, forcing me to participate in it, too.

"You know my salary isn't very much. Oh yes, I can pay your fees and for your books and hostel . . . but nothing more. No luxuries. You'll have to manage with whatever I send."

"Yes, Baba, I can manage."

At this point she forced herself into this dialogue, this two-actor drama we were enacting for her benefit.

"Do you know how much it costs to live in a hostel in Bombay? Have you any idea how much her books and clothes will cost you? And the food? How do you imagine you're going to send her that for the next five or six years?"

As steady as me in ignoring her, he went on, "Will you manage without complaining?"

Now he was a judge swearing in a witness, a leader swearing a new comrade to some mystic brotherhood.

"I will," I replied, just as solemnly.

"What's the last date for sending in your application?"

I had won. I could not believe it. I had won. But before I could speak, she burst out. "I say no, she can't go. Am I nobody here?"

Almost imperceptibly he silenced me speaking to her as mildly as he always did. "And why can't she, Kamala?" It was, I think, the first time I had heard him say her name in my presence. To me it was like a caress in public, something indecent.

"But she's a girl."

Yes, I'm a girl. But it's more than that. I'm not Dhruva.

"Well, plenty of girls go in for medicine now."

"Yes, but they're girls whose fathers have lots of money. You don't belong to that class. And don't forget, medicine or no medicine, doctor or no doctor, you still have to get her married, spend money on her wedding. Can you do both? Make yourself a pauper, and will she look after you in your old age? Medicine! Five, six, seven . . . god knows how many years. Let her go for a B.Sc . . . you can get her married in two years and our responsibility will be over."

"Is that all I am, a responsibility?"

Again he motioned me to silence. "Look, she knows how it is. I can pay either for her marriage or her studies. She chooses to be educated. Let her. It's her choice."

"What gives her the right to choose? Have we no say in the matter? And when it comes to the point, I know you'll have to spend for her wedding as well. We can't ever evade that responsibility."

"We'll meet that when the time comes. Now, let her go ahead and do what she wants. She's worked for it . . ."

"And who'll look after her in Bombay?"

"As if you care about what I do or what happens to me!"

"That's what you think. What do you know of others' feelings? When have you ever cared about anyone's feelings but your own? As long as you can have your own way, you aren't bothered about anything at all. Your own brother . . ."

"No," he said loudly.

" . . . She let him drown . . ."

"I said no!"

"She killed him."

I had won, but the victory was hers. She had managed to draw blood after all, while I had not inflicted even a scratch. I went to my room and tried to shut out the voices that seemed to go on and on. Later, the voices stopped and Baba called me out. "Let's see what certificates you need," he said. But I could still hear her voice.

She killed her brother. She killed her brother. Oh god, why did she have to say that? Why did she?

That night before going to bed, I kept my mind resolutely on the brightest visions I could think of. I was a doctor, stunning them with my cleverness. I was smart, beautiful, rich, and above all, beloved. But the nightmare came on me in spite of that, getting at me treacherously when I fell asleep and could not ward it off. There was the feeling of small hard knees and elbows prodding me, a small voice saying, *Sarutai, Sarutai.*

Oh go away. I'm sleeping.
Sarutai.
Go away. Don't trouble me. And don't call me Sarutai.
But Sarutai, I'm scared. It's so dark. Can I stay here?

No, you can't. Go away.
All right, then.

And turning large reproachful eyes on me, he turned away. No he swam away from me, for we were, for some reason, in the water. Water that was a bright green with the viscosity of oil. And now it was I who was scared. I turned round but the viscous water would not let me move. I was fighting against the cloying, sticky heaviness that was pulling me down, choking me, drowning me. And Dhruva was swiftly, silently going away from me.

Wait for me, wait for me, I screamed in panic.
I'm coming.

And I woke up.

You killed your brother.
I didn't. Truly I didn't. It was an accident. I loved him, my little brother. I tried to save him. Truly I tried. But I couldn't. And I ran away. Yes, I ran away, I admit that. But I didn't kill him.
How do you know you didn't kill him? How do you know?

I was wide awake now and full of sorrow. Sorrow so great that I could not hold the whole of it within me. So immense that it wearied me to bear the burden of it. It flowed over me like the water that had almost drowned me in my dream. And I could do nothing with the sorrow but bear it. It was mine and mine alone. I could share it with no one.

For a few years after I left home to join medical college, the nightmare ceased to plague me. But it returned to me a few days after I got married. I woke up sobbing, but he was there, hovering over me, anxious, scared, saying, "What is it, Saru?

What is it?" I could not tell him my dream. I could not speak to him of Dhruva. I could speak to no one of Dhruva.

"I dreamt that you had rejected me," I lied.

And he held me close and comforted me. So well that everything receded, my nightmare, Dhruva, my mother's anger and hatred and the burden of being rejected. And I let them go and gave myself up to being comforted and loved.

5

There had been a well at the end of their road. It was like a dream now, that distant memory of drawing water from the well. When the taps came, the well ceased to be important, except once a year during the Ganpati* festival. They had neither a river nor the sea nearby for the Ganpati immersion. And so, year after year, little processions went past their house, accompanied by the ringing of a brass bell, which sounded just a feeble tinkle in the open air. But children compensated for this with their vociferous cries of

Ganpati bappa moray,
pudchya varshi lavkar ya.

Come back soon next year. How immensely far off next year seemed as they went home; and yet how soon it was Ganpati time again.

They had celebrated Ganpati, too, with Baba bringing the elephant-trunked idol home with reverence and pride and installing it with pomp and fervour. On the third day she and Dhruva followed Baba to the well, she rather self-conscious, Dhruva not caring about anything but the bliss of ringing the bell and leading the chorus of kids who had joined them in chanting . . . *Ganpati bappa morya*. As Baba leaned forward to let the idol drop into the well, the fear would always be in her that he would fall in, too. But he would turn round calmly . . . that was the one time she admired him, thinking him enor-

mously brave . . . to say, "Come on, children, for the last time
before he goes." And to a crescendo of *Ganpati bappa morya,*
he would let go, a flat thwack and a rather horrible gurgle
telling them that he had indeed gone. Back home then, with
*puran-poli** to lift the dullness off them, and a light still burning in front of Ganpati's niche where a coconut took the place
of the idol until the next morning.

The well had been finally closed after a woman had
drowned herself in it. Nobody had expected her to die. She
had taken them by surprise. She had been ill-treated by her in-
laws and had made a habitual threat of running to the well to
commit suicide. She had always been stopped just in time, people running out in response to her screams, finding her bal-
ancing herself on the narrow ledge of the well. But one day she
had, perhaps truly desperate at last, gone to the well silently at
night and thrown herself in it. And the well had been closed,
people grumbling when they had to go a much longer distance
to immerse their Ganpatis.

It had not mattered to them, however, for by then Dhruva
was dead and her mother had given up celebrating Ganpati.
A.D. After Dhruva. When everything became bleak and dull.
But her mother had retained the other gods in the *puja* room
and performed her morning *puja* for an even longer time, sitting there for what seemed ages with closed eyes. And the
small Saru had asked herself agitatedly . . . is she praying to god
that I should die too?

Now the *puja* room was empty. There were no gods in it.
The only indication that they had been there once was the silver festoon of mango leaves that hung, black and tarnished
now, on the door frame and the oil stains on the floor where
she had for so many years lit the oil lamps.

At first she had wondered. At Baba's age most men, even
those who had boasted their dislike of religion and rituals,
turned devout. Maybe it was something to fill the emptiness of

their lives. But Baba, and the boy Madhav, the son of a priest, seemed to have dismissed gods and *pujas* from their lives with an ease she wondered at. Perhaps, the thought struck her, Baba doesn't need god because he has no stake in the future. Maybe that's why he isn't very interested in politics either, the other absorbing interest of most men of his age. It is through his children and his children's children that a man has a continuing grasp of the world, a stake in it. It is because he leaves them behind that he worries about it even when he knows his own tenure is coming to an end. But Baba isn't concerned with the state of either this world or the next. Perhaps when his son died and his daughter deserted him, he faced the fact that his life ended with him. The bleakness of the thought saddened her. And yet the old man did not seem unhappy. That was, she thought with a pang, because he had Madhav.

Thinking of Madhav she went with determination into his room. Madhav was working, bent over his book totally absorbed, his lips moving as he made some calculations. When she entered he looked up at once. There was something in his eyes which told her she was unwelcome, her entry an intrusion; but the next moment he was smiling at her, saying, "Oh Sarutai, how you startled me!"

It angered her that he was so painfully well-mannered towards her. It made a stranger out of her, whereas with Baba he was without barriers. And why do I want to force myself on him, she wondered. There was no answer to that, but the desire to shake him out of his aloofness remained. "You know, Sarutai, I was thinking . . ."

"Don't call me Sarutai," she exclaimed in sudden irritation.

His eyes flew to her face and she saw pain in them. His face flushed, and not in anger. Why, you are vulnerable after all, she thought in amazement. And then for some odd reason, she remembered the three sisters . . . the youngest only ten . . . who had been brought to the hospital suffering from syphilis. She had been only a student then and had listened in horror to the mother telling them, dully, that it was the father who had done it. He had tried the ancient prescription for his own disease, she went on, that of having intercourse with a virgin . . . the virgins being his own young daughters. And then, frightened by what he had done, he had disappeared.

To cure yourself by passing on your disease to another had seemed absurd and shocking then. But now she thought, looking at Madhav, if I imagined that by sleeping with you, I could cure myself, would I not try to seduce you? But maybe, Madhav would then look at her with the eyes of those three girls and their mother, reminding her that she had defiled innocence. And anyway, it was not that disease she was suffering from. And even your clean young body cannot bring grace back to my tired, shamed one, she thought wearily.

"I call you Sarutai because . . ." Madhav went on, trying to justify himself, as if she had accused him of a wrong, "I don't have an older brother or sister, and I thought . . . "

I could be that. An elder sister again. There was a moment of panic she struggled against.

"I thought you wouldn't mind . . ."

"Oh Madhav," and she knew she had to reassure him, "I'm sorry I said that. I don't know why I did. Call me Sarutai. Yes, call me that."

"I wish," Madhav said, suddenly switching over to English "I wish I was small. I wish I was not the biggest." Madhav painfully aware of his poor English, had asked her to speak to him in English for a short while every day.

"And correct me when I go wrong," he said.

She had smiled at his earnestness, which was so great that he had no self-consciousness at all. He laid himself wholly open to her. "If I was a sadist," she had thought, "this would have been fun." But he was quick to learn and rarely made the same mistake twice.

"Why do you mind so much?" she asked him once.

"After all, it isn't our language, and how many people can distinguish good English from bad?"

"But Sarutai, it makes so much difference when you're able to read and write good English."

She watched his struggles to improve dispassionately, as if it was a strange and incomprehensible exercise. She had already forgotten she had done the same thing once.

"Not biggest," she corrected him now mechanically. "You should say 'the eldest.'"

"I wish I was not the eldest," he repeated like a corrected child, his face glum again.

"Do you have to go home?" she asked, knowing something must have happened.

"I don't know. I haven't had any more letters. But I do wish I could have a talk with Satish. That fellow has no right to trouble mother like this. I've written to her, anyway. And to Satish, too."

"You should write to your father," she suggested.

"About what?"

"About Satish."

"But Sarutai, how can I?"

"Why can't you? And if you don't, who will? Poor Satish must not be destroyed because you don't have the courage to speak."

"It's not courage . . . " he mumbled.

"What is it then?"

"It's not right that I should tell my father what he must do."

"Oh, Madhav," and she began to laugh, "how old-fashioned you are! Don't you know now it's the young who tell the old what to do and how to do it?"

"My father hasn't heard about that," he said with a small smile. "Sometimes," and now he was solemn again, "I hate him. He sees only himself. Others don't exist in his world."

I hate him. Is it always that way . . . ? Fathers and sons, mothers and daughters. Renu and I . . . Abhi and his father?

But the very first word Abhi had uttered had been "Baba." And how pleased he had been that day. No, not just pleased. He had been happy. For a moment the memory overwhelmed her, his face suffused with happiness, laughing and saying . . . did you hear him, Saru? Did you? There had been one other time when he had looked as happy. When was it . . . ? No, she didn't want to remember, but the memory forced itself on her.

He had come to her in a state of unconcealed excitement, saying, "Saru, I have some wonderful news."

"What is it?"

"We're starting a magazine. There's somebody willing to back us at last. It's a wonderful opportunity."

"We? You and who else?"

He told her. His name was . . . what was it now? Yes, it was Bhide. Manu called him Bhidya. They had met him again, years later, during the interval of a Marathi play. He and Manu had gone through the drama of greeting each other effusively, like dearest friends. Only then he had turned to her.

"Well, Sarita, how are you?"

The words had been like a challenge. She knew then he disliked her. Well, it was mutual.

"As you see."

"Hmm, you look pretty prosperous."

"You don't seem to be starving, either."

He had laughed, a complacent laugh. "I'm all right."

They had spoken for some more time, a conversation both forced and stilted, knowing that there was nothing between them any more. They had moved too far apart. As they parted, Bhide said, seemingly casual, "By the way, Manu, my play is coming on next month."

"Your play?"

"I've had three produced so far, you know. They didn't do too well. But I have hopes of this one. It's being done by . . . " And he named one of the best known directors of the day.

"I must thank you for this, Sarita," he said to her.

"Me? Why?"

"Well, if you hadn't induced Manu to give up the magazine, I'd have been still there myself. Somehow, without him, it wasn't the same. I gave up after a year and started writing plays."

The magazine had folded up after a year, too. And she had said to Manu. "There! Aren't you glad now you didn't go into that! Imagine where you'd be now!"

They went back to their seats in silence. She knew he was, like her, oblivious of the actors on the stage. Silently she argued with him, as if she could hear his thoughts.

Why did you submit? You could have gone ahead with your plans, "you think too much about money" . . . it was you who said that to me. On the contrary, it's you who do that. You want good clothes, good food, lots of books and magazines, movies and plays, the best cigarettes. And do you get all that without money? No, you were trying to fool yourself. I never did that. That's the only difference between us. If you had really wanted to join the magazine, you'd have done so despite me. No one can stop you from doing what you really want to do. I know that.

Now, remembering that happy faced ghost who had come to her saying . . . I have some wonderful news, she thought . . . Yes, you wanted it badly enough. But you were not prepared to pay for your desire. And unless you do that, you lose the whole game. She had known this. And she had been prepared to pay.

But it was true she hadn't wanted him to go into journalism. What had he got out of it but some friends and a few published stories and poems that were so soon forgotten? And then, for a while, he had been jobless. It had unnerved her. She knew now it was her middle-class upbringing and ideas that had made her regard an unemployed husband as a nightmare, a horrible humiliation. That was why she had felt an enormous, disproportionate relief when he had managed to get a lecturer's job in a private college. With her hospital pay and his salary, they would manage. But he had not been convinced.

"It's a third rate college," he had argued. "It won't do me much good working in that place. Our magazine . . . Oh, Saru, I'm sure it'll come up fast. We'll make a name for it and for ourselves, Bhidya and I, see if we don't!"

And then she had, with cold-blooded calculation, used her strongest weapon. She had made use of Renu even before she was born. But she had had no choice.

It had truly seemed a dead end to her then . . . his writing, journalism, the amateur theatre. Teaching in a college was, if nothing else, eminently respectable. It sounded good.

What's your husband doing?
He teaches in a college.

And yet, before her marriage, she had enjoyed his friends, too. They had seemed to her different creatures, far removed from the matter-of-fact people she met in her own profession. She had been utterly fascinated by them and the world they lived in, the world they managed to create for themselves, so much more enchanting than her own.

6

How dazzled I was by his friends when I first met them! For me it was like entering a new world; an escape from my own drab world of lectures, patients, exams and results. They were a motley crowd, actually; a few aspiring writers and journalists, some stage enthusiasts, one or two teachers. But they all seemed charged by some excitement that made them more alive than most people. They were teeming with ideas, wild enthusiasm, and excitement about what seemed to me the strangest things. All of which exploded into words, more words and yet more words. God, how they talked, flitting effortlessly from subject to subject with a dexterity that impressed me and made me feel immensely dull myself.

They had accepted me easily but it irritated me that my being a medical student meant nothing to them. To them, I was just Manu's friend. At times I had to retaliate, make them aware of what I was. Wasn't everyone else impressed when they heard you were a doctor?

There was the day one of them, I think it was Vasu, speaking of a movie he had just seen, in which the heroine was a pure-minded dancing girl, went into ecstatic raptures over her acting.

"You remember," he said, "that gesture of hers, when she's dancing before the man who wants to buy her? One graceful gesture . . . like this . . ." his miming brought forth a sort of appreciative laughter, but he ignored it and went on earnestly, ". . . one gesture, but, my god, so full of coquetry, disdain, femininity, pride. And those eyes behind the veil . . . A man would give away kingdoms for such a gesture, such a look."

This time I was the only one to laugh. His face changed . . . they were all of them incredibly sensitive . . . and he asked me, "Why, what's the matter?"

"It sounds very romantic, doesn't it, when you put it that way? But remove the veil of romanticism and you'll see the ugly truth of prostitution and exploitation behind it."

"There speaks the doctor," he mocked me. "You can't see anything but dirt, disease and sick bodies everywhere, can you? Honestly, you people are terrible. In your hands is all the mystery of life, and what do you do about it? What do you think of? Nothing else but how much money you can get out of that patient!"

"Well, we have to live. We are realists, after all. We deal with the ultimate human reality . . . the human body."

"The body the ultimate reality? You're fooling yourself, doctor. It's the curtain that hides the reality from us."

"And what is the reality then? The mind?"

"About that, as your own Freud says . . ."

And so on and on and on and on. Endless conversations, interminable arguments and discussions, unlimited cups of tea, plates of fried stuff, recounting of triumphs and failures, readings of plots for stories, articles, plays, half-written poems . . .

When did the enchantment begin to fade for me? There was nothing dramatic about it, actually. It was a gradual, almost imperceptible drifting. So that I began to look on them objectively and found them slightly ridiculous. They often reminded me of cocks pecking in the field of literature and the arts. They would never get anything out of it but the small unwanted grains. (Had I already classed Manu as one of them?) Their facility with words, which had fascinated me initially, had now begun irritating me. Words, words, words, I thought. Sometimes they can obscure the very meaning of life.

They can hide the fact that there is nothing behind them. They will spend all their lives talking, these people, and never get anywhere.

But they are not failures. Perhaps it would have been better if they had been that. For their lives, as they live them now, are a travesty of what they wanted them to be.

There is Vidya who was, though the term was not so well known then, an incipient women's libber. I have forgotten, misplaced so many things in my life, but some words she once spoke are with me still. Why do they return with a distinctness and a clarity as if she had spoken them for me and me alone? How is it that, even today, I can reel off her arguments, almost verbatim? Did I know then that her words would one day have some relevance to my life?

They had been discussing Shakespeare, and suddenly she had burst out. "Oh Shakespeare . . . we all know he's the greatest dramatist of all time." You could almost see the quotation marks round the last five words. "But, shall I tell you men one thing? He has a very limited vision. Now, now, let me explain. What I'm saying is that his is a typical man's view of life; the man at the centre, the woman always on the periphery."

"How do you mean?" someone asked.

"Well, look at the way he made the women always subordinate to the men."

"But that's how it was, wasn't it?"

"But it's not just their roles. It's the way he made the woman's personality merge into the stronger colours of a man's personality. Look at Hamlet, Lear, Othello. And look at Ophelia, Cordelia, Desdemona. Poor, feeble shadows. And when you come to a conflict or a climax, the woman recedes into the background. Just look at the way he disposed of Lady Macbeth. And how splendidly she starts off, really! But so much positivity, so much action is too much for the poor female and so she bows out."

"Come on, Bhidya," Manu called out, "write a play for Vidya. Full of action, and hers the central role. We'll all stand in the winds. Okay?"

"Phoo. You think it's a joke. And where would you like Sarita to be?"

As Manu turned to me questioningly, I said gaily, "I'll be down among the audience, applauding all of you madly."

"See that you stay there," Vidya said with a mock sternness. "Or else, Manu won't like it."

Vidya was then absorbed in the theatre, loving it with an indescribable passion. I met her years later, married and a mother. She was incredibly sophisticated, with the ravaged look some women have after a certain age when they try to stay slim. She had, she told me, given up acting, because, "Ashwin doesn't like the idea of my going on the stage. His family disapproves too. They don't mind my associating with the theatre occasionally, but no acting, directing or anything like that."

And that family, I found out later, was one that had made a fortune out of producing hooks, buttons or something like that!

There's Vasu who's become a third-rate actor in third-rate movies. Raja, the radical, an executive in a publishing house. Bhide, that ardent enthusiast of experimental drama, whose latest play, a success, is full of foul words, obscenities and perverted relationships. Bhide who would argue . . . "We must break this artificial barrier we put up between the actors and the audience. They must meet, ultimately merge into each other. After all, life isn't divided into watertight compartments, is it?" And he now so despises his audience that his latest play is not only a slap in its face, but a spit on it.

Oh yes, I could weep to think of them now, but I had no time then to weep, or even to think of them. I had my work, and that intense desire to get on, to succeed, that had almost become an obsession. And Manu, after that break with Bhide, drew away from them as well. His writing, too, just petered out. "I don't have any time," he would explain. In a way that was true, because after college hours he was busy with tuitions. Trying to get English into the thick heads of boys with rich fathers. He hated it, but there was no choice. For by then there was Renu. "It's strange," he said to me once, with a small rueful smile, "I had imagined that to have a child of your own would be one of life's greatest experiences. Now I can only think of the price of baby food and baby powders." "That's how it is," I replied casually, disinterested. By the time Renu was a year old, we had reached the parting of ways with his group.

We never had any friends after that. There were just colleagues and neighbours. My colleagues, whom I never met unless it was for some purpose. Even our socialising was calculated; and worse, it had a dreary sameness about it that made a chore of a party instead of the exciting affair it had once been. But then we were, all of us, monotonously alike, our patterns of life as regimented as those of soldiers in the army. Our homes, our children, their schools, our possessions, our ideas . . . these were the drab uniforms we wore, all of the same dull colour. And we marched in step to an invisible band . . . left, right, left, right. We didn't dare to fall out, sit by the wayside and watch the other soldiers march past. We had to keep up. We were dead scared of being left behind. Those who couldn't keep up, those who faltered, were left behind and ruthlessly forgotten. I didn't want to be one of them. I wouldn't be one of them.

There were his colleagues, too. He called them, "my friends," though I knew that if he didn't see them even for a short while, he would forget not only their faces, but their names as well. In the early days we regularly visited one another, though. You visit us once, and we return the visit . . . the rule was scrupulously observed. I remember the visits. The whole occasion, the talk, the food, our very selves seemed so dreary that a yawn overtakes me even when I think of it. I could tell in advance what there would be for lunch. Oh yes, it was invariably a Sunday morning visit. With us carrying a packet of biscuits or a slab of chocolate for the children, if there were any. The children in return entertained us with nursery rhymes, for they went, we were proudly told, to a "convent school." And we smiled and smiled at the children's performance, until the muscles of our cheeks ached.

And the lunch that followed . . . I could predict each item of it. Potatoes, mashed and seasoned, with a polite covering of coconut and coriander leaves on top. Green chutney, insipid and refined. A salad of raw tomatoes or cucumber so finely sliced that that it became an unappetising mush floating in water. A pale, tasteless dal. And the treat, the centrepiece, the dessert . . . whatever you call it . . . always bananas cut up and mixed with milk and sugar. Oh massive boredom . . . the food, the talk, everything. But as we set out for home, he would be humming a tune, looking inexpressibly pleased with himself. I had always thought that it was, as it was for me, the relief at getting away. It was later, much later, that I realised it was quite different. It was the day. I saw him showing off something . . . I don't remember what . . . some possession of which he was proud. And the expression on his face, the tune that he hummed, seemed familiar. Suddenly I realised that it had been the same tune, the same expression all those years back. And then I knew. It had been complacency then, not relief. Complacency at having shown off a prized possession. His wife. A lady doctor.

I have forgotten all those friends now. Their names, their faces have blurred into one immense, dull mediocrity. But there is one family I do remember, one couple, and one woman specifically. We had been invited to tea. The man sat and talked to us. The woman came in later with trays of food, cups of tea and glasses of water. She came in silently, unobtrusively, like a shadow and went out in the same way, her husband's conversation not interrupted for even a fraction of a second by her presence. He did not introduce her to us, and so strong was the man's disregard of her presence that we ignored her, too. We ate our food, sipped the tea and gulped the water as if they had been brought to us by a nameless waiter in a hotel.

When leaving, I went in to take my leave of her. I smiled at her. She did not respond. Her face was unchanged, expressionless, as if she had fallen in with her husband's desires and successfully effaced the person that was her. At the door, I looked back for a moment. She stood under a light, a strong, unshaded bulb hanging low in the centre of the room. I looked down at her feet and saw that there was no shadow. For some reason, the words came to my mind . . . If I cast no shadow, I do not exist.

The husband took leave of us effusively. I smiled at him and hated him with a fierce hatred.

But now I wonder . . . who is the victim and who is the predator? Are the roles so distinct, so separate? Or are we, each of us, both?

7

I t was still dark when she woke up. She lay back, letting the day seep into her consciousness. She would not get up, not until the darkness had lifted. To switch on the light upon waking up in the morning always seemed to her a rejection of the day. She preferred the natural half-light, a light that defined outlines without revealing details. To see the gradual revealing of details seemed a kind of deferred enlightenment which brought its own rewards.

From outside, through the closed doors, she could hear the whistle of a train. It sounded like a forlorn cry for help. As if something, someone, maybe her own self, was trying to get across to her some emotion compounded of both grief and fear. Once, when she had been ill and forced to stay in bed, it had happened to her, a sharp division of herself, so that the woman who lay in bed followed another, hale and hearty, through all the routine chores of her day, both at home and in the hospital, until at some exhausting, painful moment, the two figures merged into one lying on the bed. And then there had been, in spite of everything, tremendous relieved. Now, she summarily dismissed the other person, frightened and grief-stricken, who was trying to pierce into her, forcibly averting her mind from the whistle of the train which receded and became pathetically faint and dim.

Meanwhile she thought of her day and its tasks, tasks which set it apart from others of its kind. There was some cleaning to be done; Baba had brought home four kilos of rice yesterday.

She would clean it, meticulously picking out the large and small black stones and the unhusked paddy, taking an almost sensuous pleasure in the final clean rice. And yes, it was but-ter-making day as well.

It was comforting to have the day dictated by only her own desires. Both comfort and security had come to her somehow, not from Baba, nor from Madhav, but from the very pattern of their life together. They were both easy to live with. They made no demands of her, nor on each other, for that matter. I sup-pose we could go on living like this forever. She saw a long vista of easy, calm days, unruffled by any complications. But Madhav will finish his education and go away and Baba will die one day and I will be left alone. Or maybe, I will die before Baba and how splendidly that will solve everything. But, in the meantime . . .

In the meantime, however, it was as if she had gone back to some time, some way of living that, seen now through the haze of the years, seemed an oasis, a haven of peace, comfort and security. The man went out to work and earn money, the woman stayed at home and looked after it, the man and their children. It was not the perfect pattern nor the best, but it was there, complete, not gnawed into bits by doubts and uncer-tainties.

There was still some semblance of this pattern around her. The men went out to work, the children to school, the women stayed at home and cooked and cleaned, scrubbed and swept. There was a kind of harmony in this that pleased her. When she sat in the backyard in the mornings, she heard sounds of women at their usual tasks. It was infinitely soothing and com-forting. Like being a child at play, and hearing the voices of adults, knowing that they are not too far away.

After all the cooking had been done, she churned the cream for butter. Butter-making had seemed a long and laborious process when she had watched her mother do it. Now, to collect the cream for days, churn it for hours, and then get some butter, seemed not laborious and time consuming, but infinitely rewarding. She rolled out pats of butter in her palm, letting the liquid seep through her fingers.

Abhi . . . he loves butter. He gouges large bits out of the packet with a spoon. It enrages me. I yell at Abhi and his father defends him. They don't understand. It's the ugly sight of the butter, like a half-eaten carcass, that infuriates me. I should be pleased with Renu who delicately scrapes the butter with a knife, and with infinite patience butters her toast, so that no corner is neglected. But that irritates me, too.

Sometimes she wondered at herself. Was she an unnatural, unloving mother? She had sworn that she would never fail her children in love and understanding as her own mother had done. That she would be to her children all that her own mother had not been to her. But the children had started off a disappointment. She had been buoyed up through all the months of pregnancy by the thought of a miracle awaiting her. The miracle of motherhood. But when, after a daylong struggle, she had felt, through a haze of pain and shock, Renu's head forcing itself out, she had been outraged at the indignity of it. Her posture, her grunts, her cries, the pain which made an animal out of her . . . was this the prelude to motherhood?

Later, too, when she held Renu in her arms, she had felt not love, but an immense fear, a terrible feeling of inadequacy. Could she measure up to all that this being, so wholly dependent on her, would expect? Would she not fail her as her own mother had failed her?

"All that pain," she had complained to Manu afterwards. "It seems cruel."

"It's necessary pain, Saru," he had said. "It's the link, the bridge you have to cross before you reach perfect love." She had thought of his words the next evening when a woman had come to the hospital, almost in the last stage of labour. The labour room was next to hers, the walls thin and the sounds came through distinctly. There had been a few fierce animal grunts, sounds of forcible expelling and then it was all over. Was this a bridge, too, to perfect love? She had been discovered by a shocked *ayah* laughing hysterically to herself.

But on the third or fourth day after Renu's birth she had woken out of a deep sleep to hear a baby crying. Frantically she had pressed the bell, saying to the tousled, resentful, just-woken-out-of-a-sleep sister . . . That's my baby crying. Get her. Her breasts had felt heavy, full and hard. The certainty had been, perhaps, *there,* and miraculously, she had been right. And when she had put the inexperienced, greedy, seeking mouth to her nipple, the satisfaction had been enormous.

The hands that had probed her body while she was in labour had been utterly distasteful. But this suckling had set up an intensely erotic response within her. So that she had, unable to control herself, forced Manu to make love to her as soon as possible after she went home. There had been a kind of withholding in Manu then . . . maybe he had been shocked by her urge, maybe he had been afraid of hurting her. But it had not worried her. Her desire had been so strong, so purely physical that he could not prevent her satisfaction. Indeed she had thought once, I don't even need him. I can satisfy myself just as well. But no, she had never done that. For her, it had been an experience inextricably linked with him. It was only through his body that she tried to find fulfilment.

The butter had been collected into a vessel of water, to be stored until there was enough to make ghee. She wiped her greasy fingers on the *chappatis* she had prepared. No point in wasting it by washing it off her fingers. Her palms and fingers felt deliciously soft and smooth. She had done this chore often as a child and Mai-kaki had teased her . . . Do this every day and your hands will be so soft and smooth, your husband will never let go of them.

Everything in a girl's life, it seemed, was shaped to that single purpose of pleasing a male. But what did you do when you failed to please? There was no answer to that. At least, no one had given her an answer so far.

The sound of schoolchildren filled the street, which meant that Madhav would soon be home. Don't wait for me for lunch, he told them each morning. But she and Baba always did. She went out and stood against the gate, watching the children go by. They were a revelation to her. All these days, the only children she had known had been her own. And the children of colleagues and friends who were like replicas of her own. On the other side, there had been patients. Sick children, suffering children, dying children. So many of them that they had become one anonymous mass. But not quite.

There was Simon, the slum child, so curious about everything, even his own deadly disease.

"Tell me what's wrong with me," he had pestered them.

"TB meningitis," she told him one day, knowing he would be able to make nothing of that.

"Will it make me die?" he had asked gravely.

And what, she had wondered, could she say to that? It was he who had patted her hand reassuringly, with the maturity of a seven-year-old who had looked after himself almost since birth. "Don't worry, doctor-bai, I'm sure you'll make me all right."

And there was that other child she would never forget. The little boy who woke miraculously out of a comatose state and smiled at his mother with his eyes, his face, his whole being.

And as the mother smiled back, ineffably happy, opening her mouth to speak, the child died. The mother, when she realised what had happened, began to scream, thin animal cries of intense pain that had pierced her through and through, twisting her insides into one painful knot. I won't, she had thought that day. I can't go on with this. But she had gone on all the same. Where had that strength come from? Was there none of it left?

Now, these children going home from school were just children. She found herself looking at them with a detached curiosity, a sense of remote enjoyment. I wish it were like this with my own children. My children . . . suddenly she found herself full of distaste for the words. How possessive they sounded. Can one ever possess another human being? The act of birth can be cruelly deceiving, making you imagine you have some claim on the human you bring into the world.

"What's the time?" one of the girls stopped and asked her. The girls with their swinging pigtails, looking at her out of large eyes full of an insatiable curiosity, while the boys, absorbed in their own world, ignored her.

"Past twelve, I think," she said. There was satisfaction in ignoring the minutes. And how proud she had once been to have a watch with a second hand.

Evening, when water ran in the taps again, was washing time. Both Baba and Madhav washed their clothes in the morning. She waited till evening to wash hers. The raised slab of stone on which they beat and scrubbed clothes was clean and dry. But the sides and the floor below were slimy. When she had finished washing, she got out the large scrubbing brush and scrubbed at the stone noticing with pleasure the hard, clean surface reappearing.

"Saru, where is . . . ?"

It was Baba. She got up awkwardly and leisurely, her wet sari clinging to her legs, one hand pushing the hair back from her face. He left his question incomplete as if something had startled him.

"Saru, why are you doing that?"

"Because it was dirty," she smiled, a smile without humour in it.

"For a moment I thought . . ." he stopped again. "You looked like . . ."

It was as if he could never complete any sentence. But she knew this time what he had intended to say. Mai-kaki had said it the other day. "Saru, do you know you look amazingly like your mother now?" It neither annoyed her nor pleased her, that remark. Nor did she imagine that it was her expression that so resembled the dead woman's . . . the eyes joyless and arid, the expression one of indifference.

It's because of the way I dress now, she thought. She had given up doing anything with her hair but tying a knot of it as her mother had done. Her saris too . . . The women she had known as a child had always had just two saris for what they called "home wear." You took one off the clothesline after your bath and wore it until your bath the next morning, when you took the other off the line. She had, on leaving home, deliberately broken out of the pattern as soon as she could, feeling a faint triumph at the thought of having got away from the two-sari routine and all that it meant. Now she had reverted to it, as if there was no other way or living. She had let herself go in other ways too. Her nails had not been cut since she came home; her palms were roughened. The soles of her feet had fine hair-like fissures blackened by the dirt that got into them when she walked on her bare feet. She wore slippers only when she went out, using them carefully, feeling she had to conserve them. It had been drilled into them as children, the necessity to use footwear carefully, since slippers were bought only once a year, and only one pair at that. Baba would buy them in Bombay (what an extravagance it had seemed then) where he had to go once a year as part of his duties in the bank.

Being measured for slippers had been a thrilling event. Baba had to take their measurements with him. They were made to stand on a blank sheet of paper, while Baba crawled round them, tracing the outlines of their feet with a pencil.

Sometimes the pencil tickled her feet and she giggled and squirmed, while Baba sat back patiently and said, "Stand still, Saru. Don't move." Dhruva never had to be told that. He stood on the paper, solemn and unmoving, until Baba said, "That's all, Dhruva. You can get off now."

With the washing done, there was a respite. Preparations for the evening meal were still some way off and she sat on the stone platform outside the house, while Baba and Madhav fussed over what they called "their garden." Together, their ignorance of the whole process of gardening was abysmal. Baba was querulous and irritable with the slow process of sprouting seeds, but Madhav seemed infinitely patient. As she watched them, the warmth of the evening sun was on her back. The stone on which she sat was warm. The sound of water flowing into the bucket, the friendly soothing voices and the warmth suffused her with an intangible feeling of peace and happiness. They sat out until darkness imperceptibly replaced twilight. Stars appeared at periodic intervals like actors who had heard their cue. And then Madhav went in to his books, Baba to his Mahabharata and she to the kitchen.

She had bought a pressure cooker for the home. On the first day, Baba and Madhav, full of curiosity and awe, had watched like fascinated children as it hissed and steamed. Later, they had stared unbelievingly at the dal cooked into a soft yellow pulp. Madhav sat back and sighed.

"My mother gets up at four in the morning to have her bath so that she can start cooking the dal. It takes nearly two hours for it to be cooked."

My mother . . . somehow the words angered her. They were like pinpricks threatening the bubble that surrounded the three of them and their life together. She now had the watchful, fearful look of a person guarding something precious. She was wary of anything that changed their routine, of any references that threatened the jewel of security she was guarding.

"I'm fasting tomorrow," Baba said at the end of the meal. She had given up eating with them. She preferred to have her meal later, untroubled by the thought of serving others, of having cooked either too much or too little. She ate whatever was left. She had put on weight, her face having lost its sharpness, but, curiously, not its ravaged look.

"So, you needn't cook for me tomorrow."

"Fasting? What for?"

She had imagined that he had given up all the ritual fasts of orthodoxy. What was it now? But he did not reply.

"Is it some special *ekadashi**?" she asked with a smile.

She thought the two of them looked at her oddly. But Baba didn't elaborate. He just mumbled, "Yes, something special," and they left it at that.

At night as she was unrolling her mattress, Madhav came to her. "Sarutai," he said, and she knew he was troubled.

"I thought you ought to know."

"Know what?" She prompted him as he hesitated.

"Why Kaka is fasting tomorrow."

"No, I don't. How should I?"

She felt unreasonably irritated as if she was being accused or wrongs she knew nothing of.

"It's your . . . it's his . . . it's Dhruva's birthday tomorrow, isn't it?"

"Is it?"

She did not know that she sounded like a resentful, sullen child. Or that her face had taken on a little girl's "I know I'm bad but I don't care" look. The boy stared at her curiously, before he realised that her words were truly a question.

"Yes," he answered her. And then she smiled at him. "I had forgotten," she said simply. "Honestly, I had forgotten all about it."

And there was a joyful lift to her smile as if she was congratulating herself on something.

8

They had named him Dhruva. I can remember, even now, vaguely, faintly, a state of joyous excitement that had been his naming day. The smell of flowers, the black grinding stone that I held in my hands . . . these are the only tangible memories that remain.

He must have been a year old, or perhaps two, when my mother had told me the story of the mythological Dhruva, the child who was pushed off his father's lap by his stepbrother, and full of sorrow and anger, gave himself up to a steadfast meditation so that he became the constant North Star. Just a day or two later I had, with a cold and calculated determination, pushed Dhruva off Baba's lap. He had fallen down, his head making a sickening thud as it hit the ground, and there was a stunned silence. He must be dead. Is he dead? Even as I stood in a terrified immobility, there was a loud outraged howl and a tumult that diverted attention from me for a while.

But soon, with Dhruva quietened and lying peacefully on Ai's lap, the question had come. "Why did you do it?" When I knew I wasn't getting anywhere with prevarications. I had replied with what had seemed to me irrefutable logic, "Because you named him Dhruva."

"What do you mean?"

"I wanted to see if he would become the North Star if I pushed him off Baba's lap."

And when I was punished, unfairly as I thought, I had asked, "'Why, then, did you name him Dhruva?"

The story had been later retailed to friends, relations and acquaintances, but without the vestige of a smile, making a major crime of my childish misdemeanour. Or that was how it had seemed to me then.

There was always a *puja* on Dhruva's birthday. A festive lunch in the afternoon and an *aarti** in the evening during which Dhruva, as an infant, sat solemnly on Baba's lap, and as a child, by his side, cap on head, fatuous smile on face, while I helped my mother to do the *aarti*. My birthdays were almost the same . . . a festive lunch, with whatever I asked for, (it was always s*hrikhand** for me, creamy, saffron-tinted and nutmeg flavoured) an *aarti* in the evening; but there was no *puja*. Birthdays were not then the tremendous occasions they are made out to be now; but the excitement of having one, of being the centre of attraction never paled. It was always a fascinating thought . . . I was born. But of my birth, my mother had said to me once . . . "it rained heavily the day you were born. It was terrible." And somehow, it seemed to me that it was my birth that was terrible for her, not the rains.

After Dhruva's death, there were no more celebrations. My birthday was passed over in silence, both at home and at school. I got used to it, so that I was more amazed than pleased when one year Smita turned up with a gift for me. It was a large packet. "Open it," she said, her face serious and grave. I removed one wrapping of newspaper to find another, then another and then yet another. Smita had lapsed from gravity into her usual giggly state as I went on and on. At last, desperate, feeling ridiculously humiliated, knowing I had been the butt of a stupid, heartless joke, I flung the thing away from me in a tantrum, close to tears I would not, could not, shed in front of Smita. But Smita ran after me calling out, "Saru, don't be silly. There is something for you inside. Open it. Just a little more. I promise you there is really something."

Angrily, looking suspiciously at her face that was still on the brink of laughter, I continued unpacking and found at the end of it a pair of earrings, cheap and shiny, nevertheless inexpressibly dear to me as the first gift I ever had. I wore them secretly, and only when I was away from home, knowing, somehow, the earrings would not be approved of. All gifts were suspect and frowned upon. If someone gave you something, it meant that they would expect something in return. Or else, it was an obligation and put you at a disadvantage. Therefore, no gifts.

But my mother gave me a pair of earrings herself on my fifteenth birthday. That birthday had somehow felt eventful to me. I would be leaving school soon, entering college, and the whole of me was in a state of restlessness, eager for something I knew not what. Part of it was, perhaps, the usual adolescent turmoil, the restrained, suppressed sexuality of a growing girl; part must have been my growing dislike of the atmosphere at home. And there was no one, absolutely no one with whom I could really talk. Smita was all right for chatting and joking with, but there were so many things she would neither understand nor sympathise with.

That day, on my fifteenth birthday, we went for a long walk, Smita, Nalu and I. Smita, the only one among us to have money with her, bought some peanuts and we sat and munched and talked so that it was late when I reached home. I found her waiting for me, her face closed-in, warning me of disaster.

"Why are you so late?"

"We went for a walk."

"A walk? Such a long time? Don't you know it's dark?"

I rarely brought my friends home, rarely went out with them after school. Whenever I did so, there was always a scene. I felt full of a sullen hatred I could not find words to express adequately. I kept silent and that enraged her even more.

"Can't you talk? Am I so much below your notice? You can talk to your friends for hours, but you can't speak a sentence to your mother. What am I? An enemy?"

"Is it such a crime to go for a walk?" I burst out.

"Walk? Didn't you think you could have helped me at home? There are the vegetables to be cut, the buttermilk to be churned. When you're working, I never ask for a bit of help. I slog the whole day all by myself. But to go for a walk . . ."

A huge anger filled me making me almost blind. What about me? It was my birthday. Did she remember that other girls had gifts and smiles and festive meals. While I?

"Give me your vegetables and your buttermilk . . ." I began sullenly.

"It's all done now."

No, she had never really expected any help from me. It was just one more stick to beat me with.

"Go in and wash your hands and feet. Finish your studies and then come for dinner."

I turned away, feeling as I always did when I came home and met her, sour and flat and dull, all the brightness gone out of everything.

Then she called me back. "And there's something for you in the *puja* room."

I didn't want anything. But I was curious. I went into the *puja* room. There was a small red box there. I opened it and found a pair of earrings twinkling at me. A red stone set in a star, two pearls dangling from it.

"Do you like them?"

I looked suspiciously at her face. Did she mean it? Were my feelings important to her?

"You're a big girl now. Time you had something nice to wear in your ears. We must make you some gold bangles next year."

So that was it! It was not for me, not to please me and make me happy, but because I should, as a growing girl, have these things to wear. I put the box down and flounced off to bed.

I don't want them. I don't want to eat. I don't want anything.

There was angry consciousness in me that it was I who was behaving badly now, but disappointment blotted out everything.

Yet I wore those earrings later. I wore them every day, even after I got married. Until the day he came to us, Professor Kulkarni, and gave me my mother's message. I took them off then and never wore them again. I had Renu's ears pierced when she was three and she already has half-a-dozen pairs of earrings. But she never wears them. I don't like wearing earrings, mummy, she complains. And for some reason I am silenced. I can say nothing.

Last year I had tried to give Renu the kind of birthday I used to have.

"No party?" she asked in consternation.

"No, but you can have anything you want. To eat, I mean. And clothes too. And a gift. And we'll do *aarti* for you at night."

"I don't want any *aarti,* I don't want anything special to eat. I want a party. I want to call my friends home and I want a cake . . . a huge cake . . . and games and all that."

It was too late. We were fossilized in sarcophagi of our own making. We could never get out now. And hadn't I been frantic to get in? Hadn't I made enormous efforts to do so? How seriously I had taken the children's birthdays! How much effort I had put into organising them and making them conform to the pattern that had become compulsory for us. I had even bought a book, I remember . . . *Party Games for Children*, or something like that . . . and gone through it with the greatest earnestness, ticking off the games I had thought were suitable. On the day of the party I read them again, making sure I had all the things the game called for.

Renu is now nine and Abhi five. So many birthdays, so many parties. Yet the one that has stayed with me is the one that was a total fiasco. Not ridiculously, absurdly, comically so, so that you can later laugh at the memory of it and your own exaggerated reactions to it. It was a frightful ruin, an ugly incident in which all of us dropped our masks. And that, more than anything else, terrified me.

It was Renu's birthday and the children were playing a game in which they passed a ball from hand to hand, while I played some music. The person who held the ball when the music stopped was "out". And then it was Abhi who was left holding the ball in his hand.

"Abhi, you're 'out.'" I called gaily, ready to start the music all over again.

But Abhi was not ready to be "out." He clung to the ball. The children laughed at him, then began to yell at him, a loud righteous chorus that only bewildered him into an even greater obstinacy. I pleaded, cajoled, argued, scolded, trying to be firm yet gentle, trying to restrain my fury. Ultimately I went to him, snatched the ball out of his hands . . . he had been clinging to it with the greatest tenacity all the while . . . and tried to haul him out of his place. It was like trying to lift a sack of coals. He had made himself into a heavy, inanimate bulk. Finding in my fury a strength to match his . . . I was no longer the gentle but firm mother . . . I dragged him out of the room, while the children watched in a shocked silence. I pushed him into his room and went into mine, panting, sweating, feeling limp and exhausted. I could hear Manu, who had watched my struggle in silence, start the children playing again. I went back myself after a while, saying, "Come on, children, let's play something else now."

Manu went away after that and I had to go through the deadly business of being gay and playful all by myself. It hurt me that Renu could go on enjoying herself as if nothing had happened. She blithely distributed the gifts and sweets I had bought for the kids and I almost hated her then.

When they had all gone, I let myself down on the carpet in the midst of all the mess twenty children can make, sticky, spilt ice cream, paper plates and cups strewn about, bits of wafers crunching greasily under me, while Renu opened her gifts and gloated over them. Seeing my indifference she called Janakibai to show them to. And then Manu and Abhi came in. They had, it seemed, gone out earlier. Janakibai discreetly vanished.

"You don't know where I went," Abhi bragged. "Baba took me out with him. I won't tell you where we went. It's a secret.'

"Don't tell." Renu was absorbed in a box of colours.

"Who cares? I had much more fun here."

"I had more fun than you. Didn't we, Baba? And we're never going to tell you where we went and what we did."

At that, Renu deserted all her gifts and ran to her father clinging, pleading, the eternal female, the thing I detested above all.

"You will take me, won't you, Baba? You'll take me also next time?"

"No, he won't. Don't take Renu, Baba. You told me it's our secret. I don't want Renu."

"Renu," I cut in sharply, "come on, put away all these things. And have you shown your gifts to Abhi?"

Of course, Abhi had to clamour for some of them.

"Give me that book. That colouring book. And I want that pen also. Give me, Renu."

"No, they're all my presents," Renu tried to gather all the things at once, putting her arms round them jealously. "It's my birthday. They're not for you. Go away. When it's your birthday, you can have your presents. These are all mine."

"I want that pen. I want it. Give me."

"Renu, give it to him. Can't you share with your own brother?"

"Why should I? He spoilt my party. Crybaby. I won't give him anything. They're all mine, not his."

"Renu, don't be selfish. You know you have heaps of pens. Can't you give him one? Must you be so greedy?"

"Why do you always scold me? You never scold him. You never say anything to him. It's not fair. It's my birthday, my presents. And he cried and spoilt everything. And now you scold me. You always scold me. It's not fair, not fair."

Not fair? How could a child so easily find the right weapon? As I looked at the passionately sobbing child, the fear returned . . . do we travel, not in straight lines, but in circles? Do we come to the same point again and again? Dhruva and I, Renu and Abhi . . . Is life an endless repetition of the same pattern?

"Renu, please," I begged her wearily.

She stopped crying and glared at me. "I won't. I won't give him anything. He never gives me anything, of his! He's got two big pencils and when I asked him for one, he didn't give me. Why should I give him anything of mine?"

"Mummy, tell her . . ."

"Mummy, look at him, look at the way he's pulling my things . . ."

"Renu!"

"Okay then, take it and get out. Go away. Go on, crybaby; get out of here. Take your pen. I don't want to talk to you."

"Mummy, she hurt me, she pinched me. Mummy!"

Howls, yells, sobs. Cries of . . . mummy, mummy, mummy. And he . . . he stood there silent, watching both me and the children with a queer expression I could make nothing of. Then he turned and walked out of the room. And meanwhile the children went on with their cries of . . . mummy, mummy, mummy.

PART FOUR

1

She was alone when the telegram arrived. The peremptory knock at the door startled her. She opened the door in a flurry that turned to fright at the sight of the khaki-clad postman.

"Telegram," he announced blandly, the unconcerned professional, caring nothing about what he was bringing, doom, disaster or happiness.

Renu? Abhi? Her mind slid backwards and forwards between the two names, stopping at each with a painful jerk. Then she saw that the telegram was addressed to Madhav. She signed for him and took it in, wondering whether to open it. Finally she threw it on the table in the hall, and went into the kitchen to go on with her cooking. When she had finished, she sat there, staring dumbly at the covered vessels of food, thinking . . . if it's bad news, he won't eat his food. It'll be wasted. I could as well have avoided cooking today. Baba is fasting so it'll be just me. I wish I had concealed the telegram and given it to him after lunch.

The thought brought back something, some memory, someone asking . . .

What's the matter?
I'm not feeling well.
What is it? Fever?
No. I have a terrible headache.
Oh! Aren't you going to eat anything then?

No. I don't feel like it.

I wish you had told me earlier. Before I started my cooking. It would have saved me some trouble.

Even if I'm dying, you'll want to know whether I'll eat my food and then die, or die first so that you needn't cook.

She brushed away the memory as if it was an irritating fly hovering round her face, a nuisance she could effectively deal with.

"Saru . . ." It was Baba now.

"Yes, Baba?"

"When did this telegram arrive?"

"Some time back."

"Oh! I wonder what's wrong?"

"Have you brought the vegetables?"

"Here. "

He gave her the cloth bag, preoccupied with the telegram, frowning over it, turning it over as if he could find some answer there.

"Do you think I should open it?"

She didn't reply. She was shaking the bag on the floor, so that the vegetables rolled out. Brinjals. A long snake gourd, green and glistening. Cluster beans, dry and dispirited. What shall I prepare for the evening? I suppose I could cook the brinjals, with potatoes and onions in a gravy . . . no, Madhav doesn't eat onions, just potatoes and brinjals . . . so that I needn't cook any dal.

Baba stood over her, the puzzled frown still on his face, as if waiting for her reply. But she went on with her task of sorting out the vegetables, putting them in the little wicker baskets, their crevices filled with the accumulated dirt of years. He wondered whether she hadn't heard his question or whether she was ignoring it. His frown deepened as he walked away, the telegram unopened in his hand.

Madhav came home at his usual time, but he didn't come inside as he usually did. She could hear Baba speaking to him, then Madhav's voice. A long silence, then voices again. She sat where she was, making no attempt to get up, to find out what was wrong. At last Baba called her, "Saru." Madhav went into the bathroom. She could hear him sloshing water on his hands, face and feet.

"Yes, Baba. Shall I serve?"

"Serve?" He seemed astonished for a moment, then recovered himself. "Yes, you can serve Madhav his lunch. He has to go home."

"What's wrong?"

She turned the plate, which she had put face down on the wooden plank, the right side up, and began to serve, being meticulously careful to serve things in their *right* places. Madhav came in, wiping his face and hands dry. His face looked disturbed out of its usual pattern of imperturbability.

"It's a telegram from my mother. She wants me to go home. Immediately. She doesn't say what's wrong. Maybe, it's Satish. Maybe, someone is unwell. Or Mrinal . . . I don't know."

"When are you leaving?"

"There's a bus at six. In the meantime, I might as well go back to my classes."

He returned a little earlier than usual in the evening and declined her offer of a cup of tea.

"No, I must hurry. If I miss this bus, there's no other bus till tomorrow morning."

He put away his books neatly, giving them, she saw, a wistful look. He had already pushed a set of clothes into a cloth bag, which he now picked up.

"I must go," he said. But he lingered as if there was still something he had to do. Then he said, "Sarutai."

"What?" Her face was impassive and untroubled.

"Oh, nothing! I'll be back soon. Maybe the day after. I don't want to miss too many classes. I have my preparatory exams in less than a month. I wish I hadn't been disturbed now."

His unwanted garrulity now dried up and he looked at her again. For the first time she seemed to realise that something was expected of her. Was there something she had to say? If there was, she could not say it, because she did not know what it was. It was as if her prompter had at last failed her, the ventriloquist had gone away, leaving her mute and lifeless.

"Madhav," Baba came in and said, "isn't it time you left? Someone was saying that buses actually leave on time nowadays."

"I'm leaving, Kaka."

And then he was gone. There were only the two of them now. The old man and she. That seemed wrong somehow. There should be three persons in the house. Three was the right number. But before her coming, there had been only two of them, Baba and Madhav, and that had seemed the right number, too.

There was a curious constraint between them without the boy. The ease and friendliness had vanished. They were like two people just introduced, the common friend having gone away, leaving them by themselves. There were uneasy silences.

"Baba," she called him at night, thankful that there was something to say, "dinner is ready."

He seemed to be, a rare thing for him, annoyed.

"You know I'm not having anything today."

He removed his glasses and rubbed at his eyes. Without those protective shutters, his face looked frightfully blank.

"Fasting? But I thought it was only in the morning." Fasting usually meant missing one meal, not both.

"You know I've always observed a total fast on this day. Both of us did . . . your mother and I."

What was it? Suddenly she remembered that Madhav had told her about it. Was that what he had tried to say to her when leaving? It was Dhruva's birthday.

Your mother and I . . . Yes, they had fasted on the day. But she had not. She had eaten her food defiantly, aggressively, knowing that her mother was looking at her in astonishment, thinking perhaps . . . how can she? And then, serving her with a vengeance, saying . . . are you sure you don't want any more? Sure you've had enough?

"I had forgotten about it," she said now as she had said to the boy last night. Sullen again as she had been with him.

"You have your dinner, anyway. No reason why you should not."

"Yes, no reason why I shouldn't."

Each year the question had come . . .

You will be eating, I suppose?
Of course. Why should I fast?
Yes, why should you?

Just because it's Dhruva's birthday, and because he happened to die, must I punish myself all my life like you do?

But that was wrong. It wasn't her own self that her mother had been punishing. It was Saru she had tried to punish. She would lie in bed, stiff and immobile like a corpse, get up and cook for Saru, serve her with an exaggerated solicitude, and then go back to bed and her corpse-like posture, like a prisoner who had earned a reprieve.

"I've forgotten him," she said now. "Completely. I don't ever think of him." Her voice rose on a triumphant note.

"I'm glad," he said quietly.

But there was something in his face which told her he didn't believe her. It enraged her. And nothing I say will convince him or the contrary. There was the same infuriating feeling of helplessness she had often had as a child.

"I used to think . . ." he went on and stopped in his irritating way of leaving his sentences incomplete.

"Used to think what?"

There was the tension of a coiled spring about her. Something wild in her face.

"What did you think?"

"It's nothing, Saru. Leave it."

His face registered alarm. It filled her with glee. So she could do that: scare him.

"No, tell me, Baba."

She was quieter, some of the wildness subdued. "I want to know. What did you think?"

"Sometimes I used to think you took your mother seriously and blamed yourself for Dhruva's death. You know she was not herself when she said that. She was . . ." he groped for the right word, " . . . hysterical. But I thought you began to believe it yourself."

"Me?" She began to laugh, a high unnatural laugh. The air of deliberate composure fell away from her. "Why should I blame myself? What did I have to do with his dying? He was a silly idiot who didn't know better than to get himself drowned in a small puddle . . ."

"I said forget it, Saru."

He made a movement as if to get up, to go away from there.

It made her frantic. He could not escape, leaving her with that monstrous thought.

"No. Baba. Tell me why you think I should blame myself. You felt that way also, didn't you? I know you defended me against her. But you felt the same way, didn't you? And you've held it against me all these years. It's not because of my marriage that you cast me off. It's this. You think I killed him."

"Saru, it's so long ago . . ."

So long ago?

" . . . Such an old story . . ."

"An old story? And every night he comes and accuses me. Yes, Dhruva. He looks at me as if I killed him. Why are you all against me? Why do you all accuse me of something I never did?"

Her voice cracked on the last word and she stopped as suddenly as a bird that loses a wing in mid-flight.

"Who's accusing you, Saru? No one."

The same voice. The voice of an adult humouring a child. Soothing a hurt child. Saying . . . it's all right, you're all right knowing very well it isn't.

"You haven't done any wrong."

"Then why do you say I blame myself? Why should I blame myself?"

"I thought . . . maybe, because you took him out with you that day . . ."

"I took him out? I . . . ?" She had regained control over her voice now. "I didn't take him anywhere. I could do nothing with him. He was utterly spoilt. He did just what he liked. He was always allowed to have his way. And I had to give in, go on giving in . . ."

All the grievance for an old but monumental injustice was in her words. She was not a wife, not a mother, not a professional woman whom others looked up to. She was the wronged child again, the unloved daughter, the scapegoat.

"Saru, please. Let's not talk about it."

"Let's not talk about it and it isn't there. Let's behave as if it isn't there and it never was. That's your way, isn't it, Baba? All these years I suppose it was . . . let's forget about Saru. And it was as if there was no Saru at all. No, there was no Saru, you never had a daughter, because she was an inconvenience, a nuisance and it suited you not to have her there. No wonder you were so shocked when you saw me standing outside your door that day."

"Saru . . ."

"No, I never took him out anywhere. It was he who pestered me, followed me. He fell in himself. And both of you found me guilty without really knowing what had happened. Did you ask me once, just once . . . What happened, Saru? Did you say just once . . . Don't think of it. It wasn't your fault. Don't blame yourself. And it wasn't. Really and truly it wasn't. Look, I'll swear it to you. Will you believe me then? I didn't take him out with me that day."

Sarutai, wait for me, I'm coming.

"He followed me. I didn't want him to come. And I didn't know he was dead. I knew it only when they brought him here. I knew nothing and still you blame me. You think I'm guilty. Oh my god . . ."

It was not just weeping, they were not just tears. It was an explosion, something that hurt with the sheer force and violence of it. Tears, and once again an indifferent stranger opposite her.

Would there never be someone who cared? Would it always be this way . . . a stranger watching her torment?

He stared at her for a few moments then walked away. She scarcely noticed his going. At last the sobs became less violent. She became conscious of her running nose, and picking up the end of her sari, blew into it.

"I didn't do it," she murmured, a plaintive murmur now, all the passion having ebbed away. And miraculously the friend of childhood was back.

"I know," said the friend.

"I tried to save him," she said.

"I know," said the friend again.

But none of these words carried any conviction to her. How could she know? She would never really know the truth herself. Had she really tried to save him?

2

Oh, the agony, the ache, of not knowing, of not being sure, of doubting. The helplessness of trying to go back into that time, that state of mind, trying to be definite about what I did and why.

If only . . . surely there can be no words more tormenting than these. Words that scrape and claw and torture, like a hopeless, incurable pain that will never let you be. They have been with me all my life . . . ugly, hated companions I can never hope to escape from.

If only I hadn't gone there that day . . .
If only he hadn't come with me . . .
If only I hadn't left him alone . . .

I should not have gone there myself. The guilt starts there. So does the fear. But am I to be punished all my life for one childish fault? Just one act of disobedience . . . isn't the punishment disproportionate to the act?

And it wasn't disobedience either, for we were never really forbidden to go there, not in so many words, that is. All that the place had, before it became a fearful terrible place to me, was a vague reputation.

Don't go there, we children warned each other in whispers. You could be kidnapped. And there were also, we heard, worse things that could happen to one, girls especially, though what they could be was beyond us then. Yes, it had some sort of a reputation all right, and was, ever since I knew it, a desolate deserted place. Some years earlier it had been the busy hub of a brick-making industry. Then there had been some kind of an accident in which a few workers had died. And operations had ceased, maybe for that reason, maybe for some other.

I had never ventured there until that day. How could I? Mine was a strictly circumscribed life. That day, however, I had gone to Smita's house to borrow a book. Smita had kept me back much longer than I should have stayed. I was scared when I discovered how late I was. And, trying to get home a little earlier, I took a short cut within a short cut. As I hurried along the unfamiliar way, I was full of a turmoil of fears . . . would this path take me anywhere? What would she say to me when I got home? Thank god, I wasn't scared of the dark like Dhruva was. That would have been one more burden to bear.

And suddenly, as I tortured myself with fears, the fragrance of the mango blossoms was wafted to me on the breeze. I stood there and sniffed like a dog, trying to orient myself. There was only one mango orchard in that area, and that one not far from home. As relief seeped in, realisation and pleasure followed. The strange place, the darkness that enfolded me in an unusual solitude, the fragrance of the blossoms, the sticky crunchiness of the leaves under my feet . . . I took it all in with delight. And then, there was a loud, harsh cry. The *Ho Ho* of the watchman who guarded the mango trees—periodic cries, whether to keep away marauders, or to keep up his own spirits, I don't know. Whatever it was, it was enough for me. I fled. The wrong way as it turned out, though I discovered that only later.

And there it was, a sudden dip that took me by utter surprise. Grassy slopes on which trees grew slanting, their branches almost parallel to the ground. In the twilight I could see white starry flowers gleaming in the some of the trees. There was an enchanting air of secrecy about the place that enraptured me, until it occurred to me that this was *that* place.

A chill ran up my spine and for the second time I ignomin-
iously fled.

I told no one about my discovery. No, I did tell one person.
The friend who was always there when I wanted someone. The
boy who was my age, maybe a little older. Even now I can see
his face, the eyes eager and understanding, straight nose,
straight brows, straight hair. If I could invent any friend at all,
why was it a boy? I don't know. Nor do I know why his name
was Hemant. I did not give him that name. It was already his
when I knew him. I could talk to him as I could to no one else.
He would listen with interest to my plans, my thoughts, my
doings as no one else did. And he would not laugh at me,
ridicule me or turn away in disinterest.

I forgot all about the place until that day, almost at the end
of the summer vacation. I had wanted to go for a movie that
day with Smita and her family.

"Tell your mother it's a good movie," Smita prompted me.

"It's about the Rani of Jhansi*. Tell her it'll help you in history."

What was the use? Smita's family was unpopular at home.
They were careless, slapdash, believed in enjoyment and therefore suspect. I could not go with them.

"We'll go by ourselves one day," I was told. I did not
believe that. It was only to put me off. Angry and sullen, I got
out of the house when she closeted herself into her room for
her afternoon nap, Dhruva being patted to sleep like a baby.

What could I do? Suddenly it occurred to me. I could go
there, the place I had discovered some time back. I'd just go
and not come back till late. And then they would get anxious,
later frantic, and start searching for me. And if I was kidnapped . . . so much the better. She would be sorry she had
refused to let me go to the movie. Serves her right, I thought
viciously, imagining her distress, her tears, her remorse,
savouring my fantasy to the fullest.

Just as I was leaving, there was Dhruva, having escaped, as he always did, the moment she fell asleep.

"Where are you going, Sarutai?"

"Nowhere and don't call me Sarutai," I said all in one breath.

"You're trying to fool me. You're going somewhere. I'm coming too."

"You go in and sleep or I'll tell Ai."

"Go and tell. And I'll tell her you're going out somewhere."

"Who says I'm going anywhere?" I replied with a calculated sangfroid. But I knew from experience I could not shake him off. I made one more attempt, however.

"Look," I said, pointing to the sky in which a few clouds drifted languidly. "It's going to rain. You'll get wet."

There had been heavy rains the last two days, harbingers of the monsoon. Now there was no rain, just a hint of a threat of it.

"If I get wet, you'll also get wet. I don't care. I want to come. I'm going to come."

His face was stubborn, the pampered child who could bear no opposition. In a moment he would flop on the ground, drum his feet and indulge in a full-fledged tantrum. I could not afford that.

"Oh, come on," I said hastily. "But don't tell Ai. You're never to tell anyone where we're going."

"Why?"

"It's a secret place, that's why. And don't ask too many questions. If you want to come, just come quietly."

Perhaps it would be nice to have Dhruva with me instead of Hemant. Someone who could talk and play as well as listen.

"I promise." He held his hand to his throat, his eyes large and solemn. "I promise I won't tell anyone." I ran on eagerly, Dhruva invariably falling behind, calling out. "Sarutai, wait for me, I'm coming." At last I held his hand so that he would walk faster. As we went past the mango orchard, he said, "Oh, have we come here to steal mangoes?"

"Don't be silly. The mango season is over. No more mangoes now. Didn't Ai make mango *barfi** yesterday?"

The *barfi* was made of the last of the mangoes, usually flat and tasteless.

As we passed the orchard, there was a rotting, putrefying smell; the kind that comes from mangoes after the rains. I remembered, with a wistful nostalgia, the earlier fragrance of the blossoms. And I wondered whether my place was as wonderful as I had imagined it to be.

It was. Just as wonderful. Better, in fact, for the rains had wrought their usual magic, tinting everything a tender green. We walked down to the hollow and the ground was slippery, tufts of grass treacherously giving way, wet mud squelching between our toes. We had come away without our slippers.

"Look, Sarutai, look at the mud. And look at my feet."

"Don't call me Sarutai. And hurry."

"Where's the secret place?"

"Here. This is the secret place."

"But there's nothing here."

I knew it. I shouldn't have brought him. Now it did seem that there was nothing. All the enchantment had fled.

"Why did you come?" I turned on him angrily. "I didn't ask you to come. If you don't like it, go away!"

"No, I like it. It's nice." Dhruva suddenly changed his tune, looking with anxiety into my face.

I put my tongue out at him, shedding my anger and disappointment. "Liar," I said good humouredly, enjoying my power.

"No, it's really nice. Look at all that water. It's a river isn't it. Sarutai?"

It was the rains, I supposed, which had turned a part of the hollow into a sort of lake. The water was muddy and had the peculiar unpleasant odour stagnant water always has; but for us it was an unforeseen find, an unexpected treasure house of umpteen games. We made faces at our own reflections, we played ducks and drakes . . . and how it annoyed me to find Dhruva's stones skimming effortlessly across the water, while mine sank in hopelessly . . . we sailed twigs and dried leaves, we played, we frolicked with such joy that it does not seem possible now that I was one of those two joyous children. Never again . . . I never had that pure joy of childhood ever again. I became all at once a sombre girl, frightened of many things, most of all of joy.

"Ai says we're going to see the Rani of Jhansi," Dhruva announced proudly and complacently during a respite. "All of us."

"Who cares?"

Yes, who cared? Not I, not now. Who was she, that Rani? Just a picture on a page of a history book. She was not real.

"Tell me about her."

"She was a brave queen."

"Brave? Like Shivaji."

"Yes, Like Shivaji."

"Let's build a fort here with this wet mud. Shivaji's fort."

"No, you'll get dirty and Ai will scold me and punish me."

"We can wash ourselves in the river. Let's swim in it."

I was suddenly alarmed. "No, don't. And it isn't a river. It's just a bit of muddy water."

Just a bit of muddy water. I didn't know it then, I found it out later, when the information was of no use to me, that the shallow water concealed a deeper pond that had been dug by the brick workers for soaking bricks.

"And we've got to go home now."

I became aware of how long we had been here. Surely she would have woken up by now, she would look for us, first for Dhruva, then for me. And when she couldn't find us, she would . . .

"Come on, let's go home," I said persuasively. "We'll come some other time to build Shivaji's fort."

"No, now. I want to build it now."

"No, you can't. We must go home. And look, it's going to rain. "

A large drop did indeed splash wetly, coldly on my arm. But Dhruva would not budge. Like all self-willed children he could not bear to let go.

"I'm going to build the fort now," he announced with a maddening persistence.

Angry, exasperated, I said, "Do it yourself then, I'm going."

I walked away with determination, knowing he would not stay there long, not alone, that he would follow me soon enough.

Climbing up was worse, much worse, than going down. I could scarcely get a foothold, my feet slipping at each step. How would Dhruva manage by himself? He could never do it. I turned round to call him, to say, "Come on, Dhruva, quick, or else I'm really going," when I saw him fall into the water. Oh no! I cursed him, more annoyed than frightened. He would get dirty and wet now and he would start howling and Ai would blame me for everything. I began to climb down hoping he would have got out of the water. I looked down once and there was no one. Just blankness.

"Dhruva," I called out, my voice high, shrill and frightened. Was he hiding somewhere? Playing the fool? Trying to scare me?

Then I saw him in the water. Just a moment and he was gone again, only bubbles left to tell me where he had been.

"Dhruva, Dhruva," I tried to shout, but something was squeezing me, a monstrous grip round my chest and throat, that would not let my voice emerge. There was a quality of desperation in my descent now, slithering, slipping, clutching. How I got down and into the water I can't remember. Only that I was there at last in the water, wading in, trying to get at him, wondering where he could be. There was exasperation, too, grappling with panic . . . why couldn't he just get up and walk out, the stupid fool! The water was not deep, scarcely above my calf at its deepest.

And suddenly, as I waded on, my foot gave way. My heart lurched into my mouth in fright. I staggered, recovered my balance, and stood there, panting and gasping. The water was deep here. And Dhruva was in it.

I knelt down now, reaching out, trying to hold on to something, feeling sure each time it was him. His leg. His arm. His shirt. His hair. Again and again I clutched at something that evaded me and finally turned out to be not Dhruva after all. And all the time there was a despairing feeling that Dhruva was trying pull me down to him. I was sobbing now in jerky gasps, gulping, struggling, frantically trying to hold on to something . . . it was incredible that he could have disappeared so totally in so short a time . . . when I felt my arms go slack, as if eased of a burden. I straightened out, relief for a moment blotting out everything else. The water became placid and unruffled once more. Even the bubbles vanished. I was quiet too, not sobbing any more, knowing with a complete certainty that this was not real, only a nightmare out of which I would eventually wake up to have Dhruva calling out . . .

Sarutai, wait for me, I'm coming.

Finally I walked away from there. Steadily I climbed up the slope, and for some reason it was easy this time. I went into the deserted mango grove, and sat there under the trees. It began to rain. I had no thought of sheltering myself. Nor did the trees give me any protection. The large drops fell through heavily, with a menacing drumming sound and I was soon drenched. I left myself get wet and sat there thinking of nothing. Some time later, I suppose, it stopped raining. I sat on, still blank, not wanting to move, to get up, to do anything that would lead me away from this peaceful, almost comatose state into something dreadful.

After a while I got up. I had to go home. They would be searching for me by now, wouldn't they? They would be frantic—wasn't that what I had planned? When was that? Some time earlier, a time so far distant that it could almost have been someone else who had had the thought. And Dhruva would, of course, be at home. He would put his tongue out at me and say with glee . . .

You're late, you're very late. Ai is waiting for you. She's going to give it to you.

He would be virtuously triumphant because he had done nothing wrong himself. Hadn't he been sleeping in Ai's room when I went out.

I stood up, my dripping frock clinging uncomfortably to me. I was seized by a violent fit of shivering. I walked home slowly, trying to put off the moment of being there. I entered through the backyard, climbing up the wall, jumping down on the washing stone, sneaking in through the back door. Strange, the house was empty. I was relieved. I could now change into dry clothes. I was undiscovered, the moment of confrontation was put off.

They must have gone out to look for me. Thankfully I changed into a dry dress, buttoning myself all wrong in my hurry so that I had to undo the buttons and do them up all over again.

And I waited. Waited stoically for my punishment. She would scold me and Dhruva would gloat. But it was Baba who came in first.

"Saru," he said, "where's Dhruva?"

"I don't know," I replied. "How would I know?"

She came in a little later and asked me the same question.

"Where is Dhruva?"

Once again I said, "I don't know."

I said those three words over and over again. I said them even when they found him and brought him home. And she . . . she turned instantly to me and said . . .

3

It was one of those moments of truth that come on the instant of waking. No, not just one truth, but the whole of it came to her then with an absolute, unshakeable certainty. (And wasn't that enlightenment after all?) She felt as if she was standing on a height, with a vantage view of humanity laid out below her. And what struck her most forcibly was the futility of the whole exercise. It seemed idiotic, moronic, meaningless. Like walking onto a lighted stage a smiling, grimacing puppet. Just one of many, all of them making the same faces, the same gestures. There was never any audience, but the puppets kept coming just the same, walking off eventually to make room for yet some more. Coming out of the darkness and going into the darkness. What for?

For some reason she remembered the woman on the motorcycle. She herself had been waiting at a pedestrian crossing that day, stalled by a traffic light, when the motorbike had gone past her, a man riding it, a woman on the pillion. The woman with her fluttering silk sari, her painted lips, her shaped eyebrows and short hair covered by the end of her sari had been like so many other women. It was the expression on her face that had caught her attention. What had it been? Complacence? Certainly? Confidence? Sure of her place in the world, of her right to exist? And suddenly there had been a sense of shock, as if she was watching the husk of herself, as if she had been hinged on herself, one part of her the woman on the motorbike, the other standing there on the pavement, watching that woman, sardonic, unbelieving, asking the question . . . am I really like that?

Now the dichotomy was complete, the hinge had broken off and there were two of her, one part, the woman on the motorbike, misplaced, the other lying here wondering . . . can I survive without that part of me?

There were sounds that told her Baba was awake. She had a dim realisation that something had changed since last night when she had fallen into bed utterly exhausted. Now, waking up, she had the feeling of having done something dreadful, of having disgraced herself in some way. She knew the disgrace, the misdemeanour, would confront her the moment she got out of bed. She lay in bed as long as possible, childishly shirking that moment. But when she got out at last, there was only Baba's mild question . . . "Awake, Saru? Will you have your tea now?"

He made it and brought it to her and it was as if they had gone back to some other time. And when he cooked the lunch and served her, again it was as if he had always done so. She had, without realising it, totally relinquished her absorption in housekeeping, like a role she had discarded and forgotten. What she did remember was that he had left her alone last night, leaving her to get out of it by herself. And yet today there was something in his face that reminded her of some other time. When had he looked at her like that? Surely, some time, once before . . . ?

The memory rushed on her with a savage force. Yes, it had been when her mother had been cruel to her after Dhruva's death.

And Baba bad said . . . Keep away from her for a while, Saru. She doesn't know what she's saying.

She knows, the child who had been her had stolidly replied, as if it didn't really matter at all. She hates me.

He came to her in the evening while she sat listlessly on the kitchen step. His normal air of hesitancy seemed intensified and exaggerated.

"I want to speak to you, Saru," he said and then paused, very obviously nerving himself to speak. "About Dhruva," he went on. "You're quite wrong in imagining that we blamed you for his death."

"Speak for yourself, Baba," she spoke dully, with no rancour. She was scraping a finger on the rough stone of the step, and did not look at him.

"I never blamed you."

He stressed the 'I' and now, for the first time, she looked up at him. As if he had declared himself to be a person at last.

"But she did?"

"Maybe. That was her weakness. Call it her fault. Can't you forgive her for that even now?"

"Did she say anything about me when . . . before dying?"

"Nothing. She died silently."

The hope that had been within her died, too, extinguished in an instant. And only now did she know it had been there at all. The hope that her mother would one day say . . . what?

"I never knew the moment of her death. I woke up in the morning and found her dead. She must have died some time during the night."

Once, there had been a ghoulish curiosity in her about her mother's death. Now she felt revolted.

"No, don't tell me," she said hastily.

"But, it wasn't . . . I mean, she had accepted the fact of her death; she was reconciled to it. And so when she died, her face was peaceful. There was no struggle, no bitterness."

She felt a bitter envy. It was like hearing that the person you most despised had achieved the one thing, the very thing, you most desired. Meanwhile Baba went on speaking. His sudden garrulity not only astonished her, it shocked her. She had felt this way when a normally composed and reticent colleague had wept and indiscriminately hugged people after a few drinks at a party. Surely there was something indecent in throwing off restraint so completely?

"You know she never was a very talkative person. It was the way they were brought up, she and her sister, in their grandfather's house. 'We always had to remember we didn't really belong,' she told me once. 'We were only tolerated.' In the last few months, she almost stopped speaking. She liked me to read to her, though. The Mahabharata. The Ramayana. It seemed to soothe her. She used to lie listening quietly, sometimes falling asleep in the middle of a sentence, a word. She had become very weak. And there were all those drugs. But one day I saw that she was listening very intently. When I finished reading, she said . . . read it again. It was that episode of Duryodhana in the Mahabharata. Duryodhana at the very end of the battle."

"What happens?" She asked idly, incurious.

"When the Kauravas* are defeated and Duryodhana finds he is almost the only one left, he leaves the battlefield and goes into a lake. He waits there for the Pandavas* to come and kill him."

"Oh yes, I remember that."

"Your mother made me read that part a second time. And then she said . . . yes, that's what all of us have to face at the end. That we are alone. We have to be alone."

To be alone? Never a stretching hand? Never a comforting touch? Is it all a fraud then, the eternal cry of . . . my husband, my wife, my, children, my parents? Are all human relationships doomed to be a failure?

"The day before she died she spoke of Madhav."

Madhav. Not me.

"What did she say?"

"'I'm glad he'll be with you,' she said to me. She knew," and he smiled a wry smile, the smile of a man revealed in a weakness, "I had not yet learned to live alone. Like she had. But she was stronger. And she died at peace with herself."

"She died peacefully!" She burst out of her inertia, surprised herself by the malice in her tone. She did not know she had been roused by the frank admiration in his tone when he spoke of her dead mother. "What about me? Did she think of me at all? She died at peace with herself, you say. How could she after what she did to me?" .

"What did she do to you, Saru?"

Why did he feign ignorance?

"Don't you know how she cursed me?"

"Cursed you? When?"

"After I got married."

"Who told you about it?"

"Professor Kulkarni."

For the first time she heard her father utter a foul word. A word of abuse so vulgar that it shocked her into an inane giggle. She felt like a child delighted to see an adult commit a wrong.

"That man! What did he tell you?"

It came back to her, suddenly, at that moment, all of it. Not only what the man had said, but how it had been when he had come to them. The dark, airless room without even a fan to bring in a semblance of coolness. The two of them lying on the bed, peacefully, passionless for the moment. And then the knock at the door.

Manu got up to answer it while she hurriedly tidied herself and the bed, trying to make it seem as if it hadn't been slept in ... On the other side of the dingy curtain that partitioned their one room into two, she heard Manu welcoming him in. She prepared some coffee for him, taking a solemn pride in the gesture. It was the first time she was entertaining a guest. The aroma of the coffee filled the room, drowning the other unpleasant odours that drifted in from outside.

"I met your parents," he said to her without any preamble, as if he had hoped to shock her into an unexpected response.

She became suddenly tense, the hand holding the cup rigidly still. Then she relaxed. What did it matter to her now? What did they matter? She smiled at Manu so anxiously watching her face.

"I feel partly responsible for you two, you know. If it hadn't been for me, perhaps . . .".

"Oh, come on, sir . . ." Manu's words, his laughter, the way he crossed one leg over another seemed to her intensely, enchantingly male. ". . . Who do you think you are? The god of love?"

"No, Manohar, I'm serious. You can't get away from the fact that it was I who encouraged you two to go ahead and get married. It seemed to me . . . and let me say I still think that way . . . absurd that two youngsters like you should be kept apart for something as trivial as caste. But perhaps it was a bit rash your getting married right now. Maybe you should have waited until Sarita graduated."

"A year and a half more? Impossible!"

"But how will you manage now, Manohar? Sarita won't be earning for quite some time more. Meanwhile, you'll have to support her as well."

"We'll manage."

"Did you go there and ask them to support me?" she asked, her voice hard, her face hostile.

"I did." He seemed unperturbed. Perhaps it was being a teacher that conferred that air of impregnability. "I thought it was their duty to see you through until you graduated."

"'God! What did they say?"

"'Your father said nothing."

"'Of course. But my mother?"

He hesitated.

"Tell me. I can take it. Don't forget. I've been through it already."

"She said . . . 'Daughter? I don't have any daughter. I had a son and he died. Now I am childless.'"

She had been expecting it and yet she flinched. Her face screwed up, her muscles tightened as if she had taken a blow. But even as the two men watched her, she controlled herself.

"You shouldn't have gone to them. Why did you?" she cried out angrily.

"But, Manohar said . . ."

"Manu, did you?" The pain of this betrayal was worse, far worse. "Did you?"

"No, I didn't. Not really," he protested. "But I thought that you would be happier if you were reconciled to them."

"I'm not unhappy now, am I? You know I'm not. I know how it would be. I'd told you. You shouldn't have . . ."

"It was for you, Saru."

And she so wanted to believe him, she did believe him.

"I know they'll never come round. She always hated me."

"Oh, come on, Saru, that can't be true. Don't be unfair."

"No, Manohar, I think Saru is right." He finished his coffee with a loud slurp and put the cup down with a clatter. "I always imagined no mother could ever dislike her own child. But Saru's mother seems to be an exception. She shocked me. Imagine saying . . . I will pray to god for her unhappiness. Let her know more sorrow than she has given me."

"She said that?" Manu's face looked like that of a loyal little boy, shocked and outraged.

"Hmm. I just couldn't reach out to her. She was frightening in her refusal to understand. To her Saru is nothing but a betrayer. "

"What else did she say?" she asked coldly.

Again the older man hesitated. This time Manu broke in with,

"No, don't tell us any more. We don't want to know. Let's leave it at this, Saru."

"She cursed me, Baba," she said now to her father. "Even

her silence at the end was a curse. And you say she died peacefully." No struggle, no bitterness. She would never forget that. No, never. "Does a death redeem a whole life? Can't you understand, Baba, that it's because she cursed me that I am like this?"

"Like this? Like what?"

"Unhappy. Destroyed."

How often had she thought of the words? But she had sworn she would never say them aloud, never admit the fact, not as long as her mother was alive. And I didn't, she thought. Yet, she had a fanciful idea that somewhere a vengeful ghost sighed a sigh of satisfaction. But she was too tired to care any more. There was only the relief that comes from surrender. Not to pretend any more, not to struggle–it brought nothing but solace. Her whole body went slack.

"Saru," he asked her, "What's wrong? Is it your husband?"

"My husband?" she asked blankly, as if she didn't know what the words meant.

"He's written to me."

She reacted as violently to the words as if they had offered her some provocation. And then panic flowed. She stared at him dumbly, her mouth working, her face utterly open and defenceless, a child caught red-handed in a wrongdoing.

"He says he's been writing to you regularly and you haven't written to him once."

She thought of all the unopened letters in her suitcase . . . she had pushed them deep down under all her clothes so that she wouldn't see them, and yet she looked at them, as if to reassure herself, each time she opened the suitcase . . . and smiled in satisfaction.

"He says you write to the children, but not to him. He says that even in your letters to them, you never speak of going back. What is it, Saru?"

"Shall I tell you?"

It was a challenge. You've always avoided things. The truth.

Facts. Life. Confrontations. Can you now take this from a daughter you thought you'd got rid of?

"Yes, tell me. What's wrong? Is something wrong between you and your husband?"

"Something? No, everything."

And now she could feel a withdrawal in him. He didn't want her to go on. He wanted to leave it at that.

But he surprised her by saying," What is it, Saru? Why don't you tell me what it is."

4

N ow she knew. It was for this that she had come home. To see his face as she told him the truth. To have him declare himself on her side as he had once done. She had the words ready. She would recite them, she had thought, as if she was reading out a clinical history of an anonymous patient. Instead she blurted out, baldly, crudely, "My husband is a sadist."

His face, even after she said the words, was devoid of all expression but the expectancy that was already there. "Don't you understand, Baba?" she asked irritably. He shook his head. She noticed that though he looked at her, his eyes were focussed somewhere beyond her. "Don't you know the meaning of the word? Was your generation luckier than ours? Perhaps such words didn't enter your vocabulary. Sadism . . . love of cruelty. How simple and clinical that sounds, doesn't it? And sex . . ."

Involuntarily he put out a hand as if he would stop her. "Shall I go on, Baba?"

"Go on," he said, withdrawing his hand, staring down at it. "Go on."

The mask had slipped only for a fragmentary moment.

"Does it shock you to hear such things? I know you're my father and I'm your daughter and there are nearly thirty years. between us, but still . . . You're a man and I'm a woman. Can we talk of such things?"

"Why not?" he said and his voice came out husky. He cleared his throat and said again, "Why not?" And then he went on, irrelevantly, she thought, "Do you know, Saru, I often feel sorry that we left so many things unsaid, your mother and I. When she lay dying I wanted to ask her . . . would you like to meet Saru? Sometimes I think she might have said 'yes.' But I never did. Silence had become a habit for us. Now . . . Go on, tell me. Tell me everything."

With an abrupt movement she got up and walked into the kitchen. She stood facing the dingy, smoke-blackened wall for a moment, then turned back to her father who had followed her in. Her face, he noticed, no longer had that unnatural composure, the look of indifference it had recently had.

"He's cruel to me . . . in bed."

The words came out with reluctance, like a child being forced to betray a friend.

The man waited for her to go on but she did not.

"You'll have to tell me plainly, Saru," he said humbly, almost apologetically. "I don't know much about these things. I don't understand, either."

"Nor do I, Baba. Nor do I. I can't understand any of it myself. Look . . . there we were, a normal husband and wife. Like any other normal couple. Absolutely like any other couple. And one day . . . Yes, what happened? A girl came to interview me. Nothing special about that, either. They were bringing out a special issue on career women and someone gave her my name. And she asked me . . Can I come? I said yes. And she came. And as we were talking he came in . . ."

"You mean your husband?"

He had the air of a man determined to get every fact right, all the data complete. Would that help him to solve the problem?

"Yes, my husband. Manohar. I call him Manu. And before we got married that man had once called him Shelley. Shelley! Oh my god!"

It was not a smile. It was a peculiar lopsided grimace that took away nothing of the sombre gravity of her face.

"And I was to be his Harriet. Harriet who died with another man's child inside her. But I didn't know all that then. I thought of him as a Shelley, too, poor fool that I was. But not for long. I soon knew what he really was. I knew he would be teaching in that college until he got out with a pension. Oh yes, I was telling you how he came in that day. I introduced him to her. And while we were having our tea . . . she knew by then what he was doing . . . she asked him . . . 'How does it feel when your wife earns not only the butter but most of the bread as well?' Do you know what that meant?" She asked him angrily, as if it was he who had said it.

"You were earning more than him," he said.

"Yes, I was. But it hadn't mattered till then. I swear it hadn't. And even then, when that girl said it, we just laughed, all three of us."

The girl, she suddenly remembered now, had looked like a lively monkey when she had laughed. She had bright sparkling eyes and hair that curled round her face. "It won't straighten out," she had said, tugging at it, making a comical face.

The silence went on for so long, he wondered if she would not go on. Her hands, he noticed, moved unceasingly, twisting and untwisting a corner of her sari round her fingers.

"And then?" he prompted hesitantly.

She looked up with the face of a person plunging into cold water. "He attacked me," she said. "He attacked me like an animal that night. I was sleeping and I woke up and there was this . . . this man hurting me. With his hands, his teeth, his whole body. "

His Adam's apple moved up and down jerkily. "I don't think, Saru . . ."

"I must tell you and you've got to listen. Who else is there? There's no one else. No one at all. You've got to listen." She seemed so frantic that he said soothingly, "I'm listening, Saru. Go on, I'm listening."

"I never knew till then he had so much strength in him."
Her voice was a dull monotone again. "I could do nothing
against him. I couldn't fight back. I couldn't shout or cry; I was
so afraid the children in the next room would hear. I could do
nothing. I can never do anything. I just endure."

"It happened again?"

"Again?" The smile scared him. Her mother had smiled
like that sometimes. "Yes, again and again and again and yet
again. I've lost count."

"But why, Saru?" It was an urgent whisper. "Why? I don't
understand. Why does he do it?"

She shrugged her shoulders, holding both her hands out in
gesture of utter helplessness.

"Have you never asked him? Haven't you asked him why
he does it?"

At that she began to laugh, as if her rigid self-control had
suddenly given way. She sat down on the ground, put her head
on her knees and shook with helpless laughter. He watched her
in alarm. The laughter ceased as suddenly as it had begun.
Looking up she caught the alarm on his face.

"No, don't be scared, Baba. I'm not crazy. Not yet, anyway.
It just amused me, your question. Have I asked him? No,
never." She met his look of astonishment calmly.

"I've never spoken to him about it. Nor has he. Why
haven't I?" She rubbed a restless finger on her foot, watching
it with intense concentration. "That first time . . . I woke up in
the morning feeling somehow different, not knowing why.
There was only a knowledge of pain. And then, suddenly I
remembered what had happened. To remember and to know .
. . it was like being battered by him all over again. No, don't
worry. I won't go on about that. I'm trying to tell you why I've
been silent. He was already up that morning when I woke. I
could hear him talking to Abhi outside in the gallery where we
have our morning tea. Abhi wanted to wake me up and he was

trying to dissuade him. Perhaps I made some sound for he called out my name. I panicked at that. I went into the bathroom and locked myself in."

She stopped rubbing at her foot and crossed her ankles, making her body smaller, more compact. She looked so small the way she sat, feet crossed, arms hugging knees close to chest that he had an illusion of seeing the child who had cowered there saying . . .I don't know. I don't know.

"But I couldn't stay there forever. I had to come out. I wondered what we would say. Would he apologise? Or explain? would he look guilty and shamefaced? But when I went out, there was nothing. He said, as if it was just any day, 'Morning, Saru. Slept well'?"

She stopped and stared at her father as if she would communicate the enormity of her statement only by silence. There was no response from him. She went on. "Do you understand, Baba?" He was his usual self. Absolutely his usual self. There was no change in him, no difference. And how could I say to that man . . . why did you do it? Had he done it at all? I began to think after a while . . . how could any man do such a thing and be so unchanged? . . . Perhaps I had dreamt it. Maybe a nightmare. I had terrible nightmares after Renu's birth. You know nothing about that. I should have been here, really," and she stared at him accusingly, "for Renu's birth. My first child should have been your responsibility. Maybe if I'd been here, I wouldn't have had that nightmare. Who knows?" She shrugged and was silent for a moment, seemingly lost in some conjecture of her own.

"It was a man in a brown scarf trying to strangle me in that nightmare. And I could do nothing then, either. Luckily I woke up before I died. I thought this was again that kind of a nightmare. But it couldn't have been because there were the bruises."

"The bruises," he repeated after her dully.

"And so I didn't know what to think. And he said nothing

about it, either. I thought . . . we'll soon forget about it. But I couldn't. How could I when it happened again and again?"

"And yet you said nothing. You were silent." It was his turn to accuse her.

"How could I? He was so normal–at all other times . . . what could I say? Each time I tried to speak, to open my mouth, my heart failed me. What if he said . . . are you crazy?" And there had been the other thing. Her feeling that so long as she did not speak, the thing that happened between them remained unreal. That by speaking she would be making it real. "And you don't know, Baba . . . I think he doesn't know it himself, what he does to me at night. That's why he never speaks of it." She noticed with faint surprise that her father looked much older than the man to whom she'd begun speaking. Had he really had an air of tranquillity about him? Had she destroyed that like so many other things?

"But . . . but how?" he stammered.

"Oh, it's possible," she said wearily, as if she had gone through this argument many times before. "I know there can be such cases. Blackouts about certain actions. Oh yes, it's perfectly possible . . ."

She got up now and began to move in a wild frenzy, hands settling hair right, legs taking her swiftly up and down that dingy little room.

" . . . And I think it's true in his case. I can swear to that. I was dressing up one day and he said . . . 'God, Saru! Have you hurt yourself? Look at that!' I swear his surprise, his concern was genuine. And if he doesn't know what's the use of talking to him?"

"All the more reason. You're a doctor, you should know. Maybe he needs treatment . . ."

"He needs treatment . . . ?" Her voice grew shrill. "It's not so easy, Baba. They'll say . . . I need treatment, too. They'll go on and on about things that happened long ago."

And once again I'll have to hear the words . . . You did it. You did it.

"I don't want all that. I won't have it."

"But you can't go on like this, Saru."

"What can I do?"

Her helplessness astonished him.

"Surely you don't mean that?"

"Why not? Maybe I deserve it after all. Look what I've done to him. Look what I did to Dhruva. And to my mother. Perhaps if I go on suffering . . ."

It's because I wronged her that I'm suffering now. And, the more I suffer, the greater the chance, perhaps, of expiating that wrong. Wasn't that what she had always thought, always told herself? Why, then, did the words sound so melodramatic, so unreal, when she said them aloud?

"And what was it that you did to your mother, Saru?"

She stared at him blankly, then stammered, "Why . . . why . . . I . . . deserted her."

"But that's natural. You have to get away from your parents some time, haven't you?"

"But it was the way I went . . ."

"And will you never realise," he went on, ignoring her words, "that your mother is dead? Your mother is dead," he repeated, raising his voice.

"Yes," she repeated, the words too "my mother is dead. And . . ." now the voice was tinged with bitterness, "she died at peace with herself. What about me?"

Surely he would help her now. Tell her what to do. She imagined him saying . . . don't worry, I'll look after you. Instead he said, "But how can I answer that question, Saru? What can I do?"

She was frantic now. "But you've got to help me, you've got to. You did it once. And because you did I went to Bombay, met him and married him. And that's why . . ."

"I helped you then because you had made up your mind. You knew what you wanted to do."

"And now?"

"Now . . . what can I do?"

She heard not helplessness in it, but mockery. Hostility. She should have expected it. Nevertheless, there was the sensation of standing against a wall blindfolded, waiting for the shot that would end it all.

"Saru," he said, putting his hand gently on hers. His hand was dry and rough. It felt strange, like the touch of an unfamiliar animal. "Go to bed now and try to sleep. Go on."

She did not see his face, exhausted and drained, a man who could take no more. She could only hear his words telling her to go. So it was true. He had nothing for her. Nothing at all.

Suddenly it came to her, a memory she had tried to evade all these years. Dhruva whimpering in the dark. And she, impatient with him.

"What's there to be scared of?" she had cried out angrily. She had switched on the light, saying, "Look, there's nothing."

"But you don't know," he had said, his eyes round, a shadow of his fear still in them. "When the light comes on, it goes away. When the dark comes, it returns."

Now, after so many years, I know, Dhruva, why you came to me to escape from the dark. And how you felt when I told you to go away.

5

She came out of a deep sleep to hear voices. A sense of catastrophe, of something unwelcome, came to her as she groped her way to awareness. *He's here. He's come for me.* It was her mind that panicked, that tried to jump up and escape. Her body, exhausted and lethargic, lay still. Then she recognised the voices. They were Baba's and Madhav's. It was like a return to some distant time waking up and hearing their voices. And yet, somehow, indefinably different from that time.

Madhav . . . had he returned? She got out of bed and walked into the hall, dragging her feet as she did so.

"Madhav?"

They looked at her in surprise as if they had forgotten her presence in the house.

"I've just arrived," he said after a moment.

"What a time! What's the time?"

"Not very late, really. Just about eleven."

As he spoke the clock wheezed out the hours with its usual reluctance.

"The bus broke down on the way. We lost nearly two hours because of that. I should have been here before nine."

"Come and have something to eat."

"No, Kaka, I'm not hungry. Honest."

"A glass of milk, then."

"All right. But don't heat it. I'll drink it just as it is. I must wash."

They went away, one to the kitchen, the other to the bath-room. She stood there alone, as if stranded, in the middle of the room. She didn't seem to know what to do next. Her sense of purpose had deserted her. She had gone on all these days, hoping for something. Now all that was left was a sense of bewilderment.

Madhav came in wiping his face on his towel. He saw her standing there and said gently, "Go back to bed, Sarutai. I'm sorry I woke you up."

She remembered the heavy, drugged quality of her sleep and said, "I'm glad you did. Is everything all right at home?"

"No," he said, putting the towel away. His face was grim. "Satish has disappeared."

"Satish?" It took her a moment to recollect that Satish was his brother. "When?"

"Nearly four days age now. My father refuses to do anything about it. 'He wanted to get away from me,' he says. 'Let him go.'

Nothing my mother says can move him. And he blames her for what Satish has done. He found out that Satish had threat-ened to run away before. That she knew of his craze for movies. 'You should have told me,' he says. How could she have done that? Can any of us talk to him? And now he's pun-ishing her in his own way."

She was suddenly curious to hear about other people's pun-ishments.

"How?"

"He doesn't eat anything she cooks."

Was that a punishment? She would have laughed, but the boy's expression made it obvious he considered it cruel. For some reason she thought of the woman in the Sanskrit story from her school text. The woman who would not disturb her husband's sleep even to save her child from the fire. A woman so blessed, it was said, that Agni* himself came and saved the child. Now she thought . . . who wrote that story? A man, of course. Telling all women for all time . . . your duty to *me* comes first. And women, poor fools, believed him. So even today Madhav's mother considers it a punishment to be deprived of a chance to serve her husband. And yet . . . if I could believe in that . . . if I could put my duty to my husband above all else . . . ?

Baba, coming in with the milk, asked, "How is your mother taking it, Madhav?"

Baba and she, as though by mutual agreement, avoided looking at each other. After what she had said, it was impossible for them to go back to what they had been before. Nor could they find, so soon, an alternative pattern of behaviour.

Madhav stared frowningly into his glass of milk. His mouth hardened. "She wants me to go to Bombay and look for Satish. How can I, Kaka? You know I have exams in less than a month. 'What do exams matter?' She says. 'Think of Satish.' But I'll lose a whole year if I do what she wants me to do. And all because of one irresponsible boy."

There seemed to be something hard and callous about Madhav as he said that. "But Madhav," she expostulated, "you can't do nothing."

"Oh, I'll write to some people from our place who're in Bombay. I'm sure Satish will go to them for help. I know he'll be all right. He's a very practical and shrewd fellow, actually, though mother seems to think he's a helpless baby." Madhav grinned. "If he's in trouble, he'll turn up fast enough, either here or at home."

Then he turned to Baba, unsure of himself for the first time. "What else can I do, Kaka?"

Baba said nothing, but the boy, as if he had some reassurance from him, went on more confidently, "I can't spoil my life because of that boy. It's my life, after all."

It's my life. It's my life. Four words forming a sentence. Go on saying them and they become meaningless, a jumble of sounds, a collection of letters. And yet, they would not leave her alone. She went back to bed, the words going on and on in her mind. It was maddening. She tried to turn her thoughts to other things, to go back to that childhood fantasy of hers . . . the friend who would never fail her. But it was no use. That friend had deserted her, too. There were only these words instead . . .

We are alone. We have to be alone. Who said that?

She did. My mother.

What did she know?

But it's true. We come into this world alone and go out of it alone. The period between is short. And all those ties we cherish as eternal and long-lasting are more ephemeral than a dewdrop.

Quite the philosopher, aren't you?

She laughed at herself, a small, short laugh. Nevertheless, the argument went on until it became an argument that had taken place sometime, somewhere, between two people, one of whom, she realised in astonishment, had been her.

Philosopher? No, I'm a realist. We are realists. We deal with the ultimate reality . . . the human body.

The human body the ultimate reality? You're fooling yourself, madam.

Then I've been fooling myself for a pretty long time.

She laughed again, this time opening her mouth and letting the laughter come out unobstructed. For days now she had held her lips together, as if sealing in something. So now, when she laughed that way, she shocked herself. As if she had done something wanton.

Wanton . . . as girls they told us never to sit with our legs apart. We wondered why. Until that first day when he said to me . . . open your legs, my love, or I can do nothing. And then I knew.

"Saru . . . " Baba called out.

"What?"

"Did you say something?"

"No, I didn't"

"I thought you did."

"No, I didn't."

It made her want to giggle. A conversation like a modern play. Like Bhide's play. No, not Bhide's play, because we haven't used any expletives.

"Maybe it was Madhav then. I thought I heard something." She heard him getting out of bed.

"Where are you going, Baba?"

"I'll just have a look at Madhav. He didn't seem too well. He told me he had to walk five miles to get the bus. And that in the hot sun."

All this concern for a boy who's nothing to you. The old man seemed pathetic. And then she remembered how he had come to her one night after Dhruva's death when she had woken out of her sleep with a cry. But once there, by her side, he had seemed uncertain about what to do next. Awkwardly and hesitantly he had put his hand on her forehead as if he suspected she had fever. Simulating sleep, had lain stiff and rigid, rejecting him and the sympathy he hadn't known how to offer.

"Is he all right?" she asked, hearing the shuffling footsteps again, feeling a sudden compunction for the man whose sympathy she had rejected all those years back.

"No, he doesn't seem well. I think he has fever. He's very hot. And look at the way he's breathing."

She could hear it now, laboured and loud. It stopped for an instant . . . perhaps the boy had just turned over. But she got out of bed in a frantic haste, throwing her blanket aside. Her sari, crumpled and crushed, irritated her, impeding her swift movements. For a moment, when she saw the boy lying there, his body under the blanket, the face inscrutable, she felt an

intruder. Then she relaxed. It was only Madhav. He lay with
the high flush of fever on him. His lips, slightly swollen and
dry, kept moving as though he was muttering to himself,
though no sounds emerged.

As she knelt by him, the room was lit by a flash of vivid, eye-
hurting lightning.

"Why," Baba said, "looks like it's going to . . . "

She heard no more as, out of where, out of a deep silence,
came a rumble and a clap, just above their heads. As it died
away, dragging its echoes with it, Baba completed his sentence.
"It's going to rain. I thought it would. It was very hot today."

And then, with a shocking suddenness it began. She heard
it coming, rushing to meet them with an eager ferocity. It beat
on the windows, the tiled roof, with a maniac fury. She thought
she heard Baba say something to her through the din, but she
could not hear him. She sat by the sleeping boy, unmoving, as
if she had become catatonic. As the rain steadied to a monoto-
nous dripping downpour, Baba's words, shouted almost,
reached her.

"What about Madhav?"

And then, she came out of it with a painful jerk. A self she
thought she had misplaced took over. She took Madhav's temperature, his pulse, gave him an aspirin, forcing it between his
dry lips, holding up his head as he retched at the dry bitterness
She put a wet compress on his forehead and sat by him.

Baba, who had watched her silently, now asked, "Will he be
all right?"

"Yes" she said, concentrating on one thought . . . he's got to
be all right. Somewhere a frightened child getting drenched in
the rain was praying, too . . . let him be all right.

Baba went away after a while. She did not know when it was
that she fell asleep, sitting there on the ground, leaning against
the wall. She dreamt she was walking along a road, going on
and on, knowing with a sinking feeling that something, some-

body awful and frightening, was waiting for her at the end of it. But it was important to go on just the same, not to stop, even though there was doom waiting for her. And then she stumbled and fell . . .

She woke up. Her back ached, her neck was unbearably stiff. She looked at Madhav. He was sleeping, lips close together now, the flush gone. The compress had slipped across his forehead, giving him a slightly rakish look. Tentatively she put out a hand towards him.

"He's better," Baba said, coming into the room. "There's no fever now."

Yes, he was cool. His skin felt damp and sticky, and the odour of stale perspiration eminated from his body.

"You've been sitting there for hours. You must be tired and stiff. Why don't you go and lie down for a while?"

"Has it stopped raining?"

"Long back. It was only a thunderstorm. I wonder if there are any mangoes left."

She could not sleep now. She went out into the backyard to wash. There was a smell of wet earth and rotting leaves. The trees, their dusty, dirty leaves, washed by the rains to a tender sparkling green, were like symbols of renewal. It's over, she thought. That's done with. He's all right. Things will be all right now.

She went in to have her tea. After she had drunk it, she washed the tea things and put them away. She had stacked the saucers as usual on the small wooden shelf that hung from the wall, and hung the cups on the hooks that protruded from the shelf, when suddenly she decided to change their place. She arranged them on another shelf and looked at them in satisfaction.

"Can I go for my bath now?" she asked Baba, who had watched her in silence. He nodded and stared after her with a troubled look on his face.

After day . . . days? no, months . . . she found herself enjoying her bath, her body responding with sensuous pleasure to
the warm water, the smell of soap. She felt lighter when she
came out as if she had washed away the ugly slough of some
disease.

She peered into the mirror to apply her *kumkum*. Right in
the middle of the forehead. No, not that way today. Between
the eyebrows. As it used to be in the old days. Who had told
her that? Her hand quivered as she applied the dot with the
utmost carefulness. She frowned anxiously at her reflection
and then drew her hair severely back from her forehead. She
looked, she thought, younger and somehow softened. She felt
the same tenderness towards herself that she would have felt
for some stranger come out of any ordeal. Poor girl, she
thought. She has had a bad time.

Madhav woke up a little later. When she went in to him he
looked clean as if he had a wash. He was sitting propped up
against the wall, reading the newspaper.

"How are you feeling Madhav?"

He put the newspaper down and gave her, as was his way,
his full attention.

"I'm all right now. Kaka tells me I gave you a lot of trouble
during the night."

"It's part of my job, isn't it, this kind of trouble?" He
picked up her light, bantering tone, though his eyes gave her a
perplexed look.

"But your patients are . . . how old? Surely, I'm past the age
to be looked after by you, Sarutai."

"Oh yes, long past the age. However, you've got to put up
with me."

"You're looking different today," he suddenly blurted out.
"Different? How?"

She smiled, a complacent, childlike smile, not knowing that
it added a piquant mischievous quality to her face.

"You look . . . " And he faltered. His eyes rested lightly, very lightly, a butterfly movement, on her face. They dropped down only to fly back to her face once more. Then he flushed deeply. He did not go on. He tore bits of the corners of the newspaper he still held in one hand. And silence grew between them . .

Her thoughts rose in a whirling column of consternation. It's not Dhruva. It was never Dhruva. I can never bring him back.

Her cruelty to Dhruva, to her mother, to Manu . . . she would never be rid of it. She would carry this ugly, unbearable burden until she died. The facade of deception had cracked so completely she could never put it together again. Shafts of the truth pierced her, causing her unbearable pain, Atonement . . . ? It was never possible. What had she imagined? What had she thought? "Sarutai," she heard the boy's voice. "What is it?"

He would never have believed it, he thought, if he hadn't seen it himself, how much a person could alter in a moment. Her face had the same suffering look her mother's had had when he saw her last. The resemblance was remarkable.

"What is it, Sarutai?"

Still she could not speak. The old man entered. Madhav turned to him in relief.

"Feeling better, Madhav? Will you have some lunch? Here, Saru, a letter for you."

"For me?"

Dully she identified the writing as Abhi's.

"Kaka," Madhav rushed into speech, covering her silence, his awkwardness, by a flurry of words. "I've been thinking . . . do you think we should advertise in the papers? For Satish, I mean?"

"You mean, saying . . . come home, mother ill, all forgiven . . . that sort of thing?"

I know you want to be forgiven.

But what if there can never be any forgiveness, any atonement?

"Yes, that's what I mean."

"Why don't you wait a day or two? It costs a lot to put a thing like that in the papers."

She opened her letter and pulled out a single sheet of paper. A small involuntary smile came over her face as she read Abhi's . . . "My dearest mummy." And then, as she went on, her expression changed. The smile remained, turning gradually into a grimace.

"For all you know, he may return in a day or two. There's no point . . . Saru, what's the matter?"

The two of them looked at her in astonishment at the sound that escaped from her lips. It was a snarl of pure rage. How dared he? How dared he? Why had he used Abhi? To think that the child's letter should fill her with terror! Was the child to become a menace to her as well? Was she to be left with nothing?

"What is the matter, Saru?" Baba asked her once again, while the boy watched her with frightened eyes.

"He's coming," she said. She did not elaborate further. Instead she walked out of the room, leaving the letter with its childish scrawl lying there where she had been sitting.

6

It has been a fiasco, an exercise in futility, her coming here at all. But what else could it have been? She should have known it would be this way. She went into the inner room where her suitcase lay, looking, even after all these days, alien and out of place. Her belongings, scattered in the room, had the same derelict and forlorn air. Swiftly, she collected them. There were only a few of her things lying about—her brush, comb and toothpaste in the window, a towel hanging from a peg, a sari on a bit of wire looped between two pegs. Opening her suitcase, she began pushing the things into it. She had come away with a minimum of clothes (why then had the suitcase felt so heavy?) and she had added nothing to her luggage since coming here.

And yet she found she could not fit everything in. Trying to cram them into the suitcase with increasing irritation, she suddenly remembered she hadn't washed the set of clothes she'd changed out of that morning. I'll have to leave them behind. I wonder what they'll do with them. I wonder what they did with the clothes and books I left back when I went away last time.

"Saru . . . "

It was Baba holding Abhi's letter in his hand. She did not look up at him. She was wondering what the bulge was that prevented her from closing the suitcase. She tore away the clothes and saw the pile of letters underneath. With an angry exclamation, she wrenched them out and threw them on the floor.

"Saru . . . "

She looked up now. Baba, she noticed, was starting curiously at the letters strewn about her.

"There!" she said triumphantly. "You can put them in the boiler tomorrow. They'll heat the water for your bath."

If she had hoped to provoke him, she failed. He only said, "Where are you going?"

His tone was sharp and inquiring. It occurred to her that he had rarely spoken to her that way before. As if it mattered to him what she did. But somehow she didn't seem to care about it any more. His reactions could not touch her.

She managed to close the suitcase. The locks snapped shut with satisfying clicks.

"Can't you see I'm going?"

"But where?"

Where? How strange, she hadn't thought of it at all! Just flight, precipitate flight. Where was she going?

"Back," she said.

No, she couldn't call it home. It was not home. Nor was this home. How odd to live for so long and discover that you have no home at all!

"Back to Bombay," she said.

"Is it because of this letter?"

He still held the letter in his hand. The rage that the letter had aroused in her had died down. All that was left was the desperation of a trapped animal.

"Are you going away to avoid him?"

"Yes, Baba, I'm going away to avoid him."

She all but mocked him, using his very tone as she repeated his words. But once again his reaction was unexpected. He ignored the mockery and said, simply, "But you can't!"

"Why not?"

She gave herself a cursory look in the mirror. It was a purely reflex action, the gesture to be done before going out. She didn't really see herself.

"But Abhi says . . . " Baba was still scanning the letter. Why was he clinging to it as if it was something precious?

" . . . that he was to leave Bombay yesterday. Which means he'll be here today. Any moment now. Actually, he should have been here by now. Maybe the mailtrain is late."

The mail is late. For a moment she saw him entering the house as she herself had done. She imagined him talking to Baba. And surely Baba would ask him . . . was the train on time? No, he would say. It was late.

And then it penetrated, what Baba had said. He'll be here today. Any moment now. Was it already too late? Her earlier sense of urgency came back. "Baba, I must go," she said picking up the suitcase, pulling her sari end out of her waist where she had tucked it in. He was standing in the door, blocking her way, so that she had to stop. Poor, ineffectual Baba. . . what was he trying to do? He couldn't stop her. He could only irritate her by delaying her.

"But where will you go, Saru?"

"Anywhere," she said impatiently.

Why, after so many years, had he decided to become tenacious, persistent now?

"I don't care where. I'll go and sit in the waiting room at the station until some train comes in. I can't meet him, Baba."

It was an appeal. Surely he would move aside and let her go. But he didn't. He stood there as if unaware of her intentions.

"You can't run away, Saru."

There was something pitiful to her about his attempt to exert his authority over her.

"Are you scared of him?"

Scared of him? Oh god, yes. But not the way you think. It's not what he's done to me, but what I've done to him."

"Give him a chance, Saru. Stay and meet him. Talk to him. Let him know from you what's wrong. Tell him all that you told me."

It was too late for him to advise her, too late for her to listen to him. It seemed like the travesty of a situation she had once imagined, with someone telling her what to do.

"I can't, Baba. I can't."

She was once more the child who had enclosed herself behind walls of negation. Once he had left the child alone behind those walls. Could he not break them down now?

"Saru," and there was angry despair in his voice. "don't do it again. "

Again? She seized on that word with avidity. What had she done? How many grievances had he piled up against her? She had always known that his silence concealed resentment and anger. But wasn't that was how it was with everyone?

"What have I done?"

"Don't turn your back on things again. Turn round and look at them. Meet him."

Her mind fastened on the word "again" once more to the exclusion of everything else. "Again? When did I do it?"

"When your brother died."

That silenced her. He went on impatiently as if he was fighting against time. But why was he in a hurry? It was she who had no time left. He would be here soon.

"But let that go. That's all past and done with. I'm speaking of now. I'm asking you, pleading with you. Have I ever said to you . . . do this or don't do that? I left it all to your mother."

A peculiar expression came over, his face as he said that.

"But now I'm appealing to you. Don't go without meeting your husband. Talk to him. Tell him what's wrong."

"And then?" she asked in a small, frightened voice. A child asking apprehensively for the denouement of a horror story. Afraid to hear it, yet unable to leave it alone.

"And then? It's up to you, isn't it?"

She did not see his face, she only heard his words. And they were, after his earlier vehemence, like an indifferent shrug of the shoulder. A few moments before she had thought . . . he cares and it doesn't matter to me at all. Now she felt desolate and terrified at the thought of his withdrawal.

She put the suitcase down and leaned against the wall as if for support.

"Baba, you don't know. I'm tired, so very tired. I really don't know how I can go on. If only I could end it all . . . " She caught his alarmed look. "No, don't worry. I won't do that. I can't. If I could, I'd have done it long ago." She scarcely knew herself how often the thought of suicide had occurred to her. But to be labelled a coward forever? She shrank from the thought. And perhaps, it still had yet to come to her, the moment when there would be an involuntary break of all strings and the only thing possible would be to let go.

"But I thought . . .maybe you would help me."

But there can never be any forgiveness. Never any atonement. My brother died because I heedlessly turned my back on him. My mother died alone because I deserted her. My husband is a failure because I destroyed his manhood.

"I told you once Saru . . . your mother is dead. So is your brother. Can't you let the dead go?"

"But it's they who won't leave me alone!"

Her tone was peevish and complaining.

"I told you . . . they're dead. They can do nothing. Why do you torture yourself with others? Are you not enough for yourself? It's your life, isn't it?"

It came over her again, the feeling of being bereft she'd had when Madhav had said . . . it's my life. She knew the words had some relevance to her life, that they held some significance for her, but she seemed unable to find the connection.

"If I let them go, there's still Manu . . . "

"Yes, there's still Manu . . . "

And though he said it mildly enough, the words held a menace. He would have said something more, maybe, but suddenly he stood still in an intently listening attitude.

"There!" he said. "That's the mail."

She heard it too, the long, shrill, forlorn whistle that had filled her with such despair when she had heard it one morning as she lay in bed.

"The mail," she repeated, her hands smoothing back her hair from her face. Mechanically she noticed that her hands were cold. "It's arrived."

"Or maybe it's leaving."

Too late anyway. Too late for anything. As if Baba had realised it, too, had sensed that now she would not leave, he moved out of the room.

"Baba!" she called out in a sudden panic.

He stood still for a moment, then turned round, unwillingly it seemed, and mumbled, "What is it? I've put the rice on the stove."

Now it was obvious. He had retreated, he had withdrawn. He would do no more. But she would not leave it at that.

"Promise me," she said, "promise me you won't open the door to him. Don't open the door when he comes."

His lips moved as if to frame a word, a question. Then he closed them and nodded. "All right," he said, seeing that she still gazed at him expectantly. And he walked away.

She was alone now. How quiet the house was. A brooding stillness lay over it as if it was waiting for something. She could hear the tick tock of the clock. She stared dumbly at the letters that lay forlornly in the centre of the room and thought . . . it's my fault again. If mine had been an arranged marriage, if I had left it to them to arrange my life, would he have left me like this? She thought of the girl, the sister of a friend, who had come home on account of a disastrous marriage. She remembered the care and sympathy with which the girl had been surrounded, as if she was an invalid, a convalescent. And the girl's face with its look of passive suffering. There had been only that there, nothing else, neither despair nor shame. For the failure had not been hers, but her parents'; and so the guilt had been theirs too, leaving only the suffering for the girl.

Now she had both, the suffering as well as the guilt. She was cornered. There was no place to go, no room to breathe. There was nothing and nobody left. Even Baba had gone away, leaving her alone. It had happened at last, what she had always dreaded. She was alone, alone in the dark like Dhruva and her mother who had died alone in the middle of the night.

But it wasn't just the dead. It was the living as well. "Baba!" she had cried out in fear and he had not understood what she was trying to say. And Baba, too. Suddenly she remembered how his back had looked before he had turned round to face her. It had looked pathetic, the back of a defeated man. Had he tried to reach her and failed as well? Would every attempt to reach out to another human being be a failure? Had she been chasing a chimera all her life, hoping for someone? Perhaps the only truth is that man is born to be cold and lonely and alone.

And now it seemed that this was the worst thing that had happened to her. To embrace this knowledge meant that she had to relinquish all hope forever. What, then, was left?

But as she fearfully grappled with this nothingness, a strange thing happened to her. She was overcome by a queer sensation, as if everything was unreal. Her own body felt insubstantial. There was a feeling of weightlessness that made her almost euphoric. Even her fears faded into insubstantial ghosts. And with this sense of unreality came the thought . . . none of this matters, not really.

How comforting it was! Like being cuddled in a soft warm blanket on a cold night, when all thought is stifled and only a sensuous feeling of well-being remains. She relaxed . . . but only for a moment. Almost immediately it came . . . she did not

know why . . . a savage impulse to throw off this blanket, this
stifling comfort. For, no, it was not true. She could not find
refuge again in such a specious argument. It was too glib, too
easy a way out. To say that it isn't real, it doesn't really matter
. . . what does one make of life then? How can it help me to go
on, she thought despairingly?

And then it came to her. It was as if she was vouchsafed a
vision, the same one, perhaps, that her mother had had when
she had heard Duryodhana's story just before she died. Even if
it is an illusion, it is the only reality we know, the only reality
we will ever know. Therefore the only thing is to go on as if it
is real knowing all the while it is only an illusion.

Queer consolation, this; but consolation nevertheless. She
had to go on. To blunder her way through this to some kind of
a life that would seem right to her.

All right, so I'm alone. But so is everyone else. Human
beings . . . they're going to fail you. But because there's just us,
because there's no one else, we have to go on trying. If we can't
believe in ourselves, we're sunk.

Now she could hear the low murmur of Madhav's voice
telling her he was back at his studies. Madhav who had so resolutely put away all that came between him and his life as he
intended to live it. My life is my own . . . how boldly he had
said the words yesterday! And Baba asking her . . . are you not
enough for yourself? Such strange words, she had thought, for
Baba to say to her. Now she asked herself . . . Am I?

They came to her then, all those selves she had rejected so
resolutely at first, and so passionately embraced later. The
guilty sister, the undutiful daughter, the unloving wife . . . all
persons spiked with guilt. Yes, she was all of them, she could
not deny that now. She had to accept these selves to become
whole again. But if she was all of them, they were not all of her.
She was all these and so much more.

My life is my own . . .somehow she felt as if she had found

it now, the connecting link. It means you are not just a strut-
ting, grimacing puppet, standing futilely on the stage for a
brief while between areas of darkness. If I have been a puppet
it is because I made myself one. I have been clinging to the ten-
uous shadow of a marriage whose substance has long since dis-
integrated, because I have been afraid of proving my mother
right.

"I told you once, Saru . . . your mother is dead." Yes, I
know it now, my mother is dead.

She could hear Baba's voice speaking to Madhav. Their
voices came to her from some immense distance. She knew
what it was Baba was telling the boy. She knew that if she did
not open the door, neither Baba nor Madhav would. And if she
didn't, how long would he stand there knocking?

And then she heard the creaking of the gate. She stiffened.
There it was . . . a knock at the door. "I can't go on. I can't."

The knock was repeated with a peremptoriness that told
her the person would not be refused. Duryodhana, she
thought inconsequently, waiting for his enemies to come and
kill him. But I have been my own enemy. Will I . . . ?

Instantly she moved, her feet taking her swiftly across the
hall and to the front door. She pushed the bolt down with such
force that her finger was jammed. She was sucking it when she
opened the door. And then she exclaimed, "Who . . . ?"

The child, equally startled by her sudden appearance,
stared at her without speaking, one hand held up as if to knock
again. He was panting as if he had been running. And then,
recognising her, he gasped, "Come quick, Sarumavshi. Oh,
come quick. Our Sunita . . . " he gulped, then went on, ". . .
she's having fits and mother says . . . "

She had managed to still the trembling of her legs. But her
face, her body, felt cold and clammy with the sudden breaking
out of sweat. She felt as if she had traversed miles, years, since
she had moved out of her room to open the door.

"Ravi!" Now she recognised the boy. A child who lived a few doors away.

He tugged at her hand as if he would drag her bodily away. "Please come at once. Mother says . . . she's crying and Sunita . . . she'll die if you don't come at once." "Of course I'm coming," she said briskly. "I'll be there in a moment. Run home and tell your mother I'm coming. I'll just wear my slippers and . . . "

He sped away from her, kicking his heels high up as he ran. She went back in to wear her slippers.

"Saru?"

It was Baba, the whole of him a question mark.

"That was Ravi. Vimla's boy. He says Sunita is having fits. I must go."

She stepped out of the door, and then, moved to compassion for the old man, turned round and said over her shoulder, "And, oh yes, Baba, if Manu comes, tell him to wait. I'll be back as soon as I can."

She hurried out of the house. The gate swung behind her with its usual protesting squeak. And now, there were no thoughts in her, except those of the child she was going to help.

Convulsions . . . ?

That could mean . . . ?

Her mind ranged over all the possibilities.

EXPLANATORY NOTES

Aarti:	A ceremony performed with lighted oil lamps.
Agni:	The god of fire.
Akbarally's:	A large department store in Bombay.
Bai:	Literally, "woman"; used also for maidservants.
Barfi:	A kind of sweet.
Benaras:	A type of silk sari, with designs woven in gold thread.
Carrom:	An indoor game.
Chanderi:	A type of gossamer cotton sari, with gold thread designs on it.
Chappatis:	Indian bread.
Chawl:	A building consisting of one-room homes.
Choli:	A short blouse worn with a sari.
Churidar:	Close-fitting trousers.
Dasara:	An important Hindu festival.
Devi:	Goddess.
Draupadi:	Wife of the five Pandava brothers, heroes of the Mahabharata.
Ekadashi:	The eleventh day of each two week period of the lunar month. Devout Hindus fast on this day.
Ganpati:	The god with an elephant's head, whose festival is celebrated in South India and Maharashtra.
"Ganpati bappa morya":	A rhyme children chant when the elephant-god is being taken for immersion.
"Haldi-kumkums":	Social-religious functions, exclusive to women. *Haldi* (turmeric) and *kumkum* (a red powder with which Hindu women dot their foreheads) are indispensable in all rituals.
Kauravas, Pandavas:	The rival clans whose clash formed the basis of the Mahabharata. Duryodhana was the eldest of the Kaurava brothers and the villain of the Mahabharata.

"Not-dirty": In orthodox Hindu homes, cooked food, left overs etc., are considered dirty; preserves, milk, ghee, etc., are contaminated if they come in contact with these. Hence the two are kept scrupulously apart.

Not just the three days: In orthodox Hindu households, women are regarded as untouchable and segregated during their periods.

Paan-supari: Betel leaf and betel nut. Together, they are essential in most Hindu rituals.

Prasad: Any eatable sanctified by being offered to god first.

Puran-poli: A sweet.

Rani of Jhansi: A queen who fought the British in the 1857 war of independence.

Shivaji: The founder of the Maratha Empire, influenced by and devoted to his mother Jijabai.

Shrikhand: A sweet made of curds and sugar.

Sita: Wife of Rama, the hero of the Ramayana.

Tai: Appellation for elder sister in Marathi, also used as term of respect.

"The King and the fisherman's daughter": A story in the Mahabharata. King Santanu fell in love with and married Satyavati, a fisherman's daughter.

The Krishna Sudama story: Sudama, a poor man, approached his boyhood friend Krishna, then King of Dwarka, with trepidation. He was, however, welcomed with great love and affection.

The Taj: The Taj Mahal Hotel in Bombay.

The tulsi: The basil plant, worshipped by Hindu women.

Thread ceremony: An important initiation ceremony for a Brahmin boy.

ACKNOWLEDGMENTS

The quotation on page 11 is from a transcreation from Pali by P. Lal (Noonday Paperback; Farrar, Straus & Giroux, New York, 1967)

I would like to thank Prof. G.S. Amur for so patiently, kindly and promptly going through *The Dark Holds No Terrors* and for offering such helpful and encouraging comments.

S.D.

About the Author

Shashi Deshpande was born in southern India and educated in Bombay (now Mumbai) and Bangalore. She published her first collection of short stories in 1978. She received the Sahitya Akademi Award for her novel *That Long Silence*. Today, author of four children's books, six novels, and numerous influential essays, she is a renowned voice in Indian literature.